Area One

Estelle Cranfield

'Area One'
Estelle Cranfield

This is a work of fiction. Names, characters, places, incidents and organisations in this book are fictitious, or are a product of the author's imagination and any similarities are entirely coincidental.

First Issue 2015
Second Issue December 2019

Book cover design by Ken Dawson, Creative Covers
Copyediting by Deborah Dove, Polgarus Studio
Formatting by Polgarus Studio

www.estellecranfield.com

This book is dedicated to Tim.

And to the ONE.

Introduction

"Have you ever as a kid, or even as an adult, wished for special powers? Like the power to make something appear out of thin air? Or the ability to see through a brick wall? To be able to read someone else's thoughts? Or the power to know when something is about to happen?

All humans who have ever walked your planet have wished for such powers, if only for a second. You have dreamt about the freedom and liberation such abilities would allow. Imagined how incredible life would be. The fun you would have living a comic-strip superhero life. You have danced with these ideas in your head, pictured the thrill and exhilaration, and envisioned all that you could become.

Well, my dear One, your requests have been answered. You have asked and although it may seem they are a long time coming, beyond your planet's space-time reality, they are materialising instantly, in the form of new Laws. And we, the Collective One, are here to help you prepare for their arrival and integration. We have been waiting for the perfect time and it is now. My dear One, it is time for you to make the jump to your next destination, a place beyond your current imagination and realisation.

The Laws of Manifestation, Thought Reading, Seeing, and Sensing are bursting forth all around you, making themselves known, giving you a hint of what is to come. Many of you have experienced these new Laws, not realising what they are. They have jumped into your lives and scared some of you senseless, leaving you bewildered. Some have seen the opportunity that these new Laws bring, but then old patterns kicked in and you pulled back with fear and trepidation. Things that you ask for coming to you quicker than ever. Senses heightening so you know how someone is feeling or what they are thinking before words are uttered. Knowing things ahead of time. Feeling the pain of others without awareness of their plight. Your intuition sharpening, becoming more acute. Blurred knowingness turning to razor-sharp focus. Holding the answers before the questions. These are the signs. You are evolving, expanding, changing, transforming. Life is speeding up. Everything stretching, further than any other time. You sense that something monumental is about to happen, that somehow things will never be the same again, but you don't fully understand it all yet. It feels overwhelmingly powerful, but you only snatch a sliver of comprehension before returning to your norm. Yes, my dear One, these are the new proliferation of human functions working their way into your existence—weaving their patterns into your environment; mixing with your energy; knitting with your neural pathways; flooding your cells and atoms; blending with your RNA and DNA.

And as they take hold, old narratives begin to crumble and collapse, traditional borders and boundaries weaken, ancient rules and regulations unravel as you give birth to the new paradigm—changing you and your world forever.

You, my dear One, are the master creator in this game called life, and there is not one situation, living being, object, or place that was not created by you. Every expansion is instigated by you. Every development and escalation of the One is constructed by you. Every evolution is birthed from you. Every ascension and paradigm shift comes from you. So when you ask for new Laws to come forth, they do so with reliability and finality. How can they not? You are the One creator here—the supreme power. This is your game. Your rules.

Did you doubt your strength? Were you unsure you had this much say? Did you disbelieve in your intense power? If so, then you are mistaken, my dear One. You are the one in charge. You have asked for new Laws and now they are here, growing inside each and every one of you. Already you have passed the point of no return. Nothing and no one can stop this.

Your world and your life will never be the same again.

Chapter One

May 2033

'What do you mean you can't get in?' Trent tried to keep his voice even, but couldn't control his steel blue eyes glaring at George, who was now hunched over the security keypad.

'They've changed the code.' George's nervous hand hovered over the buttons.

'Jeez! The first level and we're out.' Trent rubbed his hand over his face. This was his third attempt at the Chryso assessment and he was convinced, deep in his gut, that he'd sail through this time. Why, oh why did he let George volunteer to be in charge of this task? Something in the back of Trent's mind told him it was a mistake when George eagerly put up his hand to lead. *Jesus Christ! Why didn't I say something back then? The poor idiot is probably trying to impress Lily*, Trent scorned. Lily was the twenty-something Barbie-like third candidate in their group, with a penchant for pink and all things glittery. *She's well out of his league*, Trent thought as he studied George's small stature, thin face, and bucked teeth. George was as far as you could get from Trent's tall, fit physique and bad-boy good looks. *Shit! Why did I let him lead?* Trent metaphorically kicked himself, knowing that if he was on his own, he'd be through by now. But that was against the rules. You had to pass each of the seven levels of the assessment as a group of three, and the other two in your group had to be complete strangers.

In the past, the authorities had trialled the tests with just individuals and also with people who knew each other, and every time it ended with disastrous consequences. That's why entry into Area One was now strictly controlled, with candidates being assigned teammates by Uriel, the Chryso group allocation computer software.

'He's got one more attempt. We can still do it,' Lily said, fluttering her long eyelash extensions at Trent, who inwardly groaned, knowing they didn't have a snowball's chance in hell, and Lily even less so with him. She was so not his type. Trent favoured an edgier woman, someone less obvious, less smiley, less blonde and pink.

'Okay, let's try again. Last time. Take charge of your thoughts.' George's hooded grey eyes looked directly at Trent. 'And you can let go of that crap, Trent. I can feel it.' Trent's eyes shot down to the floor. George and Trent hadn't warmed to each other from the first moment they'd met, but in order to succeed, they had to let go of any animosity. It was just the sort of thing the tests were designed to pick up.

Trying to clear his mind, Trent wriggled his toes in the clompy, white issue boots. They were hot and sweaty like the rest of his body which was clad in a rather becoming all-in-one white jumpsuit. Trent hated the whole assessment get-up and was itching to rip it off. It was a far cry from his usual Kurt Cobain come Gary Clark Jr style of dress. *If my fans could see me now.* Trent was pleased that phones, tablets, cameras, and the like were banned from the assessment. Mind you, the word 'fans' may be stretching it a bit. Yes, it was true his band Dark House had some fans and followers on YouTube, although they were few and far between and mainly confined to the Isle of Wight. He'd never really got to the bottom of the Isle of Wight thing, fearing that if he dug too deep, it would all unravel and he'd find himself minus the Wighty fans. Like a tug of war, Trent battled with his thoughts, pulling his mind hard to think of music and playing his guitar. The feel of the guitar in his hands, strumming, plucking the strings, the sounds, getting lost in the rhythm. Slowly his mind surrendered, and with music now playing in his head, Trent's thoughts eased and he exhaled loudly. He wasn't stupid; he'd been here before and knew that his negative thoughts could halt their progress instantly. *God, this is sooo hard.* Trent breathed deeply while the warm, rich guitar notes moved inside him.

Over the last few months, Trent had slogged away, fighting to master his thoughts. *How do people even get into this place?* Trent was often baffled. *Maybe Area One's not for me. Perhaps I should stay where I am, living with mum in Brighton. It's not too bad. I've still got my band and my music. Maybe think about university again. Perhaps even study art and design with Jonno at Leeds.* He was a twenty-two year old creative soul and, if he took all of the assessment training and applied it, maybe he could build a good life for himself. Christ! No! What was he saying? That didn't sound right. Gnawing away deep inside was everything he'd read on the internet about this New Land called Area One. The way the whole world was raving about it, Trent knew he would never be able to get it out of his head. No, he had to keep trying, otherwise he would always be wondering, 'What if?'

The New Land, now called Area One, surfaced back in the summer of 2030 in the ancient New Forest located in the south of England. Seemingly overnight, an energy portal (or that's how people explained it) opened up and across a twelve-kilometre square space, people found themselves operating in a completely different dimension. There appeared to be no obvious warnings that anything was changing in the area, and people were taken by complete surprise as new abilities began to show up in them. One minute someone was going about their normal day-to-day business, and the next minute, they could read another's thoughts, or knew what was about to happen before it had occurred. A wish they held in their mind suddenly appeared right before them. It was both frightening and thrilling in equal measures.

In the beginning, many Thought Readers, Sensors, and Seers believed they were going mad and, in a state of confusion, sought help from doctors and mental health professionals, only to find themselves sectioned under the Mental Health Act. It was only when Manifesters began unveiling their abilities that authorities realised it was more than an anomalous wave of people crossing the borders into insanity. Things they wanted and wished for came to them in an instant. Their deepest desires suddenly materialised. Manifesters were making their dreams come true, and not in days, weeks, months, or years – it was happening the very second the thought formed in their mind. Age, gender, colour, creed, IQ, and social status were irrelevant when it came to the abilities. It was happening to all walks of life within this small rural area of the New Forest.

No, Area One was far too tantalising and seductive for Trent to forget, and for all his big talk about giving up and going to university, he wanted in on it.

Although right this second, Trent wanted to scream into George's face that he was a freaking dork and there was no way he'd get them through this most basic of tasks. But instead, Trent held back and breathed some more. It was a real effort, because as soon as he cleared his mind, up something else would jump. Another cynical and contrary thought to throw him off course. Pushing music into all four corners of his mind, Trent finally let go and relaxed. Even with months of training, Trent doubted he would ever perfect this skill.

It was the most fundamental skill that all assessment candidates needed to master, and in the early days when the assessment was lax, people entered Area One still unable to properly control their thoughts and emotions. Consequently, the new abilities were used indiscriminately with lack of awareness and little control, causing sheer and utter pandemonium. Since then, the authorities had tightened things up, and for anyone wanting to become a resident inside the revered and highly prized Area One, thought and emotion control were must-have skills.

George exhaled, closed his eyes, and took a deep breath. Opening his eyes slowly, he looked to Lily, then to Trent.

'All cleared?' he asked.

'Yes,' Lily said.

'Yeah, all cleared,' Trent said with calm in his voice and peace in his mind. George turned back to the security keypad and punched in the digits carefully and deliberately.

'Code error.' George read out the message that flashed in green neon on the small screen above the keypad. 'Yep, they've definitely changed it.' This time the trio didn't react. They stood still and grounded with clear minds – no judgements, no anger. 'We need to go back to the Prep Lab and regroup.

Do you agree, Lily?'

'I agree,' Lily said.

'Trent?'

'I agree,' Trent said.

The three walked back down the stark white corridor, through the double doors, and back into the Prep Lab, their every move recorded. Throughout the centre, the lights were bright and the walls, ceilings, and floors were coloured white. The assessment centre creators called it clean and minimal. All to help the candidates focus on themselves and their inner world. The less distraction, the easier it would be to concentrate all thought and emotion. Well, that was the theory anyway. Frankly, it gave Trent a headache. If you passed the three-week assessment, you went through an additional two-week period where they gradually introduced you to more stimuli, all the while checking to see if you could still control your emotions and thoughts. Then you went through a final phase, where they really ramped up the triggers. Anything to get you to react. They poked, prodded, and stuck metaphorical fingers in old buried pains, deep paranoias, and egotistical constructs, and didn't let up until you proved you could control yourself.

The three sat down and reviewed their strategy, taking care of their minds. Any movement or wobbles from their composed centre and the receptors taped to their bodies would pick up the erroneous thoughts and emotions, giving them an immediate fail. All candidates were allowed some leeway throughout the assessment, although Trent figured he'd probably used up all of his.

Four hours later, Trent was walking with his head down towards the exit gates, hoping to avoid any 'bad luck' conversations with anyone. The gates opened as he approached and then closed quickly behind him. Trent had failed the Chryso assessment again. They'd all failed. That's how it worked. If one in your team was all over the place mentally, it was harder still to control yourself. That's exactly why they grouped you with complete strangers who would potentially aggravate you. And that's why, after passing each level of the assessment, they mixed up the groups. Constantly testing your ability to control each and every thought, each and every emotion, with new people, over and over again.

Trent took the train home, sleeping through the long journey. As he disembarked, he pushed his hands deep into his pockets and headed straight to his local pub, The Side House in Kemptown and the place where he worked part-time. He was gagging for a proper drink and some decent food and didn't have the strength to face his mum sober. The assessment centre didn't allow any food or drink that could negatively impact your mental or physical state, so things like alcohol, cigarettes, sugar, drugs, wheat, coffee, tea, additives, and all junk were outlawed. Only fresh, plain, single ingredient foods and purified water were permitted. At times it felt more like a detox centre than the gateway to the promised land. All types of food and drink were sanctioned inside Area One. They knew it would be impossible to impose bans on people who could conjure up anything from thin air. They did, however, preach against overindulgence, knowing how reckless a drunken or gluttonous Manifester could be.

Trent salivated at the thought of a big juicy burger, with mature Cheddar and Roquefort cheese melting between two chunky beef patties, home-cooked chips sprinkled with sea salt, and a pint of dark real ale, knowing full well his stomach would have something to say about it after its enforced restricted diet.

Forty-five minutes later, feeling light-headed and as though he'd eaten a pound of lead, Trent ambled home, relieved to find his mum was out. Tuesday's were her Expressive Yoga classes, an enthusiastic combination of yoga, dance, and chanting. It was a sight to behold when she practised at home and thought nobody was watching. Trent hung up his jacket and threw his backpack on the floor. His mum, Ginger, nicknamed for her mass of wild, curly, bright auburn hair, loved yoga and all things spiritual and esoteric. Trent was forever grateful that he'd inherited his father's hair. His was blonde and fell in messy waves around his face. It suited Trent's rugged style.

Ginger would be surprised to see him home, so convinced she was that he would pass the assessment this time. Her strong confidence was supported by the messages she'd received from her tarot cards. 'The cards are never wrong,' Ginger told Trent after he found her leaping around the lounge, clutching the Nine of Cups and the Wheel of Fortune tarot cards. Trent gave her a yeah-yeah-whatever look. But sometimes her belief could be infectious and this time it percolated right through to him. *Maybe it is my time. Perhaps I will get in. I've done the assessment enough times. That's got to account for something.* Trent had walked out of the lounge, leaving his mum dancing with her two tarot cards, with a glimmer of hope in his heart.

'So much for the cards are never wrong.' Trent threw the brightly coloured sequinned cushions from the sofa and across the room, and sat down heavily.

It took Trent four days before he could shift the overwhelming feeling of failure. Much to his mum's disgust, he wallowed in his bedroom and only moved from his bed to play computer games and to use the toilet.

Armed with his favourite food and an endless supply of tea, Ginger tried to coax him out of his funk. She went on about the training he'd done and how he should be able to snap out of it. He'd been learning to control his thoughts, so why couldn't he change them to more positive ones, she wanted to know. No amount of persuasion could jolt him out of his slump. The bottom line was he didn't want to change; he wanted to be down, he deserved to be down. He'd failed the assessment for a third time for Chrissake. She threatened to kick him out of the house; that didn't work. She tried reassurance that one day he would reach his dream. That was hopeless. She offered to read the tarot cards for him again. He was having none of that. Nothing seemed to work and Ginger, with her mothering and fussing, only served to get on Trent's nerves.

Maybe if Trent had jumped on things sooner, he would be inside Area One by now. When he got that phone call from his school friend Jed, he should have gone straight away. Jed had been staying right where the portal had opened up in the New Forest. Trent sighed. *He's so bloody lucky.*

Since then, the hype around Area One had built to fever pitch and was clouding Trent's ability to gain perspective. When Jed first called and told Trent about the strange goings-on, Trent had no preconceptions. His interest was piqued, but he didn't have loads of images buzzing around his mind of what the New Land was like. If only he'd taken up Jed's offer to go there and then, he would be in. Or even if he'd been one of the first ones to register for the Chryso assessment when it was set up, he may have passed first time. The assessment was easier back then.

Now though, with all the news and gossip about how amazing Area One was, there were moments when Trent felt complete desperation to be inside. Was this pushing him further away from it? With every new piece of information about Area One and each attempt at gaining entry, it seemed to outsmart him. If only he'd jumped on it sooner.

Chapter Two

It was a sunny July day and a rare day off for Jed and his two colleagues, as they drove towards Blair's Rocks for some recreational climbing. Usually this time of year was especially busy for them as Outdoor Activity Leaders, with back-to-back trips for youngsters with working parents who were at a loss to know what to do with their offspring for the long summer break. The three intended to make the most of their precious free day by going rock climbing and white-water kayaking, and then round it off with a trip to the local pub.

After setting up the rock-climbing gear and running through the necessary safety checks, Jed took the lead. He was only halfway through his ascent when he slipped. Jed wasn't a bad climber and, like all good climbers, was meticulous about safety. So although he was momentarily shocked, Jed didn't panic, trusting that the safety mechanisms would kick in. But they didn't. *That's weird*, Jed thought. *What's going on?* They'd done the checks; he knew they had. Along with everyone else who worked at the Outdoor Centre, they were ultra safety conscious. It was in their blood. It had to be when you were teaching people to climb, abseil, and kayak moving waters.

No matter how weird Jed thought it was, he was definitely falling. Everything around him speeded, yet within his bubble, time slowed down so he was able to go through the whole safety procedure in his mind, time flexing and stretching. Everything had been done correctly, he was sure of it. Jed's mind then flicked to his life. From the beginning as a baby, snapshots blasted out in Jed's head. As a toddler, a child, growing up. His accomplishments and milestones. Did he still have things to do in this lifetime? Was he ready for it to end? In that moment, Jed knew he could choose to stay or go. He could live or die. It was his to decide. He could go; he really could. A deep peace was pulling him, calling him Home. Bliss was calling his name. It was the first time he'd ever linked the idea of death to peace and bliss. But that's what it felt like. NO! He wasn't ready to leave. He still had stuff he wanted to do, things to achieve. He was certain. Jed decided. He wanted to live. *I want to live!* Jed shouted to himself. *I'm not ready to go yet! I want to be at the top of these rocks NOW! I want to live!* The words screamed out inside him, sure and determined. In a flash, his body propelled upwards and was thrown onto the top of the rocks. Then everything went black.

'Jed, mate, can you hear me? Are you alright?' Cautiously, Jed opened his eyes and he looked up at the two anxious faces of his climbing buddies, Dave and Flynn. Their faces visibly changed when they realised he wasn't dead.

'Are you hurt?' Dave moved closer towards Jed, concern in his eyes. Flynn stood looking down at the pair, eyes wide, mouth open, both hands on his head, as though he'd seen a ghost.

'Errrr.' Jed wiggled his fingers and toes. 'I don't think so. I'm scared of moving too much.'

'Keep still, mate, we've called for help,' Dave said. Flynn shook his head, bringing himself back down to earth. He bent down and rummaged in his backpack, searching. Pulling out a space blanket, he unfolded the thin sheet of aluminium foil and began to cover Jed.

'I don't think I need that, Flynn. I'm boiling, mate. It's summer, remember?' Jed gave a half smile, worried that Flynn had started the whole first-aid routine on him.

'Have you tried to move your fingers and toes?' Flynn asked.

'Yeah, all seems okay. I think I can sit up,' Jed said.

'Lie still until the ambulance crew check you out. They might even bring in the helicopter. Neat, eh?' Dave said as he checked Jed's pulse for a third time. 'Let me see your eyes.'

'What?' Jed was suddenly troubled. Maybe he was in a bad way and didn't realise it. Perhaps he had a limb hanging off and his brain wasn't allowing him to register it as some sort of coping mechanism.

'Best to be safe than sorry,' Dave said.

'Right, before they arrive, I want to know what the hell just happened then,' Flynn blurted out. The three had been avoiding the elephant in the room and Flynn, never one to keep quiet, was bursting to say something. 'That was seriously freaking freaky,' Flynn added. As Jed gently eased himself up, he was pleased to see his limbs attached.

'I don't know.' Jed stared past Dave and Flynn, his mind working hard.

'Jed, mate, you were falling, I saw you. Then, then you... then you...' Flynn squeezed his eyes shut, trying to dispel the image in his mind. What he'd seen didn't compute. 'Then... Well, I dunno. It was like the invisible man grabbed you and threw you to the top of the rocks.' Flynn rubbed his hands through his curly brown hair. 'It was spooky, mate, like a film. Like you were being pulled up with one of those wire things they use in stunts.' Flynn struggled to put it into words. Jed rubbed his head to check he was real and this wasn't a dream. Yeah, it was real alright.

'I know,' Jed said.

'What happened? I saw you slip and fall. Then you stopped.' Flynn looked at Jed wide-eyed. 'Jed, nothing was holding you up. You weren't attached.' Jed pulled back the space blanket and all three looked down at Jed's body. The harness was intact and nothing else. No carabiner, no ropes, nothing.

'Christ Almighty!' Flynn said as he sat down heavily next to Jed. 'Jed, what on earth was that all about, mate?'

'I don't know. I felt myself falling. Then I remember thinking I don't want to die.' Jed looked from Flynn to Dave and back again. 'I wanted to live. I said I wanted to get to the top of the rocks. Then I was flying to the top of the rocks. How did that even—' Jed shook his head, and Dave and Flynn just stared at each other. All three brains ached as they tried to comprehend what had just taken place. It was impossible. What they had witnessed was inexplicable.

The ambulance turned up and even though it seemed Jed had luckily escaped with minor cuts and bruises, they took him to A&E to get him checked over. Five hours later, Flynn and Dave picked up a bemused Jed from the hospital and made their way to the Long Alice pub, with a deep need to make sense of the day and an equal need for lashings of beer.

After great discussion and debate, they concluded that none of them had a flipping clue what had gone on and made a pact never to speak of it again. Although for Jed, that was easier said than done. He'd been the one that had felt the force move his body to the top of Blair's Rocks. And two days later, Jed knew for sure he could never ignore these strange occurrences when, careering down the river, he said clearly in his head that he wanted to fly off the next large drop, affectionately called Devils Drop by the kayakers, and he did just that. He flew. It was a big gnarly drop, notoriously tricky to run, and liked to pull you under upon your landing. Jed's kayak literally launched from the top and sent him forward for what seemed like an age, before landing him gently further down the river.

Jed swore out loud as he paddled over to the bank. *Flipping heck! What on earth just happened?* He rested his paddle on the spray deck of his kayak and looked over his shoulder. *Did anyone else see?* Jed looked around; no one was there. Then Jed heard the group approaching the drop. He watched carefully as one by one they ran Devil's Drop. No one launched and landed anywhere near him. Looking at the distance now, Jed reckoned he was fifty or sixty feet away from the actual drop. *Maybe I hit a rock and it shot me forward. Yeah, must be something like that. Either that or it was just a fluke. I bet I couldn't do that again if I tried.* Jed laughed it off, all the while suppressing an uncomfortable feeling in his stomach.

'Hey, Jed, how did you get down here so fast?' Dave said, positioning his kayak next to Jed's. 'The old girl's a bit lively today, isn't she?' Jed nodded in agreement, still shocked. 'Come on, better help the rest down. Barbara's bound to swim again,' Dave said as he rolled his eyes before paddling away, leaving Jed to pull himself together.

'What is happening to me?' Jed said as he looked towards the heavens. He picked up his paddle and made his way to the bottom of the drop, where Dave was rescuing a stressed-out Barbara who had swam out of her boat prematurely, unconfident she could roll up in her kayak.

The Madness, as Jed called it, continued over the next few days and after the fifth freakish incident, it dawned on Jed what was happening. What he asked for was coming true, although sadly not all the time. And as spine-chilling as it sounded, that's what Jed was experiencing. So far, the Madness had only showed its face when Jed was engaged in outdoor activities and, apart from the first time, had only occurred when no one else was watching. Jed wasn't sure why it only happened occasionally, and his mind was doing backflips trying to work out the cause. Maybe it was specific words he used? Or perhaps it only worked certain times of the day? Was it about his state of mind? He didn't know. There didn't seem to be any obvious pattern to it. Jed was mystified as to the reason why. And after flying off a rock face – Jed was meant to be abseiling – he knew he had to talk to someone. Part of him was excited, part of him scared, and a big part thought he'd gone nuts. Jed called Trent, one of his best mates from back home in Brighton.

'Alright, mate. How's it going?' Trent asked as he picked up the call.

'Yeah, not bad,' Jed said, struggling to find the right words.

'Job alright?' Trent asked.

'Job's okay. Not sure about the location though. I think I prefer Wales. Not for the weather. It's just the terrain and rivers are better in Wales than here. Anyway, how's things your end?' Jed stalled on raising the subject of the Madness.

'Yeah, okay. I've signed up for college to get those qualifications I need for the art and design course at uni.' Trent's voice was devoid of any enthusiasm or joy. 'Thinking I might join Jonno at Leeds.'

'I thought you wanted to do music at Manchester?' Jed was shocked. If you cut Trent in half, Jed was sure you'd find 'guitar player' written deep inside him like a stick of Blackpool rock. Music and guitars were how they first met, with them both trying out for the same band while at secondary school. Trent won the place and Jed conceded gracefully, acknowledging that Trent was by far the better guitarist.

'I don't know. Not sure I want to do all that theory rubbish that goes with it. Might lose something for me, you know?' Trent loved his guitar and music, but studying it, learning its history, analysing other musicians, exploring the whys and where-fors would take away its magic. Trent couldn't care less about reciting significant musical historical dates and had no regard for the music professors' theories or the academics' hypothesis. He only knew how it made him feel and enjoyed where it could take him when he played.

'I know what you mean. You'll still play though, won't you?' Jed asked.

'Oh yeah, I'm still in the band. That does it for me, jamming and strumming out some songs. You never know, we might get picked up one day and smash it. Could knock the whole uni thing on the head then.'

'Your mum won't be pleased,' Jed reminded Trent.

'Tell me about it. She was made up when I told her I was seriously considering uni. I was her number one son.'

'Not hard considering you're her only son. And her only child for that matter,' Jed said.

'Well, you know what I mean. Meet any nice girls?' Trent changed the subject quickly.

'Some. But I need to talk to you about something much more exciting,' Jed said.

'More exciting than girls? Really? Well if it's not sex, it's got to be drink and drugs then.'

'What? No and no.' Jed laughed.

'You've found Jesus in the New Forest?' Trent asked.

'Definitely not. Seriously, mate, you've got to hear this...' And Jed proceeded to tell Trent about the strange developments. Knowing that Trent's mum was out with the fairies most nights, he hoped Trent wouldn't think he'd gone bananas. And Trent didn't. He'd grown up with his mum feeling energies, cleansing his chakras, and speaking openly to ethereal beings she claimed were her spiritual guides from the 'other side'. Trent had seen it all, especially during his mum's spiritual workshops she ran from home, where usually women, and occasionally men, sat around their lounge, learning to read the secret meanings of their dreams, regressing to past lives, healing their auras with crystals, and trying to levitate – unsuccessfully. All by candlelight and enveloped in Nag Champa and Patchouli essence. So Jed talking about his unusual episodes didn't faze Trent at all.

'That's amazing, mate,' Trent said at the end. 'Have you got special powers or something?'

'I don't know.' Jed laughed. It sounded ridiculous now and reminded him of reading superhero comics as a boy. 'Listen, why don't you come down? I might be able to show you.' Jed was eager to share it with someone he trusted.

'I haven't got the money for it, Jed.' Trent didn't get a lot from his part-time bar job. 'What's that noise?' Clicking noises on the line interrupted their chat.

'I don't know, maybe the signal's dropping out?' Jed said.

'Maybe.'

'Look, you can camp out in my room on the floor if you like. Come on, Trent. I've got to show someone, I'm going crazy here,' Jed pleaded.

'Sorry, mate, I'm broke. And I've still got work to do if I'm going ahead with this college course.' Trent was gutted he couldn't pack a bag and head to the New Forest, but his mum's voice rang in his head. She was an offbeat contradiction – a free spirit of a woman with a laissez faire attitude to most things in life who wanted a conventional education for her only child.

'Oh well, mate, never mind. I'm back in Brighton before Christmas. Maybe we can hook up then and I'll show you,' Jed said.

'Sure. Sounds great. See you then,' Trent said.

'See ya.'

That was the last time Trent heard from his friend Jed with the special powers.

Chapter Three

The government was first alerted to this enigma when a troubled single mum of four bowled into the police station at Burley, with three children trailing behind and her youngest on her hip.

Viv rang the bell on the counter impatiently, hands shaking. It was Monday evening just before nine o'clock, and the village police station was quiet. She banged the bell again, agitated.

'Can someone help me?' Viv's voice, just under a scream, highlighted her anxiety.

'Alright, alright, keep your hair on.' Police Constable Jim Cartwright came to the desk. 'What can I do for you?' Constable Cartwright studied Viv, a mere child with children, her once pretty face hardened by premature motherhood. She wore tight jeans wrapped around stick-thin legs and a baggy T-shirt covered in purple sequinned hearts. Her mousy brown hair needed a wash and was scraped back, held in place with a bright pink scrunchy band.

'I have to talk to someone about some TVs. Five of them. Big ones with curved screens. Really posh and expensive looking,' Viv said.

'Stolen, are they?' Constable Cartwright could have kicked himself for airing his assumption.

'Don't know.' Viv sniffed her disapproval. 'They just appeared.' Viv wiped the baby's snotty nose with her hand and rubbed it down her jeans.

'You'd better come through.' Jim Cartwright was seeing out his final year at Burley Police Station before his retirement. During his career, he'd held numerous positions in the police, but that was before his stress-related heart condition forced him out of the city and into the relative peace and quiet of the New Forest. The truth was, Jim wasn't cut out for the police. He was a naturally easygoing, happy guy who found the job hard on his nerves. Over the years, he had seen and dealt with the worst of humankind. Gradually, it took its toll, wearing away his positivity, grinding him down and crushing his spirit, until one day he couldn't stand it any longer. And that's when his heart problem showed up and his once thick, dark hair turned white and started to fall out. Now he was counting down the days until he left the seething abyss that was the police force.

Constable Cartwright ensconced Viv and her brood in the one and only interview room, and fetched a colleague to cover the front desk before rejoining Viv.

'Now then, let's start at the beginning, shall we? You say you've seen some TVs?' He sat opposite and pulled out his notepad and pen.

'Yeah, five of them.'

'Where are these TVs?' Constable Cartwright asked. Viv shifted in her seat and looked at her children, who were mostly sitting on the floor and being surprisingly well behaved. Constable Cartwright waited. No answer. He decided to change tack. 'Can I take your full name?'

'Vivienne Charlotte Smythe,' Viv said. Constable Cartwright looked at her with one eyebrow raised. She didn't look like a Smythe to him.

'And your full address?'

'We're in a B&B down Talbot Street at the moment. It's not permanent. Just until I get a council place. You see I had to leave the old man, me and the kids, so the authorities put us in a B&B temporary like. It's called Dolphin Lodge, Talbot Street, Burley. I don't know the postcode.'

'That's okay.' He took notes as she spoke. Constable Cartwright liked his own notes. 'So Vivienne...'

'Viv.'

'Yes, right, Viv. You say there are five TVs. Are they new?'

'I think so.' Viv nodded.

'Where did you see these TVs?'

'In one of our rooms. We've got two rooms and they're in the room that I sleep in with the two youngest.'

'So these TVs are in your room?' Constable Cartwright asked. Viv chewed her bottom lip; she wasn't sure how much to say. 'How did they get there?' he asked. Viv stroked the hair of her babe in arms as he looked at her with big saucer-blue eyes. She smiled at him and kissed his chubby cheek. 'How did the five TVs come to be in your room, Viv?' Constable Cartwright had come across these situations before; parents struggling to cope are pushed to the limit and step over the line out of desperation. Being a father himself, he could imagine how easy it was. He would do anything for his kids. Well, nearly anything. 'Why are the TVs in your room?' Constable Cartwright repeated. She had to tell him. The B&B owner, a weaselly little man, surely suspected some wrongdoing on her part, and Viv had to admit, it did look suspect.

'I asked for them and they appeared. I couldn't bloody believe it, but it's true. You see, me and the kids have got nothing now, not even a TV of our own. And I got so fed up last night, I wished for a TV. You know, one of those posh, smart ones. I turned my back for one second and blow me, there was one on the floor. I don't know how it got there I swear. It came from nowhere. Can you believe it?' Viv laughed, shaking her head in disbelief. It had stunned her when it happened.

'Came from nowhere? What, it appeared out of the ether, did it?' Constable Cartwright had heard some lies in his time, and this one was right up there with the best of them.

'Out of the what?'

'Never mind,' Constable Cartwright mumbled.

'I'm telling you. Honest. Then I thought wouldn't it be good if we had another one. You see, I could sell it and make some money. It's so hard on my own with this lot.' Viv was on a roll; she had to get it all out before she exploded. 'I know the selling bit might be wrong, but I'm telling you, I struggle to make the money go far enough. It's hard, and their useless father gives me nothing. So anyway, I carried on asking for another TV. Then another. I stopped at five because I ran out of space. Those B&B rooms they give you are so tiny. They say they're for families, but they can't be—'

Constable Cartwright held up his hand. 'Hold on; hold on a minute. So Viv, you're telling me that you wished for these TVs and they appeared? Out of thin air? And now you have five brand-new, smart TVs in your room at the Dolphin Lodge B&B establishment in Talbot Street?' Constable Cartwright asked. It sounded preposterous. *Oh, hold on, there could be some mental health issues here.* Constable Cartwright had seen it all, including the downright gut-wrenching sad stuff.

'Yeah, that's right.' Viv sighed. She was so relieved she'd told someone. It had weighed heavy on her mind all last night and throughout the day. She wasn't a dishonest person; she just wanted to do the best for her kids.

'Do you have anyone who can look after your children?'

'What do you mean? No, I've got no one.' Viv didn't like the look on Constable Cartwright's face. 'They're not going anywhere; they're staying here with me. Come here, kids.' She opened her arms to gather her children close to her. *He don't believe me. Oh no! This was a mistake. I shouldn't have come.* Knots formed in Viv's stomach. There was no way anyone was taking her children away.

'Viv, I'm going to get one of my colleagues to assist with this situation. Wait here.' Constable Cartwright stood up and walked out of the room, taking his notepad and pen. As the door closed, Viv bit her already chewed nails. *He don't believe me.* She held her children close to her and kissed baby Jacob's chubby cheek again, drawing comfort from his sweet baby smell. Then it came to her. *I know. I'll prove it. Then they'll have to believe me.*

Constable Cartwright took only minutes to get his colleague Constable Hallkirk, and as they both entered the interview room they saw it – a massive curve-screen, smart TV, all shiny and new.

'What the dickens?!' Constable Cartwright clamped his hand over his mouth to stop anything else escaping. Marigold, Viv's five-year-old girl, burst out laughing.

'He swore, Mummy. The policeman swore. Will he have to go to prison now?' Marigold asked with innocent eyes.

Commissioner Whinings pushed the button that ended the conference call and the screen on his monitor went blank. He would never have believed it unless he'd seen it with his very own eyes, and Constable Cartwright must have known that. *He looked shaken to the core, poor chap. This may hurry him to early retirement,* Commissioner Whinings thought.

Like Constable Jim Cartwright, Commissioner Sam Whinings believed it was a practical joke, even wondered if he might be on some TV show for elaborate spoofs. No doubt everyone who had escalated the situation over the past hour had felt the same. But it wasn't. And that became obvious after the sixth TV appeared, as Viv incarnated her wish over again in the interview room at Burley Village Police Station. At every step of the escalation process, she'd had to substantiate her claim and got really fed up, telling numerous high ranking officers who she was, where she lived, what she'd done, and then provided proof she wasn't lying by manifesting yet another bloody TV. She was sick of them now.

Although Commissioner Whinings was mystified as to what was going on, it was clear to him what he now needed to do as he picked up the phone. He paused, wondering how it would look to them. To him it seemed illogical, like something from the movies. But he knew the procedure. Dealing with a single mum of four who'd suddenly developed the ability to manifest smart TVs was beyond his remit and maybe it was even beyond MI5's. Still, that was their problem and thankfully, it would soon be out of his hands.

****

"Manifesting external material items such as TVs, cars, watches, shoes, hard currency, and the like, is a first clear indicator that the Manifester function is operational inside of you. Like all of these new abilities, the Manifestation power has different angles and aspects. For example, as well as external physical things, you will be able to manifest the less tangible too, like inner beliefs. So, if you think you are an excellent artist, you metamorphose into one instantly. If you believe you are a hopeless driver, you become one right away. If you see your body as healed, it is.

These new human functions have the potential for good, but in your current world-state of duality and polarity, they also have the capacity for what you define as 'bad'. Let us explain. When the Law of Manifestation is fully active, it means that you not only manifest so-called positive things, rather, you will manifest anything and everything that your mind is focused upon. And we mean anything and everything. If you are in a dreadful mood and your thoughts are centred upon something you define as negative, then that is what you will manifest, whether you say you want it or not. If you are having a rotten day and briefly wish something unpleasant would happen to your annoying friend, POW! At the speed of light, it will happen.

The same is true for all the Laws. For example, with the Law of Thought Reading, you will hear all thoughts, the good, the bad, and the ugly. Consider how it will be to hear the complete, no-holds-barred truth. People on your planet say little of what is sincerely on their mind, so as this new Law takes shape, be aware that you will be privy to everything that is usually held in secret within another. It is time to prepare yourself to hear everything, dear One. And what about the white lies you tell each day? What happens when other people have the ability to know your thoughts too?

And when the Law of Seeing is alive in you, how will you react when you can see what other people are doing behind your back? When walls and distance no longer mean anything; when closed doors become irrelevant and immaterial."

Chapter Four

'Hide it! Quick! They're coming to the house!' Terry yelled over his shoulder to his wife Faith. Peering out between the wooden venetian blinds at the lounge window, Terry couldn't tell for sure who they were. They just looked authoritative and frankly a bit terrifying. He assumed they were police, although it was difficult to say in their unmarked vehicles and without the usual uniforms on. He snapped the blinds closed and looked around at the piles of cash. It had to be over a million. Terry had been counting it, but without a money counter it was hopeless. There was so much cash, probably too much, and it was everywhere. *I told Faith to stop, but she wouldn't listen to me.* Terry's pulse quickened at the sight of the uninvited visitors hotfooting it up their pathway. *It's all her fault. She should have stopped ages ago. I told her. Strewth!*

It had become Faith's drug, an unstoppable addiction, a cruel master she could never appease.

'What?! They're coming here?!' Faith dashed around, picking up £50 notes, stuffing them everywhere and anywhere, under the cushions, in the TV cabinet, down her jeans, up her top. She pushed a pile under the sofa, barely making a dent in the small mountains that were dotted around the lounge. Hysteria surged through Faith's body and she laughed manically. It was like a comedy. Pushing back her long, chestnut hair from her face, she stuffed a note in her mouth. *Maybe I can eat them?* Faith laughed harder now. It was completely crazy. *Perhaps I can wish them all away? It could work.* Because wishing was how Faith got the £50 notes in the first place. Now that was some day.

Faith arrived back home from a hard day's slog at the New Forest District

Council. She'd worked there since leaving university and after years of climbing the greasy poll, now held the respectable position of Head of Strategic Local Planning. Endless hours of unpaid overtime, all round gut-busting, and untold sacrifices helped Faith secure the role. Two days into the job, she wondered what it had all been for. Most days she was caught in the middle with her hands tied, trying to strike an unattainable balance between local authority initiatives, property developers, community groups, the general public, the environment, and any other minority group or worthy cause the council saw fit to champion.

At forty-six, Faith felt more like eighty-six and hated her job with a passion. She loathed the politics, the rules, the regulations, the red tape, the green belt, the brown belt, her boss, and her inept colleagues who couldn't perform their way out of a paper bag and believed they were untouchable by the firing squad. Yes, she hated every last thing about it. Each day was torture, and each minute in that place sapped a little more of Faith's spark. She was drowning, slowly dying inside, and if she stayed, she knew she would end up making herself sick. Either that or she would maim a colleague very badly.

The years being employed in dull, dreary grey offices, pushing paper and attending interminable meetings, had Faith yearning for the freedom of self-employment. Her dream was to own and run a quaint village tea shop. She pictured it with vintage decor, curtains hanging at the leaded-light windows, white linen tablecloths covering old, knotty wooden tables. There would be crisp cotton napkins, mismatched vintage floral cups, saucers, and side plates. She'd serve tea in china teapots, all made with loose tea leaves, and definitely none of this tea bag nonsense. There would be homemade cakes that were freshly baked every day, wafting welcoming smells around the place. Sandwiches made from artisan breads and filled with salad from her own vegetable garden, and she would name it Rose's Tea Shop, after her mum. It would be her business, full of colour, authenticity, and comforting smells. A place to nurture one's soul.

After dumping her jacket and bag in the hallway, Faith headed straight for the kitchen to make a cup of tea – her usual after-work routine. With tea made in the white china pot, she sat herself down at the refectory-style kitchen table, kicked off her sensible black court shoes, and undid the button on her navy suit trousers. After pouring her tea, she sipped it, savouring the taste. It was never quite the same at work, or anywhere else for that matter. Faith knew that when she opened her tea shop, she would make the best cup of tea for miles around.

'Oh, I so want lots of money,' Faith whined at the ceiling. They'd been saving, but at this rate, it would be years before they had enough. 'I want piles of £50 notes so that I can leave my job and set up my own tea shop,' Faith said as she closed her eyes, imagining the day when she could finally hand in her notice at work. A sound from the hall startled her. Her eyes shot open and she looked around. 'What's that?' It sounded like the postman poking letters through the letterbox. 'That's odd.' Faith concentrated her hearing, not ready to move from her comfy position, hands wrapped around her teacup. The noise intensified.

'Is someone pushing through lots of junk mail? They'd better not be!' Putting down her cup, Faith stood up. It could be kids messing around. 'Alright, alright, that's enough,' she said as she opened the kitchen door to the hallway. 'What on earth is that?' Faith walked towards the front door, not believing her eyes. *They must be fake.* She bent down and looked at the notes. *Toy money from a game perhaps? Maybe kids pulling a stunt, trying to make people believe they'd been given piles of cash.* Faith opened the front door. No one was there. She closed the door and blinked her eyes as she crouched down. Slowly her fingers touched the pile of £50 notes scattered on the mat and spilling onto the Victorian mosaic tiles. She picked one up. *It feels real.* She held it to the light. *It looks real.* 'It's got the watermark and metal strip and everything.' Faith sat down on the floor, pulled out the band holding back her hair, and scratched her head. She knew she was stressed from work, but there could be no mistake that these notes did look real. Faith grinned. *They can't be.* Her tired mind raced as it attempted to work it all out.

'Now, let me think. I asked for money. Actually, I asked for piles of £50 notes. And now I've got piles of £50 notes.' Faith laughed. *This is stupid.* 'It must be some sort of joke.' *Maybe there are hidden cameras in the hallway.* She stood up and looked around, running her hands over the pictures, along the top of the picture rail, under the console table, inside the lamp shade. No evidence of espionage. 'This can't be real.' Her brain whirled. *Is it real? Maybe I'm dreaming.* Faith didn't know if she should feel happy or freaked out. 'Perhaps someone's won lots of money and gone round to random homes giving it all away. You do hear of people who have loads of money giving it away because it's become a burden,' she said, talking out loud, hoping it would help her make sense of it. Faith didn't understand that mentality, although it could explain the money in her hallway.

'I'm home, love,' Terry said one hour later as he opened the front door. He always said that when he came in. Terry was a man of routine who oozed kindness and honesty. And it was this honesty bit that worried Faith as she sat in the kitchen facing bundles of cash.

'In the kitchen,' Faith called out. Once Terry had relieved himself of his briefcase and suit jacket, he opened the kitchen door.

'Strewth!' Terry stared at Faith sitting at the table still in her work clothes, small stacks of money in front of her. 'What's that? Did you rob a bank?' Terry asked, now smiling as he assumed it was fake and related to Faith's work in some way. *Probably to do with that team building event she's attending soon.* The council was partial to a team building event or two. Terry couldn't stand the cringe-inducing things and did everything he could to avoid them.

'I'll put the kettle on,' Faith said more calmly than she felt. It hadn't been kids messing around or an anonymous wealthy benefactor trying to relieve their encumbrance. Faith had asked again for lots of money, for piles of £50 notes in fact, only this time, she was in the hallway when she asked. This time, she saw what happened.

In silence, Terry sat down, not liking the conclusions he was jumping to in his mind. *Has she really robbed a bank? Perhaps not a bank, that's pushing it a bit far, but maybe the local shop or post office. Oh no! She's got in with the wrong crowd, hasn't she, and started dealing drugs. Would she do that? Surely not.* Terry suddenly questioned whether he knew his wife at all. *I know she hates her job, but we've got a plan. We're saving. Perhaps she had a bad day and flipped out. You do hear of these things.* Terry's brain was in turmoil.

It took thirty minutes and a demonstration to persuade Terry that she hadn't stolen anything. Anxious to prove her innocence, Faith took Terry's hand and led him to the front door. Upon her command, more money came gushing out of the letterbox.

'Strewth! What the...?' Terry knelt down, staring at the cash flowing from the letterbox. 'This is a joke, right?' Faith shook her head. 'It's got to be some sort of prank,' Terry said. 'Oh, I know, it's like those magic tricks that Dynamo does, isn't it?' Terry opened the front door. There was no one there. Money still poured into the hallway. 'This can't be...' Terry turned to Faith with a bewildered expression. Faith shrugged.

'That's what I thought at first,' she said.

'Strewth!' Terry quickly closed the door and stood with his back pressed firmly against it, money cascading around his body. He slid down the door until he was sitting on the floor and picked up two of the notes. They felt genuine. They looked like the real deal.

'That's enough money now!' Faith said. Terry turned toward his wife, confused. 'Stop!' Faith said. The money cascade halted.

'Oh my...' Terry was flabbergasted as he watched the stream of money stop at Faith's bidding. Terry stroked the cash. 'Strewthing hell!' It was the most Faith had ever heard Terry swear.

'Come on, let's get this lot together and put it with the rest in the kitchen.' Faith began picking up the notes and Terry followed her lead. 'We'll have to take it to the police tomorrow,' Faith said, more for Terry's benefit than hers.

'Sure.' Terry trailed behind Faith with his hands full of cash, dazed.

'It's almost certainly phoney,' Faith said. All of a sudden, an idea flashed into her mind. *Hold on. If it is fake, it's no good taking it to the police, is it?* Terry unloaded more notes onto the table and sat down. He felt dizzy. 'What if I try to bank one of them? They always test the large denominations to see if they're counterfeit.' Faith couldn't stand the thought of handing it over to the police tomorrow. 'If it's dodgy, I'll feign shock and surprise, and say a tradesperson gave it to me. I'll say a plumber, or someone like that, gave it to me as change for a job they did for us.' Faith was now thinking on her feet. If it turned out to be a bogus note, she was sure she could wriggle out of it somehow. On the other hand, it could be real. *My God!* That was too much to contemplate.

Terry was quiet, mulling it over, battling with his conscience. 'I'm not sure, Faith. What if they rumble you? They might call security or the police. You could get arrested. No, it's too risky.' Terry was torn. He disliked the idea of his wife putting herself on the line, however he wasn't bold enough to do anything like that himself. And if the money was legit, could he honestly hand it over to the police? Terry struggled inside. After twenty or so minutes of Faith's gentle cajoling, Terry agreed that she would try to bank one of the notes tomorrow during her lunch break. It was a gamble, but both were dying to know one way or the other.

The next day, sweating buckets as she waited in the queue at the bank, Faith nearly fainted as the cashier called out, 'Can I help you, madam?' to her. With her heart hammering in her chest and legs wobbling, she made her way over to cashier Chantelle, who was wearing far too much orange fake tan. Everything slowed and came into sharp focus as Faith shoved her paying-in book, containing one of the notes, towards the cashier. She had planned to say she'd like to pay in some cash, but the words stuck in her throat. Orange Chantelle began the usual tests on the note. *Twinkle, twinkle little star, how I wonder what you are. Up above the world so high, like a diamond in the sky...* Faith had to do something to stop herself from throwing up.

'Anything else I can help you with today, Mrs Radford?' said Orangina as she stamped the paying-in book and pushed it back towards Faith, fake tan stains evident on her palms. Faith gripped the counter to steady herself. 'Does that mean it's okay? Has it passed the checks? Is it a real £50 note?' she wanted to ask. She couldn't. Faith shook her head and strained a smile, unwilling to trust anything else. Her heart danced in her chest, her pulse loud in her ears. She had to get out of there before she crumpled. Carefully, Faith replaced the paying-in book into her bag and walked towards the door. The door was so far away. Would she ever get out of this building? Her face was flushed and her body felt heavy. She expected an alarm to sound as she opened the door and armed guards to rugby tackle her to the ground. They didn't. As soon as Faith was a safe distance from the bank, she grabbed her mobile phone and with shaking hands, called Terry. She would have to pull herself together before she went back to work. Terry was on his lunch break waiting for the call and was relieved to hear his wife calling from the street and not a police cell.

'I've deposited the money,' Faith said as steady as she could. These were the exact words they'd agreed upon the night before.

'That's great. Shall I cook dinner tonight?' This question was code for 'Did the note pass the checks?' If she said, 'Yes', he would know it was real. 'Hold on, what's that? Can you hear that clicking sound? I think the signal's bad,' Terry said.

'Can you hear me?' Faith said. She could hear it too.

'That's better, it's stopped. I said, shall I cook tonight?' Terry asked again.

'Yes, love,' Faith said.

'Strewthing...' Terry's calm collapsed. He was less robust than Faith.

'Anyway, got to go. See you tonight.' Faith ended the call before Terry blew it.

'Okay,' Terry whispered into the phone. He stood up, feeling sick. He needed the toilet and fast. *Now what are we going to do? The money is only strewthing well real!*

For three whole days they did nothing, reeling from the shock and still trying to get their heads around everything. But slowly and surely, they allowed themselves to accept, then to believe, and finally they began to plan.

'We can pay off the mortgage. Oh, just think about that, being mortgage free,' Faith said. 'We could buy our tea shop. Terry, we could set up our tea shop now. We don't have to wait. I could leave the council.'

It was enticing, alluring, sucking them both in. Over the next fortnight, Faith continued to ask for more money and their letterbox delivered. Forget trying to do things the conventional way by working themselves into the ground. Stuff waiting until retirement to do want they wanted. Before, they had no choice; now the money was giving them choice and lots of it. Faith was determined to make all their dreams come true, and not years down the line when they were both dead on their feet, but as soon as possible.

'Just a bit more,' Faith said. 'Perhaps a few more thousand to get me through the first year of trading at the tea shop.' 'Another chunk to cover the

renovation of the tea shop. You never know what state the place will be in.'
'Oh, I'll need good staff too. They don't come cheap.' She was hooked. And
as Faith's craving increased, Terry's anxiety followed suit. It felt so good and
yet so very wrong. *Is it illegal what we're doing?* Terry didn't know, and there was
no one he could talk to. *No one must know.* Yet how would they explain away
all this extra money to friends and family? *Will the tax man be after us? How do
they classify money coming through your letterbox? Is it capital gains or earnings or a
windfall?* It was getting too much for Terry, and he vowed to speak to Faith.

They'd had a lovely weekend together and she was in a good mood, mainly
due to her recent accumulation of £50 notes, so on the Sunday evening Terry
decided to speak to Faith. Unsurprisingly, they were at odds. Faith saw the
money as their only route to complete freedom, while Terry saw it as a disaster
waiting to happen.

'Something's bound to go wrong, Faith. It can't be this easy, it just can't
be,' he argued. The discussion got heated, and Terry was beside himself. 'I
can't take it anymore!' Terry shouted. Faith had never heard her husband
shout before. He was a sweet, gentle-mannered man. Faith wrapped her arms
around him and promised she would stop. She didn't tell him she was going
to get up during the night and do one last push. Then it would be over; she
would let it go. Then she should have enough. Plenty in fact.

Faith never got the chance to do her final push.

'It's so dark,' Faith said as she held Terry's hand tight. They'd been bundled
into the back of a black van by men dressed in black who hadn't told them
what was going on or where they were taking them. Both Terry and Faith
assumed it was because of the money. Terry had pleaded their case, but with
notes showered everywhere and hanging out of Faith's clothing, it did look a
bit suspicious. Innocent people counting their savings or lottery winnings
would surely not be hiding it. Not a single word was uttered by these men in
black as they apprehended them, and that played heavy on Terry's mind.

'They're meant to tell us about our rights. You know, when they say, "You
have the right to remain silent." They didn't say anything like that.' Terry was
indignant. How dare they? 'They didn't even handcuff us. Surely they're

meant to do that.'

'I don't know. I don't know what's going on,' Faith said. As she leant closer into Terry, a crumpling noise came from her bra. She smiled sheepishly. It was a £50 note.

'This isn't right. Something's not right.' Terry put his arm around Faith's shoulder.

'I know. They didn't even have proper uniforms either. Who are they?' Faith asked. Whoever they were, they didn't want to be identified. They looked like riot police dressed in black clothing with black helmets which covered the bottom part of their faces, and they wore dark wraparound glasses. It was evening, for pity's sake. You don't need sunglasses at night. Who wears sunglasses at night?

'I've got a bad feeling about this. They're meant to show us their identification at least before they arrest us. What if they're not police?' Terry said.

'Don't say that.' Faith was suddenly petrified. They should have put up more of a fight. They believed them to be the police coming to arrest them over the money; now Faith wasn't sure who they were and what they wanted.

It was tricky to say how long they travelled with time distorting as they fretted. Both were frightened not knowing what was going on, and it was even scarier when they stopped and the back doors opened to six menacing men. Faith thought she might faint, and Terry fought hard not to wet himself. As quick as anything, four of the men jumped into the back of the vehicle, handcuffed Faith's and Terry's hands behind their backs, and put loose sacks over their heads. *This isn't how they arrest people.* Terry's heart pounded in his chest. The men in black virtually carried them out of the van and along a hard walkway. Buttons were pressed on a keypad, followed by a clicking sound, then a door opened. The difference in temperature told them they'd moved into an air-conditioned building. They were herded along through three more doors, each with security pads and keys being punched. The fourth door didn't seem to have a security pad, although Faith still heard whirling and clicks as the door opened.

Faith was guided to sit down on a cold, hard plastic chair. One of the men took off the sack and freed her wrists before he left the room. She was alone.

Where's Terry? She found herself in what looked like a cell. Or perhaps it was an interview room. She wasn't sure. She sat at a small, square Formica table with two plastic chairs positioned the other side of the table. They were similar to the ones the council had for their meeting rooms – cheap and uncomfortable. The plastered walls were painted light grey, and the floor was concrete and unforgiving. In the corner stood a seatless, stainless-steel toilet with one roll of toilet paper next to it. Faith shuddered. In the opposite corner was a single bed that looked about as comfortable as the concrete floor and on one wall, a large and obvious two-way mirror. Faith had seen enough films to know she was being watched.

Terry was in a similar room next door, but unlike Faith, Terry had used the stainless-steel toilet in the corner. He'd been busting to go since they left the house and it was either that or wet himself. He knew they, whoever they were, probably saw it all, and that only added to his anxiety and humiliation.

'What do you mean you don't know?' said one of the two men, now sitting opposite Faith. They were dressed in dark navy suits with white shirts and dark navy ties. One of them wore his tie with small red spots. *His way of asserting his individuality,* Faith thought. She'd met his type before. You didn't get to her level in the Council without meeting bags full of repressed men, who in the minutest way, offer up feeble attempts at rebellion and sticking it to The Man. *Pathetic.*

'Well, I don't, not really,' Faith said, not knowing what else to tell them. This question had been asked several different ways and she was at the stage where she might just make something up to get them off her back.

'So you're telling me the £50 notes just appeared?' Mr Nice, the red-spotted tie wearer, asked. Faith had decided he was the nicest one of the two, even with his lame attempt at dissent. He was chubby with black curly hair and had a momentary hint of a smile when he first came into the room. He'd erased it swiftly when Faith responded with her own desperate smile. Mr Nice had reassured Faith she was in no danger and wasn't under arrest, and told her she was merely assisting the government with their enquiries, which Faith thought was rather peculiar. And he had organised a cup of tea for her, horrible though it was. Anyway, Faith had named him Mr Nice. Hardly original, but it was the best she could muster under the fraught circumstances. The other one, Mr Nasty, barely spoke and mainly stared at Faith through narrowed eyes. He was tall and gangly and had a hooked, thin nose. Mr Nasty unnerved Faith with his eyes that were too close together for her liking.

'Yes, as I keep saying, they just appeared'—Faith pulled off another piece of skin from her thumb cuticle—'from the letterbox.' As the words left her mouth, she knew it sounded far-fetched.

'The letterbox?' asked Mr Nice. Mr Nasty lost his eyebrows under his lanky fringe. He kept doing that. Mr Nice and Mr Nasty looked at each other. Faith wondered how long it would be before they rang for the men in white coats. 'So you're telling me that money appeared through your letterbox?' Mr Nice stood up and paced around the room. 'Who put the money through your letterbox?'

'No one.'

'No one?'

'When I opened the door, no one was there.' Faith sat on her hands. 'The money kept coming out of the letterbox. It was like the invisible man was the other side, posting it through the door.' Faith's shoulders drooped as she sighed. She knew how it seemed.

'The invisible man? Pushing money through your letterbox?' Mr Nice asked. Faith went to smile then stopped herself. The whole thing sounded farcical. Completely bonkers. Surely she'd wake up in a minute to the sound of her alarm going off. Mr Nice sat back in his chair, his head churning as he observed Faith. They'd been going round in circles and no matter how he phrased it, her answers were the same. 'Why was the money coming through your letterbox?' Faith shrugged. So far she'd held back on telling them she'd asked for it, wished for it. *I'll have to tell them sooner or later. But what if they think I've got special powers and take me away to a secret location to perform experiments on me?*

'Faith, why was it coming through your letterbox?' Mr Nice was beginning to lose his patience, and so was Faith. She looked down. 'What did you do to cause the money to come through your letterbox?' Silence. 'You did something to cause it, didn't you?' Mr Nice asked. Mr Nasty continued to glare at Faith. Silent still.

It was no good. She would have to tell them. Faith sighed heavily. She should have known the money was too good to be true. Faith felt beaten. She couldn't win. At least if she told them the truth, they may let Terry go. He wouldn't be able to do time in prison; if that's where they were headed, it would kill him. 'Faith, we know you did something to cause it.' Steadily, Faith raised her head and made eye contact with Mr Nice. He didn't look evil. He didn't look like he would experiment on her. Something in his face was reminiscent of her old music teacher from school who was generally a big softie and constantly let them off their homework. 'What did you do, Faith? If I'm going to help you and your husband, you have to tell me what you did,' Mr Nice said, exasperated. Faith looked down at the table.

'I asked for it,' Faith whispered. Both men raised their eyebrows. 'I asked for lots of money. I wished for it. The next thing I know it was pouring through our letterbox.' There, she'd said it. Mr Nice and Mr Nasty turned towards at each other, stood up, and left the room without another word.

'Oh no!' Faith said as she rested her forehead on the table. Having never heard of this phenomenon before, she wasn't sure of her rights around conjuring up money out of thin air. Faith and Terry had found nothing on the internet under paranormal activities, the law of attraction, or bizarre manifestations. Maybe she did have special powers. Faith closed her eyes and sighed as she felt the imminence of experiments to her body.

****

"Before every evolutionary shift, elements of the future changes are always expressed and experienced incrementally. It is a preview of what lies ahead, with people gaining some functions at relatively low levels, within a small area. It makes the process, in evolutionary terms, moderate and measured. Yet for many, it will still seem extreme, colossal, and overwhelming. Like one of your sci-fi movies. The stuff of wild imaginings. And for those who fail to remember that you are the deciders in this game, it will appear to go against all logic and reason.

Shifts and leaps in consciousness are not linked to certain times or dates, as some of you have believed. So don't panic that at a predefined time, on a marked day, something catastrophic will happen in a puff of smoke. It never happens like that. It is always progressive and step by step. Yet many will still feel out of control and overwrought, drowning in something they believe they have no control over.

Remember that you and your world are made of energy with an intelligence that is evolving and expanding. Everything in your world has been, and always will be, created and controlled by you. You set up this whole game, from the beginning to the end and everything in between. There is no one else here except you. My dear One, everything that happens is all down to you.

So when all around you are losing their heads and wondering what on earth is happening, rest assured this is not being done to you. And it is not due to the chemical plants or global warming, or a displeased God punishing you for untold sins, or karma being dished out. And it is definitely not Judgement Day and the end of the world. It is you, the creator of all and everything. It is humankind, awakening from the illusion. It is You resurrecting. It is the beginning of your journey back home to Oneness."

Chapter Five

The change to the landscape of the New Forest was swift and radical. New Forest ponies, donkeys, cattle, and deer, which once roamed freely, were taken to other nature reserves and sanctuaries. Some were shot. Residents were turned out of their homes and evacuated from the area. Businesses were forced to close down. Security perimeters and checkpoints were urgently erected. What was once a thriving tourist destination was now an eerily quiet location, converted into an international hub of intrigue and speculation.

Area One encompassed most of the town of Ringwood, the village of Burley, many rivers and waterways, parts of the Kingston Great Common nature reserve, and some densely wooded areas of the New Forest.

Why it was happening, nobody was certain, although everyone had a theory. The anti-fracking movement claimed the destructive method of oil and gas extraction was to blame and demanded an outright ban on all fracking around the world. Environmentalists said it was caused by a combination of chemicals and toxins leached into the environment, destroying the ozone layer, and called for the immediate abolition of all harmful chemicals and toxins. Some extreme religious groups believed it to be just punishment for people's immorality and wickedness. The Pope preached it was the world's sins being brought to bear. A few claimed it was Armageddon. But the majority agreed, led by the science community, that an anomaly had occurred in the energetic field of the earth, causing an energy portal to open.

Up until the Manifesters surfaced, authorities believed they had an unhealthy spike in mental health issues, with Thought Readers, Sensors, and

Seers being misunderstood and misdiagnosed. Once the tangible displays of the Manifesters were witnessed, word spread like wildfire and it became a losing battle for the government and security services as they attempted to contain and manage the information. With everyone's insatiable craving for the internet and social media, it was impossible. Even before the lockdown of Area One, many had spoken out, uploading videos on YouTube, sharing stories on Facebook and blogs, and tweeting with hash tags: 'dreamscomingtrue', 'iamtheoneandonly', and 'theendisnigh' – all trending.

A wave of enraptured terror charged around the globe at lightning speed and in seconds, every country was hearing about the magical powers rising up in a sleepy part of England. Feelings ran high as people, entranced and overwhelmed, heard the news. Many disbelieved, a few were intoxicated, and most made swift travel arrangements: destination – the New Forest, England.

Chapter Six

A few nights into Faith's detention, as she lay down on the hard bed drifting off to sleep, she heard Terry speak. 'I hope Faith's okay. Please let her be okay.' His words were audible, as if he were standing right next to her. Opening her eyes, she stared at the ceiling. *That's odd.* Faith pushed herself up onto her elbows. She was still alone in her darkened locked cell.

'I think I'm losing it.' Faith sat up.

'Faith, I love you wherever you are. Stay strong.' It was Terry's voice again, as clear as anything. She got up from the bed, eyes darting around.

'Where is he? Terry? Are you there?' She went to the door. 'Terry?'

'Stay strong, Faith. Stay strong.'

'Terry?' Faith raised her voice. He was near, really near, she was sure of it. She banged on the door. 'Terry! I'm in here! Terry!' Tears pricked her eyes. He must be outside trying to rescue her. She was finally getting out of this hellhole.

The alarm screeched, making her jump, signalling to Faith they were coming in and she should go and sit on the bed. Faith did as she'd been trained. The door opened and in walked the two guards she saw most days. They were men of few words who gave her food, drink, dated benign books, and every fourth day brought her a clean green jumpsuit, folded up with four days worth of underwear. Because of this, and the fact they never interrogated her, she assumed they were kind – ish.

'Is Terry outside? I thought I heard him,' she said, eager to be reunited with her husband.

'No. No one's outside,' said Guard One. He was taller than Guard Two, and Faith had seen something in his eyes when she begged him not to look in the two-way mirror when she used the toilet for the first time. It might have been pity, she wasn't sure, but she thought he understood. She warmed to Guard One and even though he did his best to give off a stern air, his eyes were expressive, and Faith could sense his feelings just by looking into his eyes. When his mouth remained tightly closed, his eyes spoke, telling Faith that he felt for her. Guard Two had cold, dead eyes.

'I thought I heard him. It was like he was inside the room.' Faith peered into Guard One's eyes. 'Is he next door, is that it? Is that why I can hear him talking?' She saw a fleeting look of concern. 'I heard him talking. I did, honestly,' she pleaded. Guard One looked at Guard Two. *I think she's cracking up*, Guard One thought.

'I am not cracking up, thank you very much.' Faith crossed her arms. Guard One looked at her, his brow furrowed.

'I didn't say anything,' he said.

'Yes, you did. I heard you. You said, "I think she's cracking up", didn't you?' Guard One shook his head bemused. *This is getting freaky.*

'You can say that again,' Faith said.

'Say what again? What do you mean?' Guard One asked.

'You said, "This is getting freaky" and I said, "You can say that again".'

'I didn't say any—' Guard One looked at Guard Two, then nodded towards the door. They almost ran from the room.

Chapter Seven

'Jeez, what the hell are we dealing with here?' Doug Greenlake, Head of MI6 asked after being updated on the increase of Manifesters, Thought Readers, Sensors, and Seers. The heads of operation White Paradox – code name for Area One – were gathered together in Doug's office for an update. The situation was potentially catastrophic, and they knew it. No one had ever experienced anything like it. Not even the longest serving MI5 and MI6 personnel had seen the like, and they had dealt with just about everything the world had to offer, and then some.

'God only knows.' Mike Tremblay, Head of MI5, rubbed his face. Originally Mike had headed up the operation, but the whole thing was growing by the second and would no doubt have an international reach. And although they were pulling together, Mike was glad that the buck had been transferred firmly onto Doug's shoulders. He didn't envy him one bit.

'We'll reconvene again tomorrow at the same time. In the meantime, don't forget to contact me immediately with any new developments,' Doug said to the men and women in front of him. They were out of their depth.

They'd been conducting interviews with the Manifesters to try and get to the bottom of what the hell was going on, but the risk of continuing the interviews with the people who'd developed outlandish abilities had just escalated. Now there was every chance they would know exactly what the interviewers were thinking – their motives, assumptions, and prejudices. Everything would be laid bare. They had to find another way to get to the root cause of this bizarre turn of events.

A frightening thought popped into Doug's head. *It could spread.* Doug stared at his desk with grey, bloodshot eyes. He'd barely slept a wink since the situation had unfolded, getting by on strong coffee and cigarettes. His no-smoking resolution was so out of the window. Doug wasn't just on the edge, he was completely over the other side, flailing around and waiting for the next piece of bad news to whack him into tomorrow. *Someone could have heard or seen that meeting. What if they can pick up on my thoughts and feelings now? Jesus!* Doug crossed himself, bent his head, and recited the Hail Mary prayer, even though he was an atheist. After years drenched in secret service work, it was impossible to believe in any sort of God. But his mum had always drawn strength from her faith and now he was willing to try anything. After finishing his prayer, he sighed wearily, knowing he had exactly the same feelings of dread in the pit of his stomach as before. God probably gave up on him years ago.

During his career, Doug had seen the unthinkable, dealt with things that no person should ever have to deal with, and witnessed the depths of human depravity. Yet even in his darkest, toughest moments he'd known what to do for the safety of his country, for the common good. But this was unchartered territory, a totally different ball game. The Manifesters, Thought Readers, Sensors, and Seers weren't your run-of-the-mill evil, bad, or insane people. For the most part, they were everyday good citizens with normal jobs and lives, but for some unknown reason had developed remarkably gifts.

The next day the White Paradox team met and argued over how to move forward. The government heads in attendance were keen to use Area One as a marketing tool for the country.

'We could use it as leverage to gain more investment,' The prime minster said, seeing pound signs. The chancellor of the exchequer's pointed narrow face became animated as he launched into a brainstorm of how they could market Area One as the place of choice for every person and business. 'What price will that command?' the prime minister asked, smiling and nodding his approval to the chancellor, who smiled back. *Clueless, bloody clueless,* Doug thought. He had enough on his plate. How would he ever secure the resources for this? Doug and Mike had argued for Area One to remain shut down completely, with no one entering the area until they could get a complete grip on what was going on. The prime minister and chancellor disagreed.

'This could be big. Really big,' the prime minister said. Doug knew he meant the profits could be big; the revenue could be big. You could see how their minds worked. 'The deficit would be a thing of the past. The country finally in the black. We'll be able to invest in the country like never before. The electorate will love us,' the prime minister said. Blinded by the potential of pounds, billions of lovely pounds, the prime minister commanded that the area must be opened. Contained and controlled of course, but nevertheless, opened for business. Only then could they turn it into a money-making machine.

With Area One already cordoned off, residents displaced, and all known Manifesters, Thought Readers, Sensors and Seers being held at Harrow Chalk, a detention centre just outside of Bransgore village, the next step was to find a way to control and limit access.

'We need a way to determine whether people can handle it inside Area One. And we can't have people abusing the place. They have to be able to live in this privileged location without any unscrupulous agendas,' Mike said.

'How do we do that? None of us have these powers. How do we even know what it feels like to have these abilities?' Doug asked. People around the table shook their heads and shrugged.

'We need to assess the people before they enter Area One,' Mike added. 'What if we use the people currently displaying the abilities to help us set up some sort of assessment process?' Mike suggested. 'I'm not sure how though, or what the process would look like.' Faces around the table signalled their approval.

'It could work,' Doug said. The truth was, none of them really knew. They were sailing unchartered waters.

'Yes, yes, yes, great idea,' the prime minister said. 'Set it up. Whatever you need. And keep me in the loop.' The prime minister pushed back his chair, stood up, and glanced at his watch. 'Right, got to get back.' The other government ministers stood and followed their leader.

Set it up! Just like that. Jeez! Doug was irritated as he stared at the backs of the prime minister and his minions leaving the room. *He doesn't give a shit. He's only thinking about the money.* Why was Doug so surprised? He'd worked with enough prime ministers over the years. *Could they even persuade these people to work with them?* Doug thought so. The secret service had ways of compelling people to do what they wanted. They really had little choice, and Doug couldn't afford to take 'no' for an answer. *These Thought Readers may already know what we're up to.* Doug shook his head. *Christ, it's a bloody minefield.* Doug had to laugh. Crying wasn't an option.

****

"As these new functions come online, it is not only you who has to adapt, but also your whole planetary setup will need to adjust to assimilate them. It will mean deep, never-seen-before changes for you and your world, and it is critical you consider what these changes will mean.

Manifesters will ultimately no longer want or need anything from anyone else. Thought Readers will have the answers to every question. Sensors will understand what is going on inside every other soul on the planet. Seers will see right through everything and everyone.

Consider for a moment how governments and authorities will treat people when everyone can have, do, or be anything they so choose? How will large corporations deal with the fact they can no longer manipulate, lie, or cheat? When others can see to the very core of them? What will happen to industries when all their deepest, darkest methods are known? And what of the agricultural and farming industries — how will they fair when all animal thoughts and feelings can be experienced by everyone? For it is not just the thoughts and feelings of people you will experience, it is the thoughts and feelings of all living souls on your earth. And how will congregations react when they can see into their religious leader's hearts and minds, and know the truth of their bias and prejudices? What happens when the victims can read the true fear inside their attacker's mind? When they realise the absolute spinelessness, impotence, and true weakness of their perpetrator?

Do you see how tables will turn, and situations and roles will transpose?

Existing rules, regulations, and doctrines will no longer work. They will become old and redundant. Some may panic and try to cling to them, desperate to feel solidity on ever moving ground. Many existing organisations will be superfluous to requirements. Current governments not required. Law and order parameters useless. Coal, gas, and oil no longer needed. Food for all without suffering and killing. Clean water without cost. Resources without pillaging and destruction.

Every single aspect of your world will change. Nothing will escape its touch. Ways of living will alter, relationships will change, hierarchies will decay, and structures will dissolve. All reforming, reshaping, and transforming into a brand-new chapter in your game."

Chapter Eight

It was the dead of night as Trent King and Hudson Story attempted to break into Area One, dressed in black with camouflage paint smeared over their faces. Holding his breath, Trent began cutting through the metal fence. Hudson crouched alongside Trent and looked around anxiously. Pressing the button down to illuminate the face of his watch, Hudson could see they only had two minutes left. That was not good. There was no way they'd make it.

For a number of days, they'd been watching the perimeter of Area One, writing down all observations, working out patterns for the security guard patrols, locating the security cameras, assessing the three-level barrier system, and judging what it would take to cut through them. So far during their attempted break-in, things were panning out as they'd assumed, apart from the time it was taking to cut through this fence. They had severely underestimated the thickness of the metal and needed stronger cutters. It was clear it wasn't going to happen tonight. Although with each shot, they gained vital information for future use.

There were five people in their break-in team - Trent, Hudson, Devon, Will, and Ziva. They met on a forum for people trying out for the Chryso assessment. The five gravitated towards each other after Trent posted an angry question after his third failed attempt. 'Anyone fancy breaking into the New Land?' he wrote. Many slammed him, saying that wasn't the attitude and no wonder he'd failed the assessment. Eventually, a forum moderator banned Trent and closed his account. But not before the other four had corresponded via private message, saying they were up for it.

Hudson looked at his watch and then at Trent's progress.

'We're not going to make it. Let's go,' Hudson whispered, getting nervous. He knew the guard would be around soon.

'I'll speed up.' Trent upped the pace, reluctant to give in.

'We've got to go now!' Hudson said. Trent exhaled loudly. Admitting defeat, Trent and Hudson raced to their safe place in an area of thick hedging away from the perimeter. As they covered themselves with branches and foliage, an armed guard walked past.

'That was close,' Trent said smiling, a mix of exhilaration and terror running through him.

'Too close.' Hudson shook his head. 'That was too close.'

'Don't ask me how or where I got it, alright?' Devon looked at the surprised faces of Trent, Hudson, Will, and Ziva, her dark eyes warning them as she rolled out an A1-sized piece of paper on an old wallpaper pasting table. Using their mugs of tea, she held down the drawing at each corner. Having these plans of Area One was perilous, and the mere fact they were looking at them would probably mean instant arrest for all five.

Alright! What a woman! Trent thought as it became evident he was looking at a security map for Area One. Devon was two years older than Trent and to him, seemed so together. She'd done so much with her life already – dancing, theatre, spoke three languages – and he was infatuated by her toned dancer's body, cropped jet hair, flawless olive skin, and large chocolate eyes.

'What do you think, Trent?' Devon asked.

'What?' Trent hadn't heard a thing.

'Have I been wasting my breath?' Devon scowled at Trent. Even standing there frustrated, with her hands on her hips, she looked amazing. Years of ballet and dance classes gave her a grace and poise that few young people had these days.

'Sorry, miles away. What did you say?' Trent cleared his mind of all raunchy thoughts. Ziva rolled her eyes at Trent. Will winked at him, guessing at Trent's daydream. Will, with his obsession for music, classic cars, and Shakespeare, liked Trent. They were the same age and shared a love for music, drifting through life, and working part-time in meaningless jobs. Will and Trent hit it off the moment they met.

All five were driven to gain entry into Area One and whether through failure at the Chryso assessment or for other reasons, they were all now prepared to resort to illegal tactics. And that's why they were in Ziva's garage looking at a drawing of the security perimeters and scheming the next break-in.

'So as I was saying, this gives us a much better chance to plan a successful break-in,' Devon said, giving Trent a I-hope-you-were-listening look. 'I think our schedule for guard patrol is pretty spot on, and using this information, we should be able to work out more accurate timings for getting through each perimeter as well,' Devon said.

'Do we know if this is everything? What if they've updated things since this?' Ziva asked, mistrusting Devon and her drawings. She wasn't sure about Devon, too beautiful for her own good. And the way she fluttered those long dark eyelashes at the boys, completely shameful. Painful memories of Ziva's ex's betrayal were triggered every time she saw how the three guys reacted to Devon. Ziva was the oldest of the group at twenty-six and lived alone after recently splitting from her husband, Tate.

'We'll never know for sure until we try. Let's think positively though. This could get us into the New Land.' Devon smiled, hoping she was right. *She's always so bloody positive.* Ziva raged inside at Devon's go-to attitude and stunning good looks. Ziva certainly wasn't what you would call ugly; more forgettable. Her square face was set with a permanent frown, her eyes were far too small for her liking, and she made little of her unruly, curly blonde hair, which she often tied back. Mind you, Ziva was rather proud of her toned body, which came from working as a supervisor at her local gym, although that was about it and next to Devon, she felt decidedly grotesque. It was too much for Ziva. She had to get out of the garage and away from Devon before she did something stupid.

'Tea anyone?' Ziva painted on a smile. After counting the nods, she headed to the kitchen to make the tea, glad to be alone for a moment.

'This was not meant to happen.' Devon laid her head back on the clean white-cotton-covered pillow, impressed that Trent had such linen on his bed.

'I know,' Trent said. 'Is it so bad though?'

'You know the answer to that.'

'Surely the people living inside Area One do this. It can't be part of the rules, can it?' Trent sniggered and gathered Devon closer.

'Who knows?' Devon giggled at the thought of enforcing such a rule. Like Trent, she was keen to get into Area One and didn't want anyone or anything getting in her way.

'It'll be alright, you'll see.' Trent ran his hand up and down her bare back, trying to convince her.

'This can only be a one-off, you know that, right?' Devon looked seriously at Trent. He wasn't in a serious mood. 'Don't look at me like that. We can't risk it, Trent. We both want it. And this – us – is not going to help. It'll get in the way.' Devon removed Trent's arm from around her and lay back on the pillow, staring at the ceiling. 'I really want to get in Trent. So do you.' She turned to face him again.

'I know.' Trent sighed, although he honestly didn't feel bad about what had just happened between them.

Devon and Trent were part of the trio, along with Will, who would take a stab at the group's next break-in. The five had worked hard since that night in Ziva's garage and now had a plan they felt confident about. Devon, Trent, and Will had met at Trent's home and, with his mum away on one of her spiritual retreats, were doing a final run through. Will bailed on them after his mum called saying his granddad had taken a fall. Fortunately, it was only minor bruising, but it left the pair alone with two bottles of red wine. After Will left, Trent opened the wine and one thing led to another, and now they were in bed together.

Since the first time Trent saw Devon, he had lusted after her. The same couldn't be said for Devon. It wasn't that she didn't like Trent; it was more that she'd never thought of him in that way. Now she hoped they hadn't jeopardised everything.

'So this is just a one-off then?' Trent said.

'Yes. It's got to be.'

'What if we haven't quite finished this one-off?' Trent asked, a glint his eyes.

'What do you mean?'

'Well, what if we've been taking a five-minute break and the one-off hasn't actually finished?' Trent looked at the alarm clock standing on the wooden chair that served as his bedside table. 'In fact, if I'm not mistaken, we've got a few more hours to go yet.' Trent laughed and rolled on top of Devon.

'Trent!' She laughed and hit him playfully on the arm.

Looking at the perimeter fence, they could hardly believe it. The third level security was far more lax than either of them had previously thought.

'They must be hoping no one gets this far,' Devon said.

'Is that seriously it?' Trent almost laughed. Senses had been heightened for a few hours and stress-related fatigue was setting in. Plus, they were minus Will. After getting through the level one perimeter, Will heard a sound. It was like someone was walking towards them. The three took cover, with Trent and Devon holding their nerve as the noise came closer, and Will running for it. Who knew where he was now. In the middle of the night with fog all around, it was hard to tell what was moving in their direction. Thankfully, it was only a fox.

Both stubbornly determined, neither was willing to concede defeat and they pledged to go on without Will. 'Foxgate' meant they missed the perfect gap between guards, so they had to wait over an hour for the next slot. Locating a ditch, they bedded down and hid. It was dicey, especially as it would be getting light at the next safe time to break through the second perimeter. Water and energy bars were eked out, and they covered themselves in leaves and undergrowth. Then they waited. The unseasonably cool June night air penetrated their bodies, and it didn't help that Devon wet herself, making her feel cold and uncomfortable. She had tried, unsuccessfully, to have a pee lying down without moving, which for a woman was virtually impossible. Now Devon sported a large wet patch on her camouflage trousers. When the time was right, Trent and Devon made it through the second perimeter without a hitch. After which, Trent made light work of the final fencing. Now they were actually inside Area One.

Carefully, they edged around the boundary looking for a suitable route in, passing through a mass of tall tree ferns with Devon leading the way. Trent offered to lead, but she rounded on him. 'You don't have to protect me, you know. I'm quite capable, even though I'm not a man!' Devon whispered angrily. Trent shut up and let her carry on. The fog was dense, making it difficult to see and without any warning, Devon abruptly came face to face with a security guard relieving himself in the ferns. That was the trouble with fog; you couldn't see anything until you were right on top of it. For a split second, Devon and the guard stared at each other, him still urinating.

'Oh, shoot!' Devon said without thinking. She could have kicked herself. She should have pretended she was meant to be inside Area One, just one of the residents taking a very early ramble, in the fog, along the security fence. Well, maybe not. Her look told him otherwise, head to toe in dirty, camouflage clothing and wearing a guilty, frightened look on her face.

'Run!' Trent shouted as the scene came into view. He went to grab Devon's hand as he turned but missed and ran off empty-handed. Quickly zipping up his flies, but still dribbling, the guard pulled out a gun and pointed it at Devon's head.

'Don't even think about moving, missy,' said the guard. Devon held up her hands. The guard looked over her shoulder. Trent had already fled into the fog.

'Devon, run!' Trent's voice was distant now. He didn't know if she was running behind him or where she was. Devon assumed Trent was probably safe, figuring the guard was hardly likely to fire randomly into the fog. *We were so close.* Devon's thoughts turned to what would become of her. *Maybe they'll let me do the assessment. Perhaps this won't be so bad after all.* Devon tried to ease her mind and soothe herself.

'Both hands on your head, slowly now,' said the guard.

Devon caught sight of the dark urine stain on the guard's trousers around the crotch area. *Obviously hadn't quite finished.*

'Looks like we both wet ourselves,' Devon said as she smiled weakly. Somehow it made him seem less frightening.

'This isn't it,' Will whispered as he climbed down from peering through the window of what seemed to be a satellite control centre inside Area One.

'We're lost. What are we going to do?' Agitated, he ran his fingers through his hair.

'Come on, Will, chill out,' Trent said. They both ducked down and made their way back to safety behind some shrubs.

'There's only one security woman in front of about six or so monitors,' Will said.

'This isn't it then,' Trent mused.

Since Devon's capture and Trent's close call, they'd regrouped and formulated another plan. Trent wanted to go back in immediately. Both Ziva and Hudson thought he was too emotional about Devon's capture and was liable to endanger the whole operation. Trent gave no ground, and finally Ziva and Hudson opted out of the next attempt, handing it over to Trent and Will. If they were unsuccessful, as Ziva knew they would be, it was agreed that all four would go together next time. No one had heard from Devon since that fateful day, and as time slipped by, Trent became more fearful that something dreadful had happened to her. He had to get back in and find her. Nothing and no one would stop him.

'What do we do now?' Will asked, anxiety rising in his voice.

'What we do now, Will, is breathe. And calm.' Trent knew that if Will lost his cool, he could threaten their mission. 'Recite some Shakespeare,' Trent suggested and smiled, knowing this would do the trick, with Will being Shakespeare's number one fan of the twenty-first century. The break-ins unnerved Will, and his usual easygoing, chilled-out manner was temporarily lost. Mainly because he wanted it so badly. Just thinking about the sort of life that was possible, where anything he dreamt of could come true, made the whole thing a bit too intense. Will smiled at Trent, his eyes suddenly shining at the utterance of his hero's name. He closed his eyes, took some deep breaths, and muttered to himself, 'Once more unto the breach, dear friends, once more...'

The authorities constantly hammered home the need to control thoughts and feelings whilst inside Area One. The potential for suddenly developing an ability was real. With no warning, any ability could become active in you, and if your head was all over the place, it could get very messy indeed. The theory was that if you kept yourself in a perpetual state of calm, with clear positive thoughts, nothing too drastic would happen. It was easier said than done. Although with consistent practise, the majority saw a steady improvement in this regard. Up until Area One's advent, people had no cause or motivation to master their thoughts and emotions, preferring instead the drama and turmoil of reacting aimlessly to events and things happening all around them, based upon borrowed and outmoded beliefs. But the enticement and potential of Area One made people willing to change.

'Okay.' Will opened his eyes, his face serene. 'The master has worked his magic again.'

'Good.' Trent nodded, not sure whether Will was referring to Shakespeare or him.

'I've only gone and done it. Oh! My! Word! I've done it.' Will woke Trent up from his uncomfortable position under some large mountain laurel shrubs, his excitement spilling over into laughter. Rubbing his eyes, Trent tried to focus on the inanimate object in front of them.

'Holy cow! What's that?' Trent couldn't work out what he was looking at. Was it an apparition?

'I figured we'd need some wheels to get us around,' Will said casually. 'And if we can't find a place to stay, we can always sleep in it.' Will felt smug as he stroked the bonnet of the silver-grey Aston Martin DB5 car. Suddenly the penny dropped, and Trent shook his head as he stared from the shiny sleek car, to Will, and back again. Will had manifested.

'Will, this is too over the top, man. We'll get spotted,' Trent said, although he couldn't stop himself from laughing. Will was a curious fellow – a music-loving, Shakespearian petrolhead. Who would have thought? They'd both been trying to manifest since they crossed the third perimeter security fence and so far, neither had managed it, until now. 'Couldn't you have rustled up a nice family hatchback? A simple Ford or Vauxhall would have done the trick.' They'd seen a couple of these moving around the roads seemingly unhindered. With so few cars in Area One, anything like this Aston Martin would immediately draw unwanted attention. Will smiled and sighed.

'I know. In truth I didn't think I'd be able to do it. I couldn't sleep and was trying to get us some food. That didn't work. Then my mind wandered to all the luxury things I could wish for when I finally cracked it. I remembered this Aston Martin I'd seen which belonged to our neighbour back in Cornwall.' By all accounts, Will came from a wealthy family who lived in Cornwall. As he moved through his teenage years Will increasingly found Cornwall too quiet, so now he lived in the buzzing town of Brighton, with all its rich and colourful eccentricities. 'The neighbour saw me admiring the car and asked if I wanted a spin. I tell you, mate, it was awesome. So I sat here and recalled the feeling of riding around in it, the smell of the leather interior, the throaty roar of the engine. For a second, I really felt like I was in the car again. Then, upon my soul, it was here. Incredible.' Will laughed, not quite believing he'd done it. Because despite Area One and its proof of instant manifestation, in most people, there still lay seeds of doubt.

'I must admit, it is a stunner, mate.' Trent couldn't help feeling slightly jealous that Will had manifested before him.

They soon found one of the downsides to manifesting – reversing the manifestation. One of the key things to success with manifesting was mastering your emotional state. When you desired something and felt good about that thing, when you were relaxed, clear, and believed without holding on, the manifestation happened. When you were stressed, forcing it, uncertain of your ability, with your mind flitting from 'Yes I do' to 'No I don't', it rarely happened. And that's exactly what was happening to Will as he frantically tried to get rid of the Aston Martin.

'You're not concentrating,' Trent accused.

'Of course I am.' Will closed his eyes.

'Come on, Will. Get into that good feeling place again, only this time, imagine what it would be like to not have the car. As if it doesn't exist,' Trent said, not really helping.

'I'm trying. I don't think it's going to work. I'm all over the place.' Will opened his eyes. The trouble was, Will didn't want the car to go. That was another thing getting in the way. The car was lovely. Gorgeous. The best car he'd ever seen. And it was his, all his. He didn't want to make it disappear. Surely there was a way to sneak it out. Will gave it another go. Nothing. All of a sudden, he burst out laughing. 'Look at my car. That's my car. I own it. I made it, out of thin air.' Will couldn't help but see the comical peculiarity of the situation and at that point, Trent lost it too, and they both cracked up.

'We're going to have to get it together,' Trent said, wiping tears of laughter from his cheeks.

'I know. I know,' Will said. It was so funny though. Never before had he witnessed something so far out there.

'Why don't we camouflage it?' Trent suggested, and Will reluctantly agreed. Pulling branches and leaves from nearby trees, shrubs, and ferns, they gradually covered the Aston Martin.

'All that glisters is not gold in here,' Will muttered as he secured some greenery under the windscreen wipers. 'Seems sacrilege.'

'It does. I know,' Trent said. Area One was a strange place. It had captured the world's attention, but for the first time ever, Trent admitted that maybe the authorities were right when they said there were downsides to living inside Area One.

Knowing it was too dangerous to stay near the car, they set off towards the next building on their map which they hoped was the main control centre. Progress was slow as they moved from bush to tree to hedge, at times crouched down, sometimes wriggling on their stomachs, frequently creeping slowly, looking all around and occasionally running for cover. It wasn't as exhilarating as actors made it look in the movies. Instead, it was uncomfortable, tiring, and dirty, and they ended up with thorns in painful places. After travelling a few hours, they stopped.

'I'm starving. We need food,' Trent said. They found a secluded ditch and sat down. A plump, grey wood pigeon landed nearby and pecked at the ground. 'I'm not at the Bear Grylls stage just yet,' Trent said.

'Me neither.'

'Ready to give it a shot then?' Trent asked.

'Okay,' Will agreed. But feeling hollow and ravenous were not good emotional states to be in when trying to manifest food.

'Right, let's get into it.' Trent shifted position and sat upright. Will followed. 'What about focusing on some burgers?' Will nodded. They closed their eyes. 'Visualise a lovely juicy burger, with lots of bits on it ... crispy lettuce, ripe tomatoes...'

'Yeah, and garlic mayo with barbecue sauce. Oh yes. Let's make it a double, with melted cheese.' Will salivated at the thought.

'My stomach's rumbling, I'm so hungry,' Trent said.

'Don't think like that, think about eating it. The smell of it. The taste. Mmmm.' Will was getting there. 'Can you smell it?'

'I think so.' Trent was sure they were making progress.

'Me too. Do you think we've done it?' Will was reluctant to open his eyes for fear of seeing nothing.

'Maybe.' Trent's stomach groaned.

'I think they're there. Two juicy burgers. I think we've done it this time, Trent,' Will said, opening his eyes. There was nothing there. 'Rampallians!' Will punched the ground. Trent was discovering this was one of Will's favourite swear words, although he hadn't a clue what it meant. Trent opened his eyes and sighed with disappointment. Their bellies moaned in unison.

'What do you mean you've forgotten the plan?!' Ziva shouted.

'Alright, alright, simmer down everyone,' Hudson said. With his natural smiling face and gentle way with people, Hudson often took on the role of peacemaker. It had rarely been needed within the group, but just lately Ziva had turned from Ms Smiley to Ms Angry. Trent fired daggers at Ziva. Immediately Hudson put his hands out between Ziva and Trent. 'Calm down, you two. You know exactly what can happen if things get out of control.' Trent turned away, unable to look at Ziva's face a moment longer.

'We're not in the Promised Land now, you know!' Ziva's onslaught on Hudson provoked a frown from him.

'I know that, but we should practise the clear mind, positive thought thing all the time,' Hudson said. His kind grey-blue eyes failed to appeal to Ziva, who just gave him a filthy look. 'That's how it's going to be when we get in there tomorrow,' Hudson reasoned.

'*If* we get in there tomorrow.' Ziva looked pointedly at Trent. 'We need the plan and some idiot left it at home.'

'Shut up, Ziva. What's with you tonight? You've turned into the Wicked Witch of the West,' Trent said. They were in Ziva's garage again going through their strategy for what they hoped would be the final break-in attempt tomorrow. This time they were determined to get in and stay in.

Trent and Will's last effort was thwarted by hunger. Unsuccessful at manifesting food and not prepared to go to the shops in case they were found out, they had no choice but to leave. Even though they'd ultimately failed, they had gained more intelligence about the place. After retracing their steps, they escaped from Area One and headed to the nearest burger joint.

'Look, if I can borrow Will's car, I'll pop home and get it. Give us all a chance to chill out.' Trent looked directly at Ziva. She rolled her eyes. 'Will, is that okay?' Trent asked.

'Sure.' Will threw the car keys and Trent caught them one-handed. Ziva tutted her disapproval, walked out of the garage, and headed for her bedroom.

As Trent got into Will's orange Mini Cooper he exhaled loudly, glad of the air and time away from Ziva. She was doing his head in and he didn't know what had got into her. Ziva had always been so smiley and happy, willing to help anyone. Mind you, she was a little too happy for Trent's taste, a bit over the top, but she seemed harmless enough. Until tonight that is.

'What are you doing?' Ziva said. She pulled back the disorderly blonde curls from her face and stared in the full-length mirror that hung on her bedroom wall. 'Now listen to me, you have got to get yourself in there tomorrow, so enough of this nonsense. *He's* in there, remember? With *her*.' Ziva looked down at the oatmeal-coloured carpet, pained at the memory. Taking a deep breath, she looked up. Pointing a finger, she continued. 'You have to get in there and these morons are your only hope, so, young lady, you had better get a grip and make out as though you like them.' Ziva nodded her compliance. 'Make them see that you're a vital part of the team.' She nodded again. 'They can't suspect anything, do you understand?'

'Sorry.' Ziva pouted and stared at her trainers. She lived in casual gym wear.

'I should think so. Now, young lady, look at me when I'm speaking to you. You go back in there and make some excuse for your behaviour. Make them feel sorry for you, get them back on your side.' Ziva smiled, a vacant look in her eyes. 'You have to get into Area One and find Tate and that evil woman that has him under her spell. Do you hear?' Ziva nodded. She smoothed down her clothes before she left her bedroom and went to the bathroom to wash her hands three times. It was a ritual, a habit now. Because she always felt dirty after The Voice had spoken to her.

It was an hour and a half round trip from Ziva's home in Worthing to Trent's in Brighton, and by the time he pulled up outside her modern, two-bedroom terraced house, he felt so much better. Will's music in the car had been the perfect antidote. And thankfully, Ziva had sweetened up when Trent went back inside the garage.

The rest of the planning went smoothly, with the four arranging to meet the following evening at nine o'clock at Ziva's house. Not having far to come from Brighton, Will and Trent arrived early.

'Evening boys.' Ziva opened the door before they had a chance to knock. She beamed at them and did a weird double-handed wave.

'Hi.' Trent raised a hand.

'Evening, Ziva. How's things?' Will asked.

'Good. Yes, yes. Come in, come in.' She closed the door. 'All ready? All packed? All excited?' Ziva seemed a bit hyper to Trent.

'Yes, all ready.' Trent eyed her with suspicion.

'Good, good, good. Tea? Before we go?' Ziva very nearly skipped to the kitchen. Trent looked at Will and rolled his eyes. Will shrugged his shoulders. Humming the theme tune to *Mission Impossible*, Ziva made them tea. Trent looked at Will while nodding in Ziva's direction, as much as to say, 'What's with her?' Will pulled a 'Search me' face. Not for the first time, Trent wished Ziva wasn't part of their group. 'Here you are, boys. Two lovely cups of tea.' She placed the mugs of tea on the kitchen table.

'Cheers.' Trent picked up his tea then looked away. She was making him feel uncomfortable.

'Thanks, Ziva.' Will smiled at her and she beamed back, holding his gaze.

Thankfully, Will's phone broke the smiling stare-off and he glanced down to read the message he'd just received. 'Hudson's about twenty minutes away; apparently he's been stuck in traffic on the M25. Something about a lorry overturning.' Hudson had the furthest to come from Kent, where he lived with his parents and younger brother. 'That still gives us plenty of time though,' Will said. At Ziva's insistence, they had built in extra contingency time for this sort of thing. She was a stickler for timeliness.

'Great! Great! That's just great.' Ziva clapped her hands like an eager child. *Why does she keep repeating herself?* Trent thought. She was really starting to grate. With the clapping finished, Ziva took the milk from the side and placed it back in the fridge. As soon as she closed the fridge door, she opened it again. Then closed it and then opened it. She did this three times.

Threes were important to Ziva. Except, of course, threes in a relationship. Now *that* three definitely did not work for Ziva. But threes in everything else were good. They soothed, reassured, and comforted her. Three pairs of trainers sitting in her wardrobe, three mascaras in her makeup bag. Three potatoes on her dinner plate next to three sausages. Three stirs of her tea, clockwise, never anticlockwise. Threes, wonderful threes. Of course, she couldn't always control everything to ensure her threes, but this was easily overridden by Ziva clicking her finger and thumb three times. Threes made Ziva feel normal again, in control. Threes washed away the muddle in her head, they made sense, and above all, they cleansed away the debris left by The Voice.

Engrossed in his phone, Will didn't see Ziva open and close the fridge door three times, but out of the corner of his eye, Trent did. When she realised what she'd done in front of virtual strangers, Ziva turned quickly to see if they were watching her. *Good, they didn't see me.* 'You can't let them see the threes. If they do, they may not work ever again,' The Voice taunted her. Ziva didn't know how she would cope without her threes. Her threes kept her sane.

As he sat sipping his tea, Trent felt uneasy, and with each second he became less sure about Ziva. *How can I get rid of her now though?* He couldn't. Hudson would be here in minutes, after which they'd go through their plan before setting off in Will's car. *Jeez!* Trent couldn't think of a plausible excuse to offload her and resigned himself to the fact that Ziva was coming.

As soon as Hudson arrived, they talked through the plan with no arguments or bickering and Trent began to relax. *Maybe it's pre-match nerves; probably the stress of breaking into Area One.* Trent tried to put any misgivings about Ziva to one side.

'Okay, team, let's hit the road.' Hudson folded up the plan and they loaded into Will's car and set off. At this time of night, the drive to the New Forest was an easy one, with little traffic and no hold-ups. And yet Trent still couldn't fully relax and now had his mum's words from that morning replaying in his head.

Ginger had insisted she confer with her spiritual guides about Trent's impending break-in. The pair had a very open and honest relationship. From an early age, Trent decided that if she really was psychic, then it was pointless trying to lie to her. Consequently, she knew all about the break-ins. Before Trent did anything significant in his life, Ginger always took it upon herself to indulge in some sort of spiritual or psychic fortune telling. This time she consulted her guides via the medium of a crystal ball. Occasionally she was bang on with her predictions, other times completely off the mark. So who knew if it was special powers, the law of averages, or pure guess work? And although it wasn't Trent's thing, once in a while, her certainty rubbed off on him. Like this morning, when her words struck a chord.

'There will be a fly in the ointment,' Ginger said, sounding all mystical as she gazed into the crystal ball. 'Heed thy warning, son, this fly is not of sound mind.' Her words spoke right to the heart of Trent's doubts about Ziva.

Chapter Nine

'We stay together.' Trent grabbed hold of Ziva's arm a little too hard.

'Ouch, you're hurting me.' She pulled away from his grasp.

'Sorry,' Trent mumbled without meaning it. He could feel the situation getting out of hand, and as much as Trent now hated Ziva, his want to stay in Area One was greater.

'We're in now, so what's the problem if we split up?' Ziva asked. The actual break-in was the easiest yet, with everything going smoothly. As soon as they cleared the third security perimeter, Ziva announced she was heading off in the other direction. Trent lost his cool.

'We agreed we were safer together during the first day or so. We agreed to wait until we'd settled into the place before we split up.' Trent glared at Ziva and ran his hand through his surfer-dude hair, pulling it in frustration. Ziva hated Trent's hair.

'We're in now, what does it matter?' Ziva returned his dirty look.

'It's better if we stick to the plan. Our plan. The one we all decided upon and agreed to,' Trent said as though he were speaking to a six-year-old.

'Surely plans should be adaptable. Yes, I know we said we'd stay together initially, but I do think it would be okay for us to split up. It's not all about what you want...'

Trent stopped listening to Ziva's jabber and tried to calm himself. *All is well, all is well,* he said over and over in his head. *No, it's not!* His thoughts pushed back against their restraint, his anger not ready to be quashed. Trent took his focus to his breath, moving in and out of his body. *All is well. All is well.* The mantra played over in his head. *That woman's going to get us caught at this rate.* Rage poked through. *All is well. All is well.*

'So? What have you got to say about that?' Ziva folded her arms. He hadn't heard a single word she said and didn't want to either.

'Let's find a safe place where we can sit down, have some water, and talk about it, eh?' Trent knew they had to keep moving. They were only just inside the Area One perimeters and were still vulnerable.

'Mmm,' Ziva begrudgingly conceded. *I could stay with them for a bit longer,* Ziva thought. *It might be safer, until I get my bearings.* 'Don't be so stupid, girl. You know our plan. Drop them as soon as we're in. We're in, so drop them. Now!' Ziva closed her eyes and covered her ears to the sound of The Voice screaming. Trent, Will, and Hudson noticed and gave confused glances to each other.

'Ziva, are you okay?' Hudson said.

'What? Yes, fine.' Ziva fixed a smile at Hudson.

'You sure?' he checked.

'Yes, yes, I'm all good.' She smiled again. Her smile was off-putting to Trent, who thought it looked strained and unnatural.

'Let's find somewhere to lay low for a while and go through our next steps.' Trent knew they were too exposed.

'Sure. You okay with that Ziva?' Hudson said. Ziva nodded.

'Come on, let's move out.' Will was getting itchy feet.

'I'm going with them and that's that!' Ziva thought she'd said it in her head. It was out loud. Trent looked at Will and then to Hudson, his face asking a thousand questions. Will shrugged, and Hudson looked at Ziva with concern. Ziva turned away. 'Come on, let's go,' she said.

It wasn't difficult finding cover in the New Forest with its miles and acres of hedging, ferns, trees, and undergrowth. Soon they found a hidden area, tucked under a large, dense hazel tree that had low-hanging branches, touching the forest floor. They sat and shared water and flapjacks in silence, all the while their minds contemplating Ziva and her strange outburst. *I knew it. She's going to be a problem,* Trent thought. *No, don't think like that, it'll become a self-fulfilling prophecy, especially in here.* Trent tried to stop the rant inside his head.

It was hard once it had begun. *Peace, calm, breath*, he told himself.

'Do you want anymore to drink?' Hudson asked Ziva.

'No, I'm fine thanks.' Ziva smiled an empty smile. It hadn't escaped Hudson's attention that Ziva's smiles had changed since he'd known her, and it worried him. Not in the way Trent and Will were bothered, but in a three-years-of-psychiatric-training-under-your-belt type of way. With Hudson's previous study and his innate empathy for people, it meant that he was highly attuned to people's mental well-being.

Hudson had ditched his training recently after struggling with the politics and general incompetence of the so-called health professionals. The last straw came when his on-job manager, Steve Quinn, left. Steve had a notable natural way when dealing with patients and was a luminous light in an otherwise dark place. Leaving the psychiatric training course had saddened Hudson, because for years he strongly believed he could make a difference in the mental health sector. He decided as a young boy that's where his future lay after watching his parents struggle to get the right support when his younger brother was diagnosed with Asperger's syndrome. If the place had been filled with more Steve Quinns, Hudson would still be there now.

Once Hudson had dropped out, he was bitten by the Area One bug, intrigued by the fact that people were now using the power of their consciousness to manifest instantly, read thoughts, and experience other people's emotions. Hudson was blown away by the potential of the abilities showing up in people. If the mental health sector was too twisted for him, then maybe he could be part of this new wave inside Area One. He'd failed one Chryso assessment and, uncharacteristically for him, was now resorting to illegal means.

'Come on, we should head out now,' Trent said. After rest and fuel, Ziva agreed to stick with them. Standing up, Trent looked around, checking they'd packed everything away, his mind wandering back to the Aston Martin they previously left. *I wonder if anyone found it.* Trent smiled inwardly at the thought as they set off. Trent led the group to a deserted home that he and Will had passed the last time they were inside.

'It should be down here.' Trent shone the torch on the map in his hand.

At the end of the short private track stood Dovedale, an imposing Edwardian detached house with boarded-up windows and doors. It sat in an overgrown garden that wrapped around the property.

'Nice.' Hudson was impressed, even though he couldn't see its full magnificence in the dark.

'Round the back.' Trent followed the path which led to the kitchen door at the back of the house.

'Someone's already had a go at this.' Hudson looked at the bashed wooden panel covering the door.

'That was me and Will.' Trent smiled proudly at Hudson.

'Sure was,' Will said. 'We didn't get far though. We got spooked by the sound of a vehicle and legged it. But not this time.' Will reached into his backpack. 'And this should make it easier.' He held up an eighteen-inch crowbar.

'I didn't know you had that!' Hudson was astonished. 'I don't remember *that* being on the kit list.'

'No, it wasn't.' Will pretended to look apologetic. He liked Hudson, but he was a bit of a worrier at times. During planning, Hudson argued against anyone taking in items that appeared weapon-like, saying they might end up using them. He refused to be associated with violence and aggression. He'd had enough of that in the psychiatric units, and it wasn't always from the patients. It was a good job Hudson didn't know what was in Ziva's bag; he'd have a heart attack.

'Right, let's get this done.' Trent took the crowbar while Will hesitated under Hudson's silent displeasure. With a few prises, the sheet of wood pinged off the doorway. To their delight, the double-glazed door underneath was open. Trent and Will laughed at this. 'Excellent,' Trent said.

'Yes, brilliant.' Ziva was keen to get inside. She longed to be alone and wanted to find a bedroom she could claim as her own. Livened by the infusion of Ziva's extreme emotions during the break-in, The Voice had been awake inside her for ages. To counter it, Ziva had been counting threes of all sorts – three steps, three boys, three stars, three fence posts, three conifer trees, three twit-twoos from an owl in the distance, three taps on her right thigh.

Everything and anything had been counted, and now Ziva was whacked.

Like most properties inside Area One, Dovedale had been vacant and unheated for many months and felt cold inside. Using their torches, they explored the house. It was a four-bedroom house, sympathetically restored with wide bay windows, polished parquet flooring throughout the ground floor, decorative cornicing, and architraves. The kitchen and dining room had been knocked through and ran along the back of the building. The whole house was tastefully decorated in neutrals with pops of greens, browns, and purples, and was peppered with ornaments and trinkets, reminders of happy times. It was a handsome yet cosy house that had obviously been loved by its previous owners.

'I've claimed my bedroom,' Ziva called out from upstairs. The first room she opened was the master bedroom. It had pale grey walls, with accents of purples and silvers, courtesy of the soft furnishings. Linked to it was a large en suite bathroom, with a white roll-top bath positioned near the window, his and hers sinks, and a shower in the corner with a huge rain-shower head. *This will be perfect*, Ziva thought as she took off her backpack and threw it on the bed.

Hudson looked around the lounge. Family photos sat on antique pieces of furniture – holidays in the sun, twin boys next to a snowman, the parents' wedding day. He picked up a photo of the family standing in front of a massive Christmas tree. *I wonder where they are. I hope they're alright. Did they start displaying abilities, or were they one of the families that have been uprooted?* Placing the photo back on the walnut sideboard, Hudson sighed, realising there were parts of Area One that made him feel uncomfortable.

After the initial scout around, they agreed to get some sleep and regroup in the kitchen early the next morning. Hudson bagged the spare guest room, not wanting to sleep in the family's beds. Ziva was already ensconced in the master bedroom, Will took one of the twin's bedrooms, and Trent the other.

Ziva was tired and drained, which wasn't unusual after a full-on episode with The Voice. It had been with Ziva since she was fourteen, arriving soon after her dad was killed in an accident at work and her mum became locked in her own world of grief. Ziva's younger sister was packed off to live with their aunty, leaving Ziva alone with her mum. Over the years, Ziva developed coping mechanisms and ways to deal with The Voice. None of it was easy. But Ziva never once let it stop her finishing school or securing a job at her local gym. In many ways the gym job was perfect for Ziva, with the physical activity helping to soothe The Voice. When she was pushing herself physically to the limit, The Voice was often silent.

After a welcome rest and longed-for showers, courtesy of the electric shower in the family bathroom and the fact the water and electricity were still on, they sat in the kitchen finishing their make-do breakfast of tinned delights raided from the cupboards, washed down with black tea and coffee. Most of it was out of date, a fact they chose to ignore. Trent and Will had prised off a few pieces of boarding from the windows and doors at the back of the house, and with the skylights unboarded, the morning light flooded in.

'I have to find him and see that he's okay.' Ziva held out her hands, pleading to the others. 'I have to. He took it quite badly. The split,' she said by way of explaining her need to go off on her own.

'This wasn't part of the plan, Ziva. We agreed to stick together until we got the hang of it in here. Then we can go our separate ways.' Trent tried to remain composed. 'We only got in last night, and now you want to go tracking down your ex-husband.'

'Technically, he's still my husband.' Ziva drained the dregs of black tea from her mug.

'Anyone want another drink? I need more coffee.' Trent got up from the kitchen table. Ziva was riling him.

'I'll do it. Got to keep busy. Idle hands and all that.' Ziva jumped up and launched herself at the kettle. Trent looked at her and sat back down, shaking his head. She was in a smiley hyper mood this morning. Trent wasn't certain what mood he preferred; they all seemed to have a side that he wasn't sure about.

'Anyone else for tea or coffee?' Ziva held up the kettle and beamed at the three sitting around the table.

'No thanks, Ziva, I'm done.' Hudson wrinkled up his nose thinking about the concoction he'd just consumed for breakfast – baked beans, mackerel fillets in tomato sauce, tinned peaches, and black tea. Yuck!

'I'll have another coffee please,' Will said as he scooped up the last few beans from his plate. Ziva busied herself making coffees for Trent and Will. With the drinks made, she placed them on the table and sat back down.

'Look, I know it's not what we agreed, but I think I know where Tate's staying and it's right on route for us this morning.' Ziva's voice was steady. Trent said nothing and drank his coffee. 'This area has our favourite B&B, Farm Cottages. We used to come down here every three months or so, for a short break. We loved it. Tate especially.' Ziva cleared her throat. 'As I say, he took the split pretty badly. He left the house that same day – when I said it was over.'

'What went wrong?' Hudson asked.

'I won't get into all of that now.' Ziva patted Hudson's hand. 'Anyway, I didn't know where he'd gone. Eventually I got hold of his mum who lives in Scotland and she said she thought he was inside Area One. He went for the Chryso assessment and that was the last she heard of him.' Trent weighed it up, still unsure. 'The thing is, I'm really worried about him. If he did manage to get in, I'm not sure how long he can hold it together, and in here that could be critical.'

'That's true. If he is in here, he could be a danger to himself and others.' Hudson could see Ziva's reasons for tracking down Tate. He'd probably want to do the same if he were in her shoes. Will was easygoing and wasn't bothered if they stuck rigidly to the plan or not.

'If he's not at Farm Cottages, which we have to pass this morning anyway, then fine, I'll leave it at that and resume my search later. What do you think?' Ziva looked at Trent, knowing that where he went, the other two were liable to follow.

'I'm not sure it's a good idea, Ziva. I know you want to find him, but still,' Trent said.

'It really is right on the way. Look.' Ziva reached for the map, opened it up, and pointed. 'We're here now. This is our route this morning. And here's Farm Cottages.' They looked at the map.

'That doesn't seem too bad.' Hudson was swayed and could understand

Ziva's concern for Tate. He looked at Trent, who now appeared to be their unelected leader.

'Mmmm.' Trent shook his head. 'I'm still not sure we need to do this now. This morning.'

'You want to search for Devon, don't you? And we all said we'd help where we can, so what's the difference?' Ziva said. Trent shifted uncomfortably.

'She's got a point,' Hudson said.

'We have to go that way anyway. What if I go and check to see if he's there? You guys can hide out close by. That way if anyone gets caught, it'll only be me,' Ziva said. This last bit of information was the clincher for Trent. *What a dream if Ziva disappeared,* Trent thought. Even though they had agreed if one was captured, they would all commit to finding them, on this occasion, Trent knew he would renege on his promise.

'Okay then.' Trent tried to quell his joy at the prospect of losing Ziva. 'Does everyone agree?' It was an afterthought; he knew they would.

'Sure,' Will said.

'Fine by me. Makes sense if we're going right by it anyway,' Hudson said.

'Good girl,' said The Voice to Ziva. It had worked. Ziva had pushed for this route when they were planning it back in her garage. 'Great. Let's get ready.' Ziva stood up from the table, wanting to jump up and down. She refrained from any celebratory dance until she was alone in her bedroom.

****

'I've done it. I've done it!' Annetta came running out into the garden where Tate was stretched out on a lounger, writing in his A4 pad and enjoying the warm, sunny, still day. It was Tate's favourite weather and perfect for writing outside.

'The migraine, it's gone. Completely.' Annetta gave Tate a wide smile. He looked at his girlfriend with her short, feathered, dark hair framing her pretty face and thought how lucky he was. She looked so much lighter, her eyes twinkling.

'That's amazing! You're really getting the hang of it now.' Tate was pleased. Since being inside Area One, she'd suffered with occasional migraines. The place affected some people that way. It was all to do with the changes in energy and frequency. Recently she'd been working on clearing them with her Manifestation ability.

Tate and Annetta met during the Chryso assessment, hours before they both gained residential status for Area One. They were surprised about passing the assessment and even more surprised to fall for one another. Following a messy break up, Annetta had sworn off men for good, and Tate's desire for a relationship after Ziva was at zero. However, neither resisted, and now they couldn't be happier. Area One had been complete bliss for both of them, with Annetta producing her best ever painting and Tate his most creative writing. And if things couldn't get any better, they'd both experienced the Manifestation and Sensing abilities within days of entering Area One.

Tate put down his pad and pen, stood up, and pulled Annetta towards him.

'I love you,' Tate whispered into her hair.

'I love you too,' she said. It was one of those glorious moments where they felt glad to be alive. Tate took Annetta's hand and they walked around their cottage garden, admiring the vibrant pink and orange gerberas, blue cornflowers, purple delphiniums, white roses, and plum irises. It was a riot of glorious colour and a source of inspiration for them both.

****

'Ready? Let's go.' Ziva was first out the back door. They'd seen a few people going about their business inside Area One and no one seemed to be wearing any obvious identification, so they felt comfortable leaving the relative safety of their temporary house. Apart from lots of boarded-up properties and more security personnel patrolling, it looked like any other quiet rural English area. Steering clear of the roads, the group made their way across fields, farmland, and through the forest. Thirty minutes into their journey, Ziva stopped and looked at the map.

'Yes, that must be it. Farm Cottages. Over there.' She pointed towards a row of charming terraced cottages.

'Must be people living there legally. There's no boarding at any of the windows or doors,' Trent said.

'We need to be careful. We don't fully know how it operates in here,' Hudson said. 'Do you still want to do this?' he asked Ziva.

'Quick, get down! Two people outside that end cottage,' Will said. They all ducked out of sight.

'Ziva, do you still want to do this?' Hudson repeated. Ziva didn't hear him the first time; she was transfixed on the two people entering the end cottage through the side door.

'Yes, of course. Look, you guys can hide towards the back of the cottages. Do you see that hedging there?' Ziva directed their attention.

'Yeah, that should be okay.' Trent said.

'We won't be far away if you need us, Ziva; just shout,' Hudson assured her. Trent knew that if Ziva shouted, he'd run in the opposite direction.

'I'm going to knock on that end cottage,' Ziva said.

'Are you sure this is wise?' Hudson suddenly had second thoughts.

'I'll be fine. Come on.' Ziva stood up and marched off towards the cottage, leaving the others to catch her up. She waited until the three were hidden before knocking on the door. 'This is it,' said The Voice. 'Don't let me down.'

'Has she gone in?' Hudson asked.

'I can't see properly.' Trent didn't care what was happening to Ziva as long as she didn't get them into trouble.

'I can't see either,' Will said.

'I think I heard a knock and then some muffled voices. Now I can't hear anything. Should we go and see?' Hudson was regretting this risky deviation from the plan.

'No, stay here.' Trent didn't want to move. *If something has happened to her, good riddance.* Then came raised voices, shouts, a piercing scream. The three flew out of their hiding place and ran to the side of the cottage, where they stumbled upon a terrible sight.

'What have you done, you stupid woman?!' Trent yelled at Ziva as he reacted to the scene in front of him. He knew he should be cool, calm, and collected in this place, but Ziva had totally and completely crossed the line.

'I can't find a pulse.' Hudson anxiously tried to find a pulse on Annetta's wrist and neck. With trembling hands, he was having no luck. Hudson looked at Tate, who stood staring at Annetta's still and silent body lying on the grass, blood pouring from the stab wound that Ziva had inflicted.

If Ziva had hoped this act would muzzle The Voice, she was sorely mistaken. 'What have you gone and done now? It's all wrong, don't you see? It's all uneven. You'll have to kill two more people to balance it up.' The Voice laughed out loud at her, its high-pitched cackling persecuting her. 'You know you have to have threes. You know nothing else will do.' Covering her ears with blood-soaked hands, Ziva backed away from the body.

'I can't find one.' Hudson was overcome with emotion and couldn't keep his hands still.

'Let me try,' Trent said. 'Will, hold here.' Trent had been applying pressure to the wound to help stem the flow of blood, not knowing if it was making any difference. Will took over from Trent. 'I bloody well knew that woman was unhinged,' Trent said, not caring if she heard. And as if someone had splashed cold water over him, Tate came to and gasped.

'Don't let her die, she can't die. She just can't.' Tate bent down and took Annetta's hand in his.

'I'm sure she won't. Look, the wound is shallow and it's right at her side. See here? I don't think it went anywhere near her vital organs.' Will was making it all up, trying to comfort Tate and himself.

'Hang on! I think I've found a pulse,' Trent said, his face suddenly relieved.

'Let me see.' Hudson needed to know for sure. 'Yes! She's alive! See here.' Hudson looked visibly lighter. 'Right, we need to get her some help. Where's the nearest hospital, Tate?'

'What? There isn't one.' Tate looked baffled.

'None?' Hudson said.

'No, we don't need them,' Tate said.

'What about a doctor or nurse, someone like that?' Hudson asked.

'They have them working at the Bruce Temperance Institution and there could be one or two in general practice, but none that I know of. Mostly we don't need them,' Tate said.

'What?' Trent was shocked. 'No hospitals, doctors, or nurses?'

'We don't need them in here...' Realisation spread across Tate's face. 'Flipping hell, I totally forgot where we were for a minute.' Quickly Tate bent down next to Annetta and lifted her into his arms. 'She'll be alright,' Tate said, all traces of fear evaporated. Trent, Will, and Hudson looked at each other, perplexed. 'She can do it.' Tate still wasn't making much sense. 'Annetta, if you want to live, you need to heal your body. See your body as healed, healthy, and perfect,' Tate whispered in her ear. 'Mend the wound,' Tate instructed. 'Heal your body, Annetta. See the wound closing and all the damaged tissue repaired and regenerated.' Annetta's chest began to move and gradually her breathing became more pronounced. 'Come on, you can do it. Just like you do for the migraines.' Air began drawing in and out of her body. Each breath that Annetta took got deeper and fuller, more steady and rhythmical. 'That's it, darling. You're doing it. Keep going,' Tate said. The blood flowing from the stab wound stopped abruptly. Annetta's eyelids fluttered.

'Holy smokes!' Trent stared in disbelief. Will had his mouth open and Hudson blinked away salty tears. They were watching the power that was Area One.

'Breathe, darling. That's it. See your cells regenerating. Slow deep breaths.' Tate gently placed Annetta back down on the grass. 'She's healing. She's coming back.' In a matter of seconds, Annetta opened her eyes and looked around at the four guys staring down at her. She lifted her hand and felt around the stab wound.

'Did I do it?' Annetta asked as she looked intently at Tate. He nodded and gave her a love-filled smile. 'Oh my God, it's healed. I've done it,' Annetta said. Even though she lived in Area One, she was still in awe of its brilliance. Tears ran down Tate's face.

'That was...' Hudson was stunned. 'That was ... incredible. Bloody incredible!' He couldn't stop his mind thinking how wonderful the world would be if everyone had this ability. No more hospitals, no more mental health units, no more ambulances needed. Families would no longer have to witness the unbearable pain and suffering of their loved ones. No one need suffer physically or mentally again. *This could change the whole world.* The colossal nature of this one ability hit Hudson square between the eyes. He thought about his younger brother healing himself of Asperger's and the patients in the psychiatric units soothing, healing, and repairing their own minds. *Oh my God. This could change everything.* In that moment, the whole universe shifted for Hudson. With this new reality, he could see everything changing. *Oh. My. God!* His brain worked hard as it contemplated the new world they were all stepping into.

With Tate's help, Annetta slowly sat up. He gathered her into his arms and they both cried openly with relief. Trent, Will, and Hudson also shed tears as they watched the touching scene. With everyone so wrapped up in the extraordinary miracle, they failed to notice Ziva had gone.

After settling Annetta into bed, Tate made the four of them fresh coffee. The end cottage was Annetta and Tate's home, a small, one-bedroom, shabby-chic cottage that felt both warm and welcoming, with its white-painted walls and floorboards and bright colours that came courtesy of Annetta's paintings, which hung on every wall. Sitting in the lounge on the beat-up, brown leather sofa and chairs, Tate filled them in on his relationship with Ziva. It had been a whirlwind with them marrying after only eight months.

'Far too quick,' Tate said, shaking his head with the memories. 'I noticed changes in her leading up to the wedding. Her mood was all over the place. One minute she was massively down and depressed, the next, she was high as a kite and over-the-top happy. She said it was the excitement and nerves, and I believed her.' Tate took a sip of coffee; the others followed. 'After the ceremony, it went badly wrong, starting on the wedding night. I won't go into details.' Tate cleared his throat. 'I tried everything, spoke to our doctor, gave her the information he'd given to me. Looked on the internet. Printed off stories from people that seemed to be going through the same thing.'

'It's not easy if someone doesn't want to be helped.' Hudson had seen enough of it during his psychiatric training.

'Tell me about it. I did try. She didn't want to know. This went on for a while, and to cut a long story short, I left after she came at me with a knife.' Tate stared into his coffee.

'Jeez!' Trent said. Everything Tate was telling them confirmed what Trent believed from the start – that Ziva was stark raving mad.

'Were you alright?' Hudson asked.

'Yes, no damage done, although that was it for me. If she wouldn't get help, I could do no more. I wasn't prepared to live like that.' Tate rubbed the back of his neck; it had been a stressful morning. 'I told her mum and sister, but it doesn't seem like either was able to help. I thought Ziva may be suffering with bipolar or schizophrenia, or something like that. I did lots of reading on the internet. Who knows, I'm no expert.'

'It could be something along those lines.' Hudson was contemplative. 'It won't help her being in here.'

'No, I don't think it will. If and when you get the abilities, they can really freak you out, even if you only experience them for a second or two. You need to be so strong and together to pull it off. Even watching someone else using their abilities can be a bit unnerving until you get your head around it.' Tate looked at them with serious eyes. 'It's just very different to outside,' he said.

'We've got to find her,' Hudson said as he looked at Trent, who promptly looked away.

'I'll make us another coffee.' Tate stood up, collected the mugs, and headed to the kitchen.

'I knew she was deranged,' Trent said. Hudson scowled at Trent's turn of phrase.

'What I don't understand is how on earth she got through the assessment,' Tate said minutes later as he walked back into the lounge with four fresh coffees on a tray. The three looked at each other.

'Tate, we'll come clean,' Hudson said. He wasn't one for secrets. He then proceeded to tell Tate how the five had met, their attempted break-ins, the disappearance of Devon, and now this successful break-in.

'That explains it.' Tate shook his head. 'Look, I'm not going to shop you or anything, but you have to understand I can't get involved anymore.'

'We understand, Tate.' Hudson drank his delicious fresh coffee with its full fat milk and sugar.

'It's different in here. Those who are Thought Readers may already know you're in here; might even know where you're staying. It's hard trying to conceal anything in here. Just be very careful,' Tate said.

'We will.' Hudson began to seriously doubt his own judgement about breaking into this place. What was he thinking?

Trent drained his coffee mug and stood up. 'Tate, thanks for everything. And I'm sorry about Annetta.' Trent held out his hand to Tate and they shook hands. After saying their goodbyes, the three made their way back to Dovedale in silence. Once back inside, they congregated around the kitchen table.

'What Tate told us changes everything,' Hudson said. 'Ziva can't be left to her own devices in here. We've got to find her.'

Trent wasn't so sure. He stood up and headed for the kettle, then changed his mind and began opening cupboards until he found what he was looking for.

'Yes! I think we need something a bit stronger after the morning we've had.' Trent held up a bottle of single malt whiskey.

'Great idea.' Will rubbed his hands together in anticipation.

'Not for me; can't stand the stuff.' Hudson screwed up his nose as he remembered the first and last time he drank whiskey. Needless to say, it involved lots of vomit. Trent went back inside the cupboard.

'Brandy? Vodka? Oh, hold on, what about this?' He turned around, holding up two bottles – one was gin and the other was Indian tonic water.

'I'll have that,' Hudson said, remembering it was his beloved Aunt Lyn's favourite tipple. Although not being much of a drinker, he'd never actually tried it himself.

'Cool.' Trent pulled out three glasses, poured the booze, and sat down at the table. Silently they sipped their drinks, trying to assimilate all that had happened that morning. It turned out that Trent's suspicions about Ziva had been right all along, and he was damned sure he wouldn't let Ziva take him away from finding Devon. She was his priority now, not some crazed woman he barely knew.

One drink led to another, then another, and before they knew it, they were five large drinks down and all comatose. Hudson dragged himself to the guest room, while Trent and Will were out cold in the lounge. That's why none of them heard Ziva sneak in through the back door.

Seeing that no one was in the kitchen, Ziva carefully opened the lounge door to find Trent and Will both asleep. Trent was snoring loudly in front of the unlit fire and Will was in one of the armchairs, legs draped over the arm, catching flies with his mouth wide open.

'There's your two,' said The Voice. 'These two, plus the girl, makes three.'

'I can't kill these two; they helped me get in here,' Ziva whispered.

'You know it has to be three. Three of everything. You started it with Tate's pretty new girlfriend.' The Voice hadn't stopped torturing Ziva. Threes were her thing, but somehow The Voice had got in on the act and was demanding threes for itself. *That's not how it works,* Ziva thought angrily. It was all getting so mixed up.

'Anyway, she's not his girlfriend,' Ziva said.

'I think we both know she is,' The Voice said.

'I can't kill these, they're together in the same room. They'll hear me.' Ziva closed the lounge door.

'Do Hudson then.'

'Not Hudson. He's the sweetest of them all.'

'Do Hudson! Do Hudson! Do Hudson!' The Voice shouted in her head.

'Alright, alright. Stop it.' Ziva put her hands over her ears. 'I'll do Hudson.'

'Then one more. I have to have threes.'

'What are you talking about? I have to have threes, not you.' Ziva's head was splitting.

'I am you, so I have to have them too. We both do,' The Voice said. 'In fact, that will make six, three each.'

'No, not six. Three! Just three!' Ziva rubbed her hand over her forehead.

'Very well, just three.' The Voice laughed at her. Ziva crept to the bottom of the stairs.

'After Hudson, then one more.' The Voice would not shut up.

'Then one more.' Ziva's shoulders slumped forward. She didn't stand a chance against The Voice. It was far more powerful that she was.

Taking a deep breath, she tiptoed upstairs, clearing her mind as she went.

It was better not to think too much about what The Voice made her do. With no hesitation, she walked to the guest bedroom door and carefully opened it. Shards of daylight pierced through gaps in the wood boarded over the window. There was just enough light for her to see Hudson's shape lying in bed under the duvet.

Gently, she took off her backpack and put her hand into the front pocket. It was still there. She grabbed the handle of the knife and pulled it out. She would aim for his heart. Hudson didn't deserve to suffer. She wanted it to be quick and painless. As she moved closer to the bed, Hudson turned quickly, his eyes wide open.

'Ziva!' he cried out. She jumped, convinced that he'd been fast asleep like the other two. Hudson saw what was in her hand. 'Ziva, it's me, Hudson.' Hurriedly, he pulled back the duvet and, fully clothed, leapt from the bed. She lunged at him with the knife and he dodged the blade. 'Ziva, what are you doing?' She went for him again, but this time caught his arm, the sharp blade penetrating deep into his flesh.

'Arrgh!' Blood poured from the wound. She stopped as he dropped to his knees clutching his arm, blood running through his fingers. Hudson looked at her, puzzled. 'Ziva, it's me, Hudson.' *Does she know it's me?* All of his psychiatric training on violent patients deserted him. 'Ziva, it's me. Put the knife down.' Pain seared up his arm and through his body. Ziva stared at the knife in her hand, surprised it was there. She looked at Hudson as though seeing him for the very first time.

'Oh no!' Ziva flew out of the room, down the stairs, and out the back door.

'Coward! Coward! Coward!' The Voice jeered as she ran from the house. 'I still need two more.'

'No! No more!' Ziva screamed.

'Help! Trent! Will!' Hudson shouted. Will, who'd already woken from the sound of Ziva crashing down the stairs and banging the back door, made his way to the stairs, still groggy from the alcohol.

'Hudson?' Will called out.

'Quick! Upstairs.'

'Trent! Get up!' Will's adrenalin kicked in and he ran up the stairs. 'Trent, come on!'

'What?' Trent opened his bleary eyes. He thought the shouting was in his dream. Clearly not. Trent pushed himself up, wishing he'd stopped after the first very large whiskey. Hudson joined Will at the top of the stairs.

'I think I'm gonna...' Hudson's knees buckled, and Will caught him just in time.

'What's going on?' Trent was now next to Will, helping Hudson down the stairs.

'Let's get him into the kitchen,' Will said. Once Hudson was sat in a chair, Trent ran around the kitchen opening cupboards and drawers.

'Get his arm above his head. And press firmly on the wound with this.' Trent threw Will a tea towel.

'Where am I?' Hudson felt lightheaded.

'It's alright, mate. You've had a bit of an accident,' Will explained. Hudson looked at his arm and remembered Ziva.

'It was Ziva. She tried to kill me,' Hudson said, not quite believing Ziva, or in fact anyone, would want to kill him.

'I don't care what excuse you give her, Hudson, the girl is looney tunes.' Trent pulled a length of bandage from a first-aid box. This time Hudson didn't scorn at his description of Ziva, because after his near-death experience, Trent may just be right.

'I'm going to look. See what we're dealing with here.' Trent took Hudson's arm and removed the tea towel quickly, glanced at the wound, then put the tea towel straight back on it. 'Right, time to see what this place is made of.' Trent looked at Will and nodded. 'Hudson, you're going to heal this. I want you to close your eyes and see the cut closing. Imagine it disappearing.' They knew what Trent was doing as he recalled the words that Tate had said to Annetta earlier. Hudson was resolute. He didn't want to die or be incapacitated, so he imagined and affirmed his desire to be healed, whole and complete, and within seconds that's what he got.

'Upon my soul, it's only freaking well worked!' Will said as he sat in wonder, observing Hudson's body changing at his command. Hudson, wide-eyed in amazement, put his arm in his lap and rubbed it. The wound was healed. All that was left was Hudson's blood drying on his clothes.

'This place is freaking awesome.' Trent sat down and stared at Hudson and his perfectly healthy arm.

'Hudson, we can't tell anyone about Ziva. I know her being on the loose is not good, but we'll get caught and I'm not risking that. Who knows what will happen to us,' Trent said. The three were sitting in the candlelit lounge, drinking hot chocolate made with hot water.

'You must realise, she could be a danger to others and herself,' Hudson argued.

'Well, not so much in here after what we've just seen.' Trent was still bowled over by the two miracles he'd witnessed that day.

'You know what I mean.' Hudson frowned. Now that death and arm amputation had been averted, Hudson was back to his usual understanding and empathetic self. 'She clearly has mental health issues and she's in an unfamiliar place. Back at home with her normal routine, she can probably cope. In here, it's all different.' Hudson drank the last bit of concentrated chocolate from the bottom of his mug. 'I can just about get my head around it. Who can say how Ziva's fairing?'

'I know what you're saying, but I'm not going after her. Sorry, mate,' Trent said. 'I've got Devon to find.'

'Yeah, he's right Hudson. We've got to at least find out what happened to Devon if we can,' Will said, feeling more loyalty towards Devon now that Ziva had turned into an attempted-murderer-on-the-run. 'Sorry, Hudson, I'm with Trent on this one,' Will said. Hudson sighed. He could see their point, yet he was worried about Ziva. She shouldn't be alone as a fugitive inside Area One.

'Okay, we'll leave it for now. But let's keep an open mind, shall we? If I see an opportunity to help or find her, I'm going to take it,' Hudson said.

'Fine by me,' Will said.

'Sure,' Trent said, knowing full well he would never actively help or go looking for Ziva.

Little did they know, Ziva was now heavily sedated in a locked cell inside the Bruce Temperance Institution.

****

"Duality is a key component of the game you have set up on planet Earth, whereby everything has an opposite — success and failure, sick and healthy, rich and poor, negative and positive, happy and sad. And as humans, it is your choice which one you revel in.

In your game, duality gives you predicaments, dilemmas, decisions, and quandaries, and has accorded you the wildest ride ever. It offers you the chance to experience the full spectrum of all-that-you-are-not, before remembering once again the deliciousness of all-that-you-are. It has allowed you to play at one end of the spectrum and then launch yourself to the other end for a completely different escapade — alcoholic embraces sobriety; man becomes woman; rich child becomes a broke, homeless adult; villain turns reformer; victim into killer.

In your energetic state prior to coming to Earth, and after you leave, you exist in a realm that has no contrast or duality. You choose to enter this game on Earth, over and over again, so that you can experience this difference. This surging from all-that-you-are-not into all-that-you-truly-are has you completely hooked. Because as you do so, you experience the most delectable and blissful remembrance. A moment that some call coming home. And it is so joyful to you, so uplifting, so very thrilling. Like discovering you've won the lottery when you'd forgotten you purchased the ticket. Like falling deeply in love when you weren't looking for it.

Many of you also find excitement in holding yourself away from all-that-you-are, knowing that you will ping right back at some point. You find pleasure in the tension, in the orgasmic build-up that comes before you launch yourself back to all-that-you-truly-are.

But know that while the seeds of these game-changing abilities have been planted and are sprouting, so too have the seeds of the complete opposite of what they can bring. Because in the current set-up of this game, you cannot have one without the possibility of the other."

Chapter Ten

'It should take a few minutes for the sedative to wear off.' Dr Irving Pratt checked the monitors connected to Ziva. They seemed to indicate she was slowly regaining consciousness.

'Can you hear me?' Nurse Carole Kennard asked. She was a petite lady with a kindly, heart-shaped face.

'Mmmmm,' Ziva murmured.

'I think she's coming back to us.' Nurse Carole smiled with relief.

'Good, I'll leave you to it.' Dr Irving walked towards the door. Nurse Carole was pleased they were bringing her back. She didn't like to see patients that way. Ziva had only been out for a day, unlike some of them. It was the part of her job she disliked, treating people like experiments. But Carole knew she must quash such thoughts in here.

'It's as much for their own safety as it is for the people living inside Area One,' Dr Irving had explained the first time Nurse Carole watched him sedate a very distressed man during her first day on the job. 'Don't forget, we're dealing with unknown factors, so we have to be extremely cautious. I know it's not ideal, and as soon as we find a better way, we'll use it. I promise you, Carole.' Dr Irving smiled at Nurse Carole and touched her kindly on the hand. For a few seconds, her doubts about how they treated the patients and detainees inside Area One dissipated.

Nurse Carole Kennard had followed the man she loved, Dr Irving Pratt, into Area One. They'd worked together at Kings College Hospital in London for three years before they gave in to a mutual attraction. Their affair continued for eight months until, unable to stand the pressure of leading a double life, Dr Irving applied for a post inside Area One and got it. Hot on his heels was Nurse Carole.

'Can you hear me?' Nurse Carole asked.

'Mmm.' Ziva slowly opened one eye. 'Who are you?' She was still groggy and muddled from the sedation.

'I'm Nurse Carole Kennard. I've been looking after you. Do you remember?'

'No.' Ziva closed her eye.

'Do you know where you are?' Nurse Carole asked. Ziva rolled her head from side to side, then opened both eyes and glanced around the room. 'Can you remember how you got here?' Ziva rolled her head again.

'Water,' Ziva said. Nurse Carole poured water from a plastic jug into a plastic cup and, holding Ziva's head up, helped her to drink.

'My, you were thirsty,' Nurse Carole said.

'Another,' Ziva said, and the nurse obliged. After Ziva gulped that one down, she said, 'One more.'

'Alright, one more.' Nurse Carole wondered how she'd react when she realised her limbs were shackled to the bed. After drinking three cups of water, Ziva laid her head back on the pillow while Nurse Carole checked all the monitors.

'How are you feeling now, Biba?'

'No! Ziva. Name Ziva'

'Oh, I'm sorry. Ziva'

Ziva nodded and closed her eyes.

Ziva had come into the unit with no identification and making little sense. They'd tried to find out who she was, but all she gave was a mumbled name that sounded like Biba and something about a voice.

'How are you feeling, Ziva?' Nurse Carole asked again.

'Sleepy.'

'Why don't you get some rest?' Nurse Carole suggested. 'When you're ready, I'll get your favourite – macaroni cheese. How does that sound?' Ziva had demanded macaroni cheese when she first came in and didn't stop going on about it until the sedative kicked in.

'Okay.' Ziva closed her eyes. Nurse Carole left the room and went outside where Dr Irving was watching through the two-way mirror.

'I'll keep an eye on her. You get some rest.' She touched his arm.

'I should be here,' Dr Irving said.

'You look done in. Use one of the rooms to get some sleep. I'll come and get you as soon as she's fully awake,' Nurse Carole said. Dr Irving looked unsure. 'You need rest. I promise I'll come as soon as she's up and about,' she reassured him.

'Okay.' He kissed her lips. 'Any problems come and get me.'

The workload inside the Bruce Temperance Institution for doctors, nurses, and specialists was unreal. Anyone who went into these jobs thinking it would be easier than the National Health Service was in for a rude awakening. They were operating in a space where boundaries and parameters kept changing, dealing with endless unusual situations, and generally flying by the seat of their pants. Their senses were on full alert around the clock, and stress hormones reached levels that none had ever known before. It was overwhelming and taxing to say the least, and they were far from on top of the situation. The methods they used were not ideal, and to cope, they avoided thinking too long and hard about what they were doing. Many yearned for the day when everyone knew how to use the abilities with compassion and for the greater good. But until that day came, they would continue to fight fire with fire. It was neither pleasant nor pretty.

Nurse Carole looked through the two-way mirror at Ziva sleeping. She looked peaceful now. Nothing like when she first arrived covered in blood and in a right state. The two security men who brought her into the unit said little, as was often the case. 'No known injuries. Mental disturbance, cause unknown.' Then they proceeded to turn and walk out.

Since working at the Bruce Temperance Institution, Nurse Carole Kennard had seen a number of people lose it, finding it impossible to get to grips with Area One. They knew Ziva was a break-in, but as yet, were unable to determine the cause of her mental disturbance. Had she seen someone displaying an ability and flipped out? Was she struggling with her own abilities, or was it a previous condition? Nurse Carole sighed with a heavy heart. How to tell the difference, now that was the tricky part. They may have a long journey ahead with Ziva.

Once Nurse Carole was sure Ziva was sleeping, she went off to make herself a cup of tea. Upon her return, she glanced through the two-way mirror and was surprised to see an apparently empty room. *Someone must have taken her somewhere. Maybe it was Irving.* Nurse Carole put down her tea and walked over to the door. Peering through the glass pane, she saw Ziva standing in the corner of the room, looking out of the barred window in her white gown, barefoot.

'How the devil...?' Nurse Carole unlocked the door and entered the room. 'Ziva, you're up. How are you feeling?' Nurse Carole furtively looked around. There was no one else in the room. The straps were still attached to the bed, undone.

'Better now those straps are off. I had to open and close them three times. What a nightmare!' Ziva rubbed her wrists.

'How did you...?'

'Easy. I focused on them undoing and they undid. It's amazing in here, isn't it?' Ziva said.

Nurse Carole immediately had an answer to one of her questions. Ziva had used one of the abilities. Unaware if she had access to others, Nurse Carole knew she had to play it carefully. She also understood it would be hopeless pressing the alarm or doing anything hasty.

'Well, now that you're up, how about a nice cup of tea? I've just made one for myself.' Smoothing the covers on Ziva's bed, she considered how best to handle the situation.

'Yes, please. And what about that macaroni cheese you promised me?' Ziva smiled sweetly. *There are no flies on her*, Nurse Carole thought.

'You're right there.' Ziva agreed.

Nurse Carole fixed a grin and tried to clear all thoughts from her mind. Ziva had started to Thought Read.

'Right, tea and macaroni cheese coming up.' Nurse Carole got out of the room quickly.

As Ziva slowly came to, it dawned on her what had happened. Remorse for

Hudson filled her body. *I hope he's okay.* She still felt befuddled from the sedative; and something else was different. 'Oh, my word! Yes!' she whispered. The Voice was asleep. These were her favourite times, when she was free from him and alone in her head.

Undoing the buckles had surprised Ziva. You read and hear about the abilities, but boy, when they came alive in you, it could near enough knock you over. Ziva didn't think it would work and laughed out loud when she felt the straps unbuckle. And just now hearing Nurse Carole's thoughts, that was hilarious. For a split second Ziva thought it was The Voice, but the voice she'd heard was female and kind. Nothing like The Voice, which was male and definitely not kind. Then after seeing the horror on Nurse Carole's face when Ziva replied, she knew it had to be her. And the way she had fled the room, only confirmed to Ziva she had indeed read her thoughts.

Now with The Voice quiet, Ziva had space to think. One thing was certain; she had to get out of this place. Although where could she go? She'd built herself into such a frenzy about confronting Tate and his girlfriend, she hadn't contemplated what to do afterwards. Regret and guilt washed through her as she sat on the bed thinking about what she'd done. She hadn't meant to harm them, either of them, not really. But it was always so hard when The Voice was awake and screaming in her head, screwing everything up. The Voice had a lot to answer for, that was clear. Suddenly Ziva missed home, her job, and all that was familiar. Her home was her safe place and her job gave some semblance of control over you-know-who. Tears welled up in her eyes. 'I'm not a bad person,' she said as she wiped away the tears with her hand. *If only The Voice would stay asleep forever.* Her tummy rumbled and reminded her how hungry she was.

'I'm starving. What's Nurse Carole doing with my macaroni cheese?' Ziva rubbed her stomach. 'Hold on, what am I waiting for?' Ziva giggled and then made herself comfortable on the bed. She took her mind to a piping hot dish of creamy macaroni cheese with bacon lardons sprinkled on top. Picturing it in her mind's eye, Ziva made the image come alive as she added the details: a brown glazed earthenware dish, grilled cheddar cheese bubbling on top and melting down the sides, the bacon crispy where it had caught under the grill.

Ziva's mouth watered. 'It's so real. I can smell it.' Slowly, Ziva opened her eyes and there on the side table was a dish of piping-hot macaroni cheese with a dusting of bacon bits over the top. 'Oh, my word! Yes!' Laughing, she jumped off the bed and made for the food. With no utensils, she stuck her fingers into the dish. 'Yow! That's hot.' Ziva licked the creamy cheese sauce from her fingers. 'Yummy!' Looking around, she spied a box of wooden spatulas along with other medical paraphernalia. She grabbed a spatula and loaded up as big a portion as the spatula would allow and popped it into her mouth. 'Mmmm, that's heaven.' Ziva tucked in. 'This is probably the best I've tasted.' She was astonished. Manifested food was scrumptious and it being her favourite comfort food of all time, Ziva knew a thing or two about macaroni cheese.

After devouring the first dish she manifested another, and it was while she was munching her way through the second dish that Nurse Carole came back. She peered through the glass pane of the door and saw Ziva eating the macaroni cheese.

'Oh, my giddy aunt!' Nurse Carole hurried away to wake up Dr Irving. She hadn't wanted to disturb him, but with Ziva displaying an array of abilities, she had to. This could get very dangerous.

****

"As you wish for something for yourself, you also wish on behalf of everyone in your world. When you pray for something to happen in your life, you activate the possibility of that in the lives of others too. As you desire, you do so for others. Everything you have asked for is then always available to every other human being on your planet. It is how the game is designed. Because you are all connected and bound together. So what one gets, the others can have too."

Chapter Eleven

'Do you want tea?' Devon asked Katie.

'No, I'm fine, thanks. I've got to go in a minute.' Katie stood by the doorway of the kitchen, dressed ready for work in her unflattering, dark security uniform. It did nothing to enhance her voluptuous figure.

'Are you going to be okay?' Katie asked.

'Yeah, sure.' Devon leant against the kitchen side, cradling the kettle in her arms.

'Promise me you won't do anything rash?' Katie looked at Devon, who glanced down and sighed.

'I won't.'

'We'll talk when I get back.' Katie pulled her bag over her shoulder and turned to leave. 'See you later.'

'See you.' Devon filled the kettle, switched it on, and reached for a mug from the shelf. Katie worked for the Area One security services and yesterday she found out they had a group of three males and one female under surveillance. From what Katie had told her, Devon was sure it was Trent and the others.

After Devon was arrested, she was taken to a building called Harrow Chalk which sat outside the village of Bransgore and was one of the central buildings for the Area One security services. They first met when Katie was tasked with taking Devon a cup of tea and making sure she was in a calm and stable state. As Katie entered the cell, she instantly knew what Devon was going through, because unlike many security personnel in Area One, Katie was a Thought Reader and Sensor. Devon's thoughts and feelings filled every millimetre of the cell. Katie could feel Devon's fear in every fibre of her own body. She knew how petrified Devon was, being held in the locked cell, not knowing what would happen next. Devon's thoughts and feelings washed through Katie as though they were her own. And in that moment, Katie felt inextricably connected to Devon. It was as if the two of them had become one. Devon was now a part of Katie. Overwhelmed with the intensity of the experience, Katie was compelled to act; she had no choice. To keep Devon locked up would be like locking herself up, so Katie not only helped Devon escape, she also gave her a place to live in her two-bedroom cottage on the outskirts of Ringwood Village.

Katie told her boss that Devon was missing when she took in the tea. It had happened on a couple of previous occasions and with the organisation's mammoth workload, Devon's disappearance gradually got pushed further down a long list of priorities.

****

"Have you dared to push your mind to explore the edges of where these new Laws are taking you? Have you thought about the subtleties and nuances that these Laws will bring to your relationships, and how they will change the dynamics of all interactions?

Let us take, for example, the impact of the Sensor and Thought Reading functions. Imagine, for a moment, what it will be like to experience your parents' emotions as though they are your own. Feeling their sadness and guilt, their regrets and disappointments. Consider how it will be when you know how your child feels inside. To know the unbridled truth about who they really are. To sense when they are saying 'yes' only to please and gain your approval. How will it change your relationships with the people you work with when you can share their sorrow and fears, and experience the suffering and pain beneath their facade?

To truly know what is inside another, to understand their hopes and dreams, fears and nightmares, enables you to appreciate them in a manner that is beyond your current comprehension. All the surface irrelevancies are bypassed and you are able to get to the heart of who they are and what they're about. When you journey to this new place of understanding, you will realise that the core of every single person on your planet is the same.

You have spent millennia playing your game of differences and individuality, of uniqueness and originality, of separation and segregation, of disconnection and detachment. But the deepest truth dear One, is that you are One and the same. You are everyone and everyone is you. You are every soul that is, has been, and is yet to be. You are One; the only One. In your game, you have created the opportunity to experience many different aspects of the One at the same time, but behind the curtains of this play, it is all you, dear One. And as these Laws take hold, they will take you closer to this knowing. And closer still to the awareness and comprehension of your Oneness.

Chapter Twelve

'We've got to rethink our next steps,' Hudson said. 'So much has happened since we set out the original plan.'

'You're telling me. Ziva's turned into a killing machine,' Will said as he scanned the cupboards. He picked up a can of tomato soup and a packet of wheat-free penne pasta, both out of date. 'Killing was certainly not in the original plan.' Filling a saucepan with water, Will placed it on the hob.

'On the plus side, we've tapped into the abilities.' Hudson held up his arm. 'That could make a huge difference.' Like everyone, they hoped and dreamed they would eventually become Quarternaters and be able to access all four abilities. 'Perhaps we should try to expand on the abilities before we go any further,' Hudson suggested. After his first taste of Manifesting, he'd been awake for most of the night thinking about all the positive things he could do in the world with this wondrous gift.

'I think you're right,' Will said. 'What if we can manifest food and drink? Or even sense where Devon is? It could change everything.' Will looked at Trent, who was sitting at the kitchen table, nursing a mug of black coffee.

'Yeah, you're right. Let's do that,' Trent agreed. Will opened the tin of tomato soup and got three bowls out of the cupboard.

'Hudson's well on the way, though.' Will nodded towards Hudson's arm.

'So are you. Don't forget the Aston Martin,' Hudson said. Will laughed as he remembered.

'How could I forget?' Will said.

Trent forced a smile, realising he was the only one that hadn't experienced any of the abilities. Doubt plagued all three. Trent worried that he would turn out to be a Sterile, the name given to a person living inside Area One that couldn't muster any abilities, and Hudson and Will feared they would never be able to duplicate their first successes.

After encountering the first ability, and once the initial euphoria wore off, it was common for people to go through a period of doubt. Would they be able to do it again? Did they deserve this ability? Could they be trusted to use it for good? Lack of faith always blocked the expression of abilities. Invariably the person would give up trying and put it down to a lucky one-off. And as they let go and relaxed – WHAM! It would come back again. They would be shocked and amazed, followed by doubt and unworthiness, the ability would go away again, they gave up trying and let go, and then it returned. It was a typical cycle that had the benefit of allowing people time to adjust to the new Laws.

The three tucked into their bowls of tomato soup and wheat-free pasta, made better with the addition of fresh thyme and rosemary picked from the overgrown herb bed in the back garden.

'Do you think you can manifest on all parts of the body?' Will asked, spooning up his last piece of pasta.

'You must be able to,' Hudson said. 'What were you thinking of?'

'Well...' Will paused. 'If you wanted to be taller or bigger in some way.' Will looked down at his empty bowl, colour coming to his cheeks.

'Oh, I see Mr William.' Trent laughed.

'What?' Hudson looked from Trent to Will and back again. Trent held up his little finger and wiggled it, nodding at Will.

'Wouldn't that be hilarious?' Will said. The three burst out laughing.

The next morning after a breakfast of tinned cherries, custard, and black tea, the three went in different directions – Trent to the lounge, Will to his bedroom, and Hudson to the back garden.

As Trent sat on the lounge floor in front of the fireplace, he felt the pressure of being the only one who hadn't managed to mobilise any of the Laws, and it rankled him. He was determined to master at least one of the abilities. Resolute, he closed his eyes and decided to start with something small, figuring it would be easier. It was a natural assumption people had – that size was important when manifesting. Honestly, there was no difference between manifesting a mug or a mansion, a penny or a billion pounds. It was the same process, and neither was harder nor easier, unless the Manifester's mind believed it to be so.

Trent began by visualising a Braeburn apple in front of him on the oriental rug. He coloured the apple in red tones with a yellow streaky background. He saw the skin glossy and firm. Imagined the creamy, pale flesh, crisp and juicy, the taste bursting in his mouth as he took a bite. He intensified the image and the colours, cranked up the aroma and flavour on his tongue. Held it in his mind's eye for as long as he could. *It must be there,* Trent thought. He squinted through one eye. Nothing. Without skipping a beat, he tried again, only this time for longer. Still nothing. He switched the Braeburn apple for a Valencia orange. Nada. Switched it for a walnut. Zilch.

Meanwhile upstairs, Will wasn't having much success either. He was going for a rare ESP guitar he'd seen on the internet. It was so frustrating because he'd managed to manifest a freaking Aston Martin for Chrissake. Why the guitar was proving so hard was beyond him. His mind leapt all over the place. *I'm not sure I can do it again. What if none of us can do it and we have to leave Area One?* His brain threw up endless fears, and each time Will dragged it back to the guitar. Then before he knew it, his mind had jumped again. *I wonder where Ziva is. What if she's been caught and tells them where we are?* Back to the guitar. *The Aston Martin may have been a one-off. What if I turn out to be a Sterile?* It was hopeless.

Outside in the overgrown back garden, Hudson's experience was different. Despite the weeds, brambles, and nettles, Hudson could tell the garden had been maintained and well cared for in its time, with its brick-edged borders, a dedicated area for vegetables with raised beds made from thick railway sleepers, a cedar-framed glass greenhouse, painted sheds, and winding cobblestone paths. After pushing back some long grass, Hudson found a wooden bench to sit on. He turned his face towards the sun and immediately felt relaxed. He was reminded of his grandparent's garden, which was always packed with cottage-style plants and had a large prolific vegetable patch bearing multiple vegetables and fruits. The growing part was his granddad's job, and the cooking was his gran's. They had a huge rhubarb plant that she turned into endless rhubarb crumbles, pies, and tarts. Plump juicy strawberries, blackcurrants, and gooseberries were transformed into delicious jams and jellies. All manner of vegetables were roasted, made into soups and stews, and of course, served with his gran's famous Sunday roast dinners. The memory was enough to make Hudson's mouth water. And let's not forget his granddad's potting shed. Hudson smiled. It was his granddad's treasured retreat from the world, where he kept a battered, threadbare tartan armchair and an old Bakerlite-style radio tuned permanently into Radio 4. Warm, comforting memories flowed through Hudson, and his heart filled with love for them both. *Such kind, sweet people.*

With his eyes closed, Hudson imagined a raised bed free from all weeds, the soil rich, nourished and well dug. He pictured neat rows of creamy parsnips, bright orange carrots, round lettuces, plump purple beetroots, red radishes, and tall salad onions. Alongside he added mini cane wigwams with peas entwined, bursting from their pods, and three staked tomato plants bearing heavy, juicy fruit. Hudson filled in the green hues of the foliage and imagined the distinct textures of each plant. He saw himself picking the fully-grown vegetables from the earth, holding them in his hands, tasting their delicious, homegrown, organic flavours. How proud his granddad would be. Hudson sighed, enveloped by the beautiful memories of his grandparents and their garden. *I love you, Granddad Bince.*

A couple of amorous pigeons flapped in the flowering cherry tree and brought Hudson back down to earth. As he came to and opened his eyes, it took him a second to remember where he was. Hudson blinked rapidly. *You've got to be joking!* Hudson stood up, hands on his head. In one of the previously overgrown beds now stood rows of perfectly formed vegetables, ripe and ready for picking. He walked over to the bed, bent down, and pulled out one of the sweet-smelling carrots. Hudson bit into the side of the vegetable. It tasted strong and earthy, with a hint of soil. Absolutely divine. Like no other carrot he'd ever eaten before. *I've only gone and bloody done it!*

After Trent's failed attempts he'd given up and lay on the floor thinking about his top ten favourite songs of all time. Over the years, his top ten had inevitably changed. While thinking about number three, a voice interrupted him, 'I love you, Granddad Bince.' It was Hudson's voice. Trent sat up and looked around the room. He was still alone. His brain churned. *That was definitely Hudson. But I'm in the room on my own.* 'Did I just read Hudson's thoughts? Did I just do it?' Trent said out loud, excited. 'You've got to be joking!' *That's Hudson again. That was definitely him.* Trent stood up and peered into the hall. It was empty. Then he checked the dining room. That too was empty. *I know I heard him. Where is he? I've got to find out if I did it.* Anticipation bubbled inside Trent as he rushed around the house trying to locate Hudson. Then something caught his attention in the back garden, and he banged on the kitchen window. Hudson turned with a partially eaten carrot in his hand and soil around his mouth.

'What the—?' Trent said.

After gathering in the garden, the three stared at the chock-full vegetable bed, Hudson still holding his partially eaten carrot, mud smeared around his face where he'd made an unsuccessful attempt to wipe it off.

'This is freaking awesome!' Will looked up and down at the vegetables bursting from the top of the soil. 'That's the food sorted.' Will rubbed his hands together, happy and relieved. The tinned food was wearing a little thin and running out. Hudson nodded, still dazed.

'I wonder if I can do more. Different veggies, you know?' Hudson said.

'I'm sure you can, mate.' Will patted Hudson on the back.

'Oh, yeah, before I forget, I think I heard something.' Trent had been distracted with Hudson's manifestations.

'Heard what?' Will said, worried someone was coming for them. His senses were heightened since the Ziva debacle.

'Thoughts.' Trent looked at Hudson. 'Hudson, I think I heard your thoughts.' Hudson dropped his carrot. What had he been thinking and was it anything to worry about, or be ashamed about, or apologise for? 'It was something like, "I love you, Granddad Vince", and then, "You've got to be joking" or something like that. It was definitely Hudson's voice.' Trent looked at Hudson, hoping he was right. Either that or he was following in Ziva's footsteps.

'Yes.' Hudson stared at Trent. 'I said that! It was Granddad Bince. We used to call him that. He loved his garden and was fanatical about growing fruit and vegetables.' Hudson looked at his hands covered in soil and rubbed them down his jeans. 'I was thinking about him when I was trying to manifest this lot.' Hudson glanced at Trent and then to Will, the penny slowly dropping even further. 'You've got to be joking!'

'That's it, that's what I heard.' Trent punched the air, overjoyed that he'd finally experienced one of the abilities. He was hoping for a manifestation first, but it was a start. 'Yes!'

'Huzzah! We. Are. On. Fire!' Will laughed, amazed and yet also worried about how he would get himself back in the game.

'Blimey!' Hudson said, suddenly aware that someone else had heard his thoughts. 'That's totally weird.' Hudson wasn't sure how he felt about it. Thoughts were normally private, for you and you alone. No matter what words and sentences you held in your head, they were only ever for you. No one else would ever know them unless you chose to share them. You could put on a brave, happy, or professional face and all the while something entirely different could be going on inside. And that was fine, because only you knew about it. Area One was turning out to be very unsettling, and Hudson wasn't sure he liked it anymore.

****

"Currently in your world you have speech to convey thoughts and feelings, but do you see how such a communication method will become useless as the Laws of Thought Reading and Sensing expand?

Speech is a very primitive way of exchanging information in the multiverse space where your universe sits. To date in your game, speech has amused you. You have used it to exert your thoughts and feelings of judgement, praise, discrimination, love, and hate. It has been a way to control and manipulate others, to externalise your fantasies. It has given you a method for receiving data in a totally different way to how it was intended. You have used speech to share words of love and support, and also to mislead, lie, and bring others to their knees.

Compared to Thought Reading and Sensing, speech is extremely slow and erratic, usually unreliable, seldom truthful, and often fickle.

Fresh ways of expression will emerge and your outdated modes of communication will become obsolete. Phone calls, texts, messages, emails, letters, and cards will all dwindle, along with speech. Every person becoming an open book. There will be no more hiding behind a cloak, no more concealment or whitewash. The truth will be exposed, brought out into the light. Everything known, everything understood. Without ever speaking a word."

Chapter Thirteen

It wasn't easy for Devon being a fugitive inside Area One – the constant worry about being found out, living on her nerves, praying that the people she came into contact with were not Thought Readers or Sensors. But now she was in, she was adamant she would stay until she'd gained the abilities. So far, they had escaped her. Trying not to get too down, she practised every day, not for her own benefit but rather for Eli, her mum. Eli had raised Devon single-handedly, and five years ago was diagnosed with multiple sclerosis. Throughout Devon's life, Eli worked two jobs to ensure Devon didn't go without and could attend her much-loved dance and drama classes. Eli sacrificed so much and now being struck down with a debilitating illness seemed so unfair. And although Devon hated leaving her mum, she was certain that if she could just gain the abilities, she'd be able to figure out a way to help her. Yes, Devon knew what people said about the abilities not working if you tried to inflict them on others, but she was convinced there must be a way round it.

'I'm home,' Katie called out as she hung up her uniform jacket and took off her comfortable and very sensible work shoes.

'Hiya. In the kitchen,' Devon said. It was as though the pair had known each other for years. Part of that was to do with the situation; the other part was because Katie was able to pick up on some of Devon's thoughts and feelings. Katie had always been a caring person, and receiving the abilities had opened her up in a way she never expected.

'Cup of tea?' Devon asked as Katie came into the kitchen.

'Lovely, thanks.' Katie plonked herself down at the kitchen table. It was a ritual for the pair to enjoy a cup of tea and a chat in the kitchen after Katie's shift.

'How was your day?' Devon asked as she made the tea.

'Not bad. I got some more information for you, but I had to stop asking questions in case Tom got suspicious. I've got a feeling he's changing.' Tom was a colleague of Katie's who was a Sterile, although today Katie sensed something unusual about him. Knowing that the abilities could strike at any time, Katie couldn't risk Tom finding out the real reason for her questions.

'Really? What makes you say that?' Devon poured boiling water onto the Earl Grey tea leaves sprinkled in the bottom of the teapot. It was Katie's favourite tea, and slowly, Devon was getting used to the smoky, fragrant taste.

'I'm not sure. He looked strange. Something in his eyes maybe. Or his face.' Katie struggled to put her finger on it. 'Anyway, I got some information from him. Then felt a strong urge to shut up.'

'I don't want you getting into trouble, Katie.' Devon put the pot of tea on the table along with two floral bone china cups and matching saucers. Granny cups Katie called them, after her two grandmas who had crockery just like them. After fetching the milk from the fridge, Devon joined Katie at the table.

'The girl is being detained at the Bruce Temperance Institution. I'm not sure what wing though. Ziva Drake, is that her name?' Katie asked.

'That's her.' Devon poured tea into the two cups and pushed one towards Katie.

'Thanks.' Katie sipped her tea, savouring the citrus flavours. 'That's all I could get, sorry.'

'No, that's fine.' Devon splashed milk into hers, subduing the flowery taste. 'I don't want you pushing it and getting into trouble.'

'What are you going to do?' Katie asked.

'I'm not sure there's much I can do for Ziva.'

'No, probably not.' Katie wrapped her hands around the warm teacup. Devon was desperate to see Trent again. He'd been on her mind since their night together, and even though she didn't know him well, she missed him. Katie read her thoughts.

'I'll try and find out more about the three guys,' Katie said. *She's doing it again* Devon thought. *It's not easy being in here.* Devon sighed.

'I know,' Katie said and gave Devon a sorry-about-that smile. 'And at the same time, it can be glorious and totally out of this world.' Devon smiled, because she knew Katie was right.

Two days later, Katie took advantage of Tom's empty office and sneaked in. Quietly, she closed the door and moved over to his desk, reports and graphs strewn all over it. A file buried in his in-tray had the answer. Flicking through the contents, she scanned the documents and came across photos of the three guys and an address for the property where they were hiding out. It was clear from the file they were on the radar and under surveillance. If they hadn't already, no doubt they'd be picked up soon. Writing the address on the palm of her hand, Katie closed the folder, but not before having a peek at Trent in a surveillance photo. *Very nice.* She could see what Devon saw in him. Katie walked out of Tom's office nonchalantly.

Back home later that evening, during their catch-up, Katie pushed a piece of paper across the table to Devon.

'They're staying here,' Katie said. She knew Devon would be pleased.

'Really?' Devon said. 'They're definitely still inside Area One then?'

'Yeah, seems that way. I didn't have time to find out why Ziva is in the BTI, but from the pictures, it looks like the guys are at that location,' Katie said. Devon studied the piece of paper.

'Dovedale. Sounds nice.' Devon picked up her tea, thinking.

'When will you go?' Katie asked. Devon raised a quizzical eyebrow at Katie, who just smiled.

'I'm not sure.'

'Be careful, they're being watched. I'm not sure how consistent the surveillance is, and I don't know when they'll be picked up. It seems from the file that they're still on the loose. But for how long, who knows?' Katie said.

'Hopefully I can get to them before they get caught. I could at least warn them,' Devon said.

'I'm sorry I couldn't get any more details for you,' Katie said.

'You've done so much for me, Katie.' Devon thought about everything Katie had risked for her. 'Thank you,' she said as she placed her hand on Katie's arm.

'Are you going tomorrow morning then?'

'Blimey! Is nothing sacred?' Devon laughed, yielding to the Area One ways. Katie smiled mischievously. She didn't want Devon, or anyone else for that matter, feeling uncomfortable with her being able to read their thoughts and feelings. Although she had to admit, it truly was something else.

'Sorry,' Katie said, not really meaning it. 'Isn't it magnificent though?' Katie laughed. *Not for me*, Devon thought. 'I heard that.' Katie laughed harder, and Devon joined in.

****

'Not for me.' A voice sounded in Trent's head just as he was waking up. 'Devon?' Trent said. After the thrill of Hudson's manifestation, Will had cooked up a medley of vegetables and the three washed them down with a celebratory drink or two, followed by a snooze in the lounge.

'What? Where?' Will woke, disorientated.

'Devon?' Hudson roused.

'I heard her.' Trent sat up and rubbed his hands over his face to wake himself. 'It was her.'

'You must have been dreaming, mate,' Will said.

'No, this was different.' Trent thought back over what had happened. 'I was waking up. It was like when I heard Hudson. Yeah, it was just like that.'

'Do you think you were reading her thoughts?' Will asked.

'Maybe.'

'It might mean she's nearby,' Will said.

'She could be.' Trent relished that idea.

'What did you hear?' Hudson was still glowing in the aftermath of his spectacular foodie manifestation.

'She said, "Not for me." It was really distinct.' Trent said.

'If it was, it must mean she's alive and well,' Hudson said.

'Where though?' Trent asked. He now had an overwhelming urge to see Devon.

'How did she sound? Happy, sad, annoyed, captured?' Will thought she was probably still incarcerated somewhere. Trent looked at him, his bubble burst.

'Yeah, I know,' Trent said. 'But she did sound okay. More than okay. It was as though she was laughing.'

'That's got to be a good sign. They may have allowed her to go through the assessment and she could be living happily in here somewhere,' Hudson said.

'Maybe.' Trent wasn't sure what to believe. He only knew he had to find Devon and prayed she was alright.

****

'You ready then?' Katie looked up from stirring the Bolognese sauce. Devon was wearing some of Katie's dark clothing and had a backpack filled with essentials. 'Be careful.'

'I will,' Devon said. Katie put down the wooden spoon, walked over to Devon, and hugged her.

'Thanks for everything, Katie,' Devon said, returning the hug.

'Come back here if you need to. You know the drill.' They had worked out a plan for Devon to return safely to Katie's house if she needed.

'I do.'

'Good luck.'

'Thanks. I hope I won't need it.' Devon opened the back door and walked out into the night.

Chapter Fourteen

With daylight breaking and after a second uncomfortable night of sleeping rough, Devon decided to make her move. She'd been watching and walking the area around Dovedale, and so far had seen no signs of surveillance. She wasn't sure if it meant they were currently not being observed, or the boys had left the house, or worse still, they'd been caught.

Scanning the area one last time using Katie's binoculars, she confirmed the area was clear. Pulling the hood tight around her head, she hoisted up her bag and set off towards the back of the house. As she got closer to Dovedale, she sighed. It was the type of house she saw herself in one day with a wonderful husband and some adorable children. Although right now, that idea seemed extremely remote.

Pushing her way through overgrown laurel hedging, she crouched down. She noticed the back door had the boarding removed; she would try that. Devon kept low and close to the hedging as she made her way to the door. She peered through the glass. All was still. *I hope it's the right house.* Devon only had Katie's word for it. She hadn't seen anyone go in or out of the house while she'd been watching, although it was impossible to keep an eye on every entrance all the time. Devon tried the handle. It was open. *Thank goodness!* She didn't fancy knocking. Slowly pushing the door open, she stepped into a large open-plan kitchen-diner. As she took in the room, she could tell it had recently been used, with crockery and mugs laying around and unwashed pots in the sink. Someone was definitely living here or certainly had been here in the last day or so. 'They must have running water and electricity,' Devon whispered as she looked at the remnants of what was perhaps last night's meal. Her mind jumped to how wonderful it would be to stand under a hot shower and drink something other than lukewarm bottled water. Walking over to the fridge, she opened it. A plethora of colourful vegetables filled the shelves. *Wow! How did they get all of this?* Devon's eyes gazed at the overflowing fresh produce. She went to close the fridge door and got the fright of her life as a gun was jabbed hard into her side.

'Hands up!' came the voice. Devon's heart leapt into her mouth. Her arms flew into the air. 'Turn slowly.' *Hold on, I recognise that voice*, Devon thought.

'Trent, is that you?' Devon risked turning her head and pulled down her hood at the same time.

'Devon! Jeez! What are you doing here?' Trent was stunned, and now Devon saw he'd been holding a fire poker to her. Dropping the poker on the floor, he stepped forward and pulled her into his arms, kissing her passionately. A couple of seconds later Devon pulled away.

'I'm sorry, I haven't had a shower for a couple of days. I must absolutely stink.' Devon was suddenly self-conscious and stepped back.

'I don't care.' Trent pulled her to him again. When he finally let her go, he took her hand and led her to the kitchen table, pulling out a chair for her. 'It's so good to see you.' Trent walked over to the kettle. 'I've been worried about you.'

Devon sat down, relief and happiness flowing through her. 'I've been fine.'

'Tea or coffee? We haven't got any milk though.' Trent filled up the kettle and switched it on. 'Or there's hot chocolate.'

'Black tea is fine, thanks,' Devon said. They sat for ten minutes drinking tea and updating each other on what had happened since Devon's arrest in the ferns. Upon hearing the chatter and occasional laughs, Will and Hudson woke and came downstairs.

'Devon, how did you get here?' Hudson said. He was pleased to see her safe and well.

'Where did you come from?' Will was equally pleased. They all exchanged hugs.

'Kettle's just boiled. Tea or coffee, guys?' Trent said, feeling happier than he'd been in a long while.

'Coffee please,' Will and Hudson said together.

There was a crash on the front door, as though someone was smashing it down. A split second later, the back door flew open and four men dressed in black ran into the house.

'Freeze everyone!' shouted the first man through the door. Devon quickly stood, knocking back her chair, hands shooting up in the air. Will made a run for it with one of the four men chasing. In sheer panic, Hudson followed Will's lead and bolted with another of the men in close pursuit. Determined that Devon would not be caught again, Trent whacked the lead man over the head with the kettle, boiling water splattering over him and his colleague. The men shouted from the shock and pain, and one dropped to his knees in agony. Trent grabbed Devon's hand and ran out of the back door.

Will and Hudson headed for the front door and remembered too late it was boarded up. Hudson changed course and went for the lounge, but was seized by one of the security men, who tackled him to the ground. Will hardly climbed any stairs before he was grabbed around the legs. Will and Hudson, defeated and restrained, were led out through the kitchen. They passed the other two security men – one with a tea towel pressed against his head, blood running down the side of his face, the other splashing cold water onto his scalded skin. There was no sign of Trent or Devon, and Will hoped it meant they had escaped. Hudson's mind was filled with worry about where they would take him. Both were bundled into the back of a black van and the door slammed closed.

'They must have got away,' Will said, leaning against the side of the van. 'Trent and Devon.'

'Yeah.' Hudson's brain tried to process everything. *I've got to be clever. That's the only way I'll survive this. I've got to think my way out. Be careful what I say.*

'How are we going to get out of this?' Will asked. 'Shall we make a run for it as soon as they open the doors the other end? Wherever that is.'

'Dodgy. They could shoot us.' Hudson wasn't enamoured with that idea.

'We've got to do something,' Will said.

'Maybe we can talk to them. Reason with them,' Hudson suggested.

'Anyway, we don't know how much they know. They may only be pulling us in for breaking into Area One.'

'I guess.'

'They must have people doing it all the time. We might even get off with a caution.' Hudson covered his fear with false optimism. Neither were criminals; surely they couldn't be in that much trouble. The more Hudson thought about it, the more he was convinced the legal system would realise that soon enough and spare them.

'Can't you do your thing on these cuffs?' Will was suddenly animated.

'I've been trying, but my mind is all over the place.' Hudson gave it another shot. 'No, it's not working.'

'Flamming horrors!' Will said. 'What are we going to do?'

'We'll have to go with it and as soon as we can, ask for a lawyer. They'll sort it out I'm sure.' Hudson, like so many, assumed the legal system inside Area One was the same or, at the very least, similar to the rest of the country. Sadly they were wrong. Area One, with its virgin territory and complex mysteries, was a law unto itself. 'With any luck we'll only get charged with breaking in.'

'Yeah.' Will was sceptical. They'd come so far, and after Hudson's vegetable mania and seeing Devon in the kitchen, he thought they were home and dry. Now though, it seemed like everything was crumbling around them.

'Even if they do know about our connection to Ziva, we're not responsible for her actions. They can't pin that one on us.' Hudson was building his case. 'She tried to kill me.'

'That's true.'

The journey was relatively short. By the time the van stopped and the doors opened, they'd talked each other into believing they would get lawyers who would invoke all the powers of the justice system and work their magic to free them. They were escorted out of the van to a security door a couple of steps away, frogmarched along a corridor, and put into separate rooms adjacent to one another. Neither had a chance to look around them for any clues as to where they might be.

Chapter Fifteen

'So you can manifest?' The woman asking the questions didn't seem impressed with Hudson's description. She had droopy eyes and reminded him of a cartoon. The other one taking notes seemed even less aroused, although it was hard to tell only seeing the top of her head with her thinning parting. Hudson had just finished detailing his amazing fruit and vegetable manifestation. Well, he thought it was amazing anyway. He'd decided on that example instead of the one where he'd healed his arm after Ziva had tried to kill him.

'Yes, I can manifest.'

'And?' Like all personnel communicating with detainees, she was a person of few words. It was part of the training.

'Nothing else.' Hudson looked at the two stony-faced women sitting on the other side of the table, weighing up if he should ask to see a lawyer again. It hadn't worked the first or second, or even the third time, why would it work a fourth? All they seemed to want to do was question him.

'Any unusual thoughts?' Droopy Eyes asked.

'No.' Hudson knew what she was getting at and didn't know if it was a good or bad thing revealing you had the abilities alive and well in you. Should he make out he had them all? Perhaps it would frighten them into getting him a lawyer. 'Not yet anyway,' Hudson added. He couldn't resist it. Droopy's left eye twitched and for a nanosecond, Thinning Parting's pen paused. Most wouldn't have noticed, but Hudson did. He also knew the shorthand used in the mental health field and tried not to look startled when the codes for 'lock-up', 'restrain', and 'sedation' were written down by Thinning Parting next to his name. Hudson tried to keep a lid on the hysteria that now surged through his body and threatened to erupt.

'Look, there's something I need to tell you. Outside I worked on the mental health stage.' *Stage? What are you talking about? Idiot!* His mouth ran away, heading down a track without him. 'Did my time with the NHS, you know. I worked with a lovely doctor called Steve Quinn. He's moved on now to head up the R & G Health Group.' Hudson was thinking on his feet, desperate to avoid being drugged and tied to a bed in a locked cell. Droopy Eyes and Thinning Parting glanced at each other. 'I did try to get a job inside Area One you see. I wanted to make a difference, if you know what I mean?' Hudson looked at Droopy Eyes, her robot-like features softening slightly. 'I've been passionate about working in this field ever since my younger brother was diagnosed with Asperger's.' Hudson ploughed on, unclear where he was going. Thinning Parting stopped writing, which Hudson took as a good sign. 'Anyway, when I tried, they weren't recruiting at the time,' Hudson lied. Droopy Eyes's face showed a glint of confusion. 'I really wanted to get in here, so I broke in. I know it's naughty and wrong of me. I've never done anything like this before.' Hudson paused. 'Mind you, I did steal Jerry's lunch one day at school and blamed it on another friend. I was young though. Eleven actually. Jerry wasn't very nice either. A bit of a bully if you ask me.' Hudson was unable to stop his prattle. 'This place gets under your skin. I couldn't get it out of my mind once I knew about it. The potential and everything,' Hudson babbled. 'I know it's not the usual way, but maybe there's something I can do in here to help or assist. I'd give anything to work here. And if it's anything like the National Health Service, I know you'll be snowed under. Perhaps you could use an extra pair of hands.' Hudson held up his hands, showing them he had a pair. The two women looked at each other in silence, saying plenty with their eyes. Thinning Parting stood up and Droopy Eyes followed suit.

'Hudson, we'll come back to you,' Thinning Parting said with a sliver of a smile. She opened the door and before she left, said to Hudson, 'I'll get some tea and biscuits brought to you.' As the door closed, Hudson exhaled.

Five hours later, Hudson was surprised to see Thinning Parting enter his room alone. He stood up expectantly.

'Hudson, please take a seat.' Thinning Parting sat at the table opposite Hudson. 'I've spoken to a few people, pulled some strings.' She nodded and looked at him in a way that meant you-owe-me-buster. Hudson was on tenterhooks, heart pounding in his chest. Thinning Parting considered him for a moment. *Is he really cut out for this place? I guess it's his choice.* 'You will have to go in front of my boss and pass a medical and so on. If those things go well, then we may be able to find you some work within the Bruce Temperance Institution.' Relief flooded Hudson and he felt like crying.

'Thank you. Thank you. I won't let you down.' He restrained himself from kissing her balding head.

'You'd better not,' she said, 'or it will definitely be curtains for you.' Hudson didn't like the sound of that.

'I'll work hard, I promise,' he said. Thinning Parting laughed at his naivety, knowing that this was the only thing all employees ever did inside Area One.

'We may be able to use your manifesting ability.' Thinning Parting didn't tell him that the majority of staff were Steriles.

'Sure, no problem.' Hudson hoped he wasn't going to regret agreeing to that, although he had little choice. Thinning Parting stood and walked towards the door.

'Tomorrow morning at nine o'clock my boss Dr Emmett Brown will see you.'

'Oh, like the—'

'Yes, the film, *Back to the Future*,' Thinning Parting interrupted Hudson. 'Ironic, eh?'

'Yeah.' Hudson gave a nervous laugh. Maybe he'd wake up in a moment back at his parents' home in Kent.

'Anyway, if all goes well, we can get you started soon after.' Thinning Parting raised the corners of her mouth in deference to a smile before leaving the room. Hudson sat on his bed and put his head in his hands, tears catching at the back of his throat. Was he finally getting out of this prickly situation or getting further in?

Hudson barely slept that night and was ready early the next morning wearing a borrowed suit, trying not to think too deeply about the poor soul who'd donated it. At one minute to nine, the door opened and in walked a short, rotund man wearing thick-lens glasses. The only similarity he had to the Dr Emmett Brown in the film was his mop of receding, untamed, white hair. Waddling towards Hudson, he held out his hand.

'Dr Emmett Brown, head of the Mental Health Division for Area One. Good to meet you, boy.'

'Hudson Story, good to meet you too.' They shook hands and sat down at the table. Hudson had hoped to be going to Dr Emmett Brown's office. He wanted to see outside the room, to get a sense of the place so that he could tailor his answers.

'Now Story, Dr Sandra Knutt tells me you have experience working in mental health and want to work for us?' Hudson wanted to snigger at Thinning Parting's real name. *You can't make this stuff up.*

'Yes, that's right,' Hudson said.

'Well, Story, bit of a strange way to go about it. Nevertheless, beggars can't be choosers.' The last few words were mumbled, but still Hudson heard them, and his spirits lifted. *They're desperate; they need me. They must be weighed down with work.*

'I know, sir. I'm sorry about that. I've never been in trouble before, and Dr Steve Quinn will vouch for me.'

'Yes, Story. He already has.'

I wish he'd stop calling me by my last name. It was annoying Hudson, although he didn't dare say anything.

'I contacted him yesterday and I must say he spoke very highly of you. Told me I'd be a fool if I didn't employ you. So there you go. There are a few bits and pieces to sort out, medical and so forth. I can't see any problems though.' Dr Emmett Brown stood up and held out his hand. 'Welcome aboard, Story.' Hudson shook his hand, dumbfounded.

'You will initially report to Knutt...'

Jeez! Does he do this with everyone?!

'...I have my assistant, Judy Payne, sorting out some temporary accommodation for you.' Dr Emmett Brown looked at his watch. 'Payne should be with you within the hour.' *Chrissakes, this place is insane,* Hudson thought before quickly picking himself up on his bias, worried he was losing himself in the freakishness of Area One.

'She'll take you around and show you where everything is. Report to me nine o'clock sharp tomorrow morning and I'll take over your induction.'

'Sounds great. Thank you.' Hudson gave an over-the-top smile.

'I'll get some tea and biscuits sent to you, Story.'

'Thank you.' *What's with the tea and biscuits all of a sudden?*

'Good O.' Dr Emmett Brown left the room, and Hudson stood there for a few moments trying to absorb it all with very mixed feelings. He wondered what Dr Steve Quinn had said. He must have known Hudson was in some type of trouble and knowing him, wouldn't be opposed to a little white lie or two, to help out. Who knew what was ahead for Hudson, but thankfully he'd averted the narcotics, leashes, and locked rooms. For now at least.

Chapter Sixteen

'Rampallians!' Will shouted as they shut the door and he heard them lock it. He'd asked for a lawyer again and they'd laughed at him. Things weren't looking great. And when the two women who questioned him left his cell later that evening, he was sure no lawyer was coming. *Why didn't we run when we had the chance?* Will thought, forgetting there had been no chance. *I shouldn't have listened to Hudson and all his talk about lawyers.* Will sighed and sat down on the hard, single bed.

After three days, they stopped the intense questioning. Perhaps Will should have been relieved, but it merely spooked him and put him on edge. Unfortunately, Will didn't have the same sort of ammunition as Hudson and opted to go with the less-is-more theory by not telling them about the previous break-ins, the manifestation of the Aston Martin, and the murderer on the loose he was associated with. As far as they were concerned, he was just a break-in, which thankfully meant only the code for 'lock-up' was written on his sheet. Unbeknownst to him, Will had escaped the tethering and sedation.

Sporadically, they checked to see if Will had developed any abilities, and whether through laziness, being swamped with work, or ambivalence, their questions were no longer cloaked, insinuated, or sophisticated, but direct and obvious. 'No,' he would say each time they asked if he'd got them yet. It wasn't for want of trying though. With little else to occupy him, Will had been practising round the clock, sadly with no success. He consoled himself by counting down the days, believing that by the time his case did get to trial, he would have served his entire sentence and be let out immediately. Will made a couple of common suppositions here; firstly, that his situation was deemed a case and secondly, that he would get a trial.

Chapter Seventeen

It was a long time before Trent and Devon dared to stop.

'I think we're alright now.' Trent gasped for air as he bent over with his hands on his knees. Devon was exhausted too. She couldn't have managed much longer at that pace.

'Where are we?' Devon asked.

'No idea.' Trent came up and looked around. Hot, searing pinpricks of pain drew his attention to his left hand, now covered in small, angry scald marks made by the boiling water from the kettle he'd used as a weapon.

'Let's look.' Devon took his hand. 'I think you've got away lightly.' She rummaged around in her bag.

'I didn't know you had that.'

'I nabbed it just before you grabbed me.'

'Quick thinking.' Trent was impressed. Devon pulled out a small tub of clear Aloe Vera gel. It was one of her must-never-be-without items.

'Here, I'll put some on.' Unscrewing the top, she dunked her fingers into the refreshing gel and gently rubbed it over Trent's burn marks. 'It should help. Oh, unless of course you can sort this yourself?' It was so instinctive to reach for a plaster, painkiller, or bandage.

'I'm not sure I've got that one yet, although...' Trent looked at Devon and wondered whether he should tell her about hearing her thoughts.

'Although what?' Devon returned the gel to her backpack and pulled out a bottle of water. Trent took the proffered water.

'Let's find somewhere to sit a while and I'll tell you.' Tucking themselves away from view, they sat down. Devon did her utmost to leave a space between her and Trent, figuring she must stink to high heaven, especially after that long run. After some much-needed water, Trent told Devon about hearing her thoughts.

'It was definitely your voice,' he said.

'I did say that. Gosh!' Devon smiled. This place never failed to amaze.

'I've heard Hudson's thoughts as well. Just a few of them. When he manifested loads of vegetables in the garden at the back of the house,' Trent said. A smile spread over his face as he remembered.

'That's what was in the fridge,' Devon said.

'Sure was.' Trent smiled smugly. Devon's mind went to work, thinking about how she felt now that Katie and Trent could read her thoughts. She couldn't decide.

Chapter Eighteen

His name was Jocky 'The Untouchable' Diamond, a forty-three-year-old tall, skinny man with an obsession for 1920s gangsters and one of the first five people to pass the assessment for entry into Area One. Slipping in at a time when the authorities were still ironing out the creases in the assessment process, Jocky was a man in the know and had heard about the creation of Area One long before the masses. Instantly his interest was piqued, and he knew he had to get in. He pictured himself as top dog, creating all manner of riches and extravagancies. Hungry to reach Quarternator status, he wanted to be hailed the best, the untouchable.

Weeks after gaining Area One citizenship, Jocky tasted all four abilities and was completely hooked on the hedonistic sensation. Frustratingly for him though, it took a further few months before he could use the abilities more fully. Jocky had big plans, and now with the abilities coming online more consistently, he turned his attention to the next step in his master plan – to take control of Area One. He would start by building a loyal following, an army who would acquiesce to his command. His recruitment campaign began under the guise of teaching the abilities to other Area One residents. Normally teachers of the abilities needed authority approval, but Jocky, unused to abiding by rules, conveniently ignored this fact.

In the basement room of Jocky's house, he was holding the second session of his clandestine eight-week training programme. Not wanting to scare off the beginnings of his Diamond Army, the first session the previous week had been a gentle ease-in as he covered Thought Reading. Now as he listened to his four students drivel on about how they'd progressed with their homework, his mind feverishly lurched to what he had up his sleeve for that night.

'Right, that'll do,' Jocky interrupted Joan, rubbing his hands together impatiently. Joan, in her late fifties, wearing a floaty, multi-coloured skirt with a bright orange top, stopped mid-sentence, her mouth open. In her world of fluffysville, people didn't cut in so abruptly.

'Well done, Joan. You're doing great.' Jocky quickly backtracked, not wanting to get off on the wrong foot with his subjects. As all good politicians know, you do anything to curry favour, but once in power, well, anything goes. He couldn't wait.

'I want to show you another ability this week. The art of manifestation.' Jocky's eyes grew black. The four people sitting in front of him lit up and nodded to each other. It was the ability that most wanted to master. 'The art of manifestation – with the body,' Jocky added, his smile exuding threat. Justin looked confused and turned to his friend Dog sitting next to him. Dog smiled knowingly.

From under a white silk handkerchief on the table behind him, Jocky took out a large hunting knife, nestled snugly in a leather sheath. Joan gasped and grabbed the amethyst pendant that was burrowed between her ample bosoms. Justin shifted uncomfortably in his seat. Pulling the knife out from the sheath, Jocky held it up for all to see. His mouth opened and he licked his dry, cracked lips. Slowly, he brought it down and caressed the steel blade. For a second, his eyes glazed as he was transported into his own little world of fantasy. Joan's coughing brought Jocky back and he held the knife up again. Betsy, the thirty-something woman with tattooed arms and legs sitting next to Justin, stared aghast.

'What in heaven's name?' Joan said, now deeply regretting her choice of teacher. Jocky Diamond took the knife and brought it up to his left cheek, locking eyes with everyone in turn. Justin swallowed, Joan let out a little shriek and hid behind her hands, Dog smiled, and Betsy continued to stare as Jocky pushed the blade into the flesh of his left cheek and brought the blade down, cutting deeply. A gush of crimson blood traced tracks down his face, dripping onto his white shirt.

'Gordon Bennett!' Justin muttered, wondering whether to get out now. He looked at his mate Dog, who put his hand on Justin's arm and mouthed, 'It's epic, watch.' Justin wasn't sure about epic.

'Umm ... I don't think this is for me,' Joan said as she wrapped a pink shawl around her, picked up her patchwork bag, and ran from the room. Immersed in his own world, Jocky never heard her go. Betsy sat transfixed. It was hard to tell if she was dazzled or disturbed.

Justin, the twenty-year-old new Area One resident, hadn't warmed to Jocky Diamond with his arrogant air. It had been Dog who had suggested the class, and Justin, being the trusting person he was, thought he was going to a normal run-of-the-mill authority-approved session. Now he seriously doubted the authorities knew anything about it, let alone approved of Jocky Diamond's training programme.

Jocky seemed to stay in his bleeding position for hours, and Justin started to get scared he would have to administer his rusty first-aid skills.

'He's going to bleed to death,' Justin whispered to Dog, who mouthed back, 'Just watch.' Jocky's chest rose and fell with deep, deliberate breaths. Then closing his eyes, he leant his head back. After what seemed like a lifetime and buckets of lost blood, Jocky opened his eyes and stared to a place beyond the back wall, the knife still in his hand, glistening with blood.

'Watch,' Dog said. The stream of blood stopped, and then as if someone had an eraser, the cut began to vanish from one end to the other.

'Gordon Bennett!' Justin said.

'Yeah.' Dog leant back in his chair folding his arms. 'Epic, right?' he said to Justin.

'Wicked,' Betsy finally concluded. Jocky took the white scarf from the table behind him and wiped the blood from the blade, all the while scrutinizing the three in front of him, his eyes black and intimidating.

'Your turn...' Jocky said as he held Justin's gaze. Dog and Betsy nodded enthusiastically, but Justin had a sudden urge to run. '...next week,' Jocky finished, his mouth hinting at a smirk. There was no way Justin was coming back next week.

Talk about being thrown in the deep end with weights around your ankles.

As far as Justin knew, none of them attending the session had this particular ability. Surely they should get the ability first, shouldn't they? The whole thing sat uneasily with Justin, and he was anxious to get out of Jocky's basement.

Justin and Dog had met when they passed the Chryso assessment and became fully fledged Area One citizens at the same time. The rhapsody of knowing you were going to live in the Promised Land was overwhelming, and it was typical for people to project those inner feelings onto the ones sharing the same experience. Many friendships were formed this way. Outside, Justin and Dog would probably never have become friends. They were like chalk and cheese. Justin was more likely to play by the rules, but Dog had a rebellious edge and liked to see what would happen if you stepped outside of those rules.

There was no question about Justin opting out of the following week's session, although Dog still went. Justin was keen to get the low-down and popped round to Dog's one-bedroom flat, located above a thriving artisan bakery. The aroma pouring out was mouth-watering. As Dog's front door opened, Justin did a double take.

'What on earth happened to you?' Justin asked. Dog, a normally good-looking guy, had a top lip swollen to five times its normal size, with a nasty cut running along it, and his left eye was black, blue, bloodshot, and half-closed with swelling.

'Come in,' Dog mumbled, trying not to move his lips. Justin followed Dog into a small kitchen that was stuck in the eighties.

'What happened?' Justin asked. Dog pointed to the kettle and Justin nodded. They were both silent as Dog made coffee and then grabbed a straw for himself.

'Stops dribbling.' Dog held up the straw. After Dog had a few awkward sucks of coffee, he proceeded to regale Justin with the story of how he got his injuries. Apparently Jocky, as promised, had stepped up the session. It was only Betsy and Dog that week, and Betsy jumped at the chance to have a go at invoking the manifestation ability, just as Jocky had demonstrated the previous week.

'Couldn't do it,' Dog murmured.

'What, couldn't cut herself? That's understandable,' Justin said.

'No, did that. Easy.' Dog remembered how Betsy did not stall or shy away from cutting herself, and although Dog was far from shockable, something about it didn't seem right somehow. 'Forearm,' Dog said, keeping his words to a minimum. 'Couldn't heal.'

'Oh my God, what happened?'

'Sent to nurse he knows,' Dog said and sucked up some more coffee, wincing with pain.

'Did you do it? You know, the cutting, healing routine?' Justin asked. Dog shook his head. 'So what happened, mate?'

'After Betsy, Jocky tamed it.'

'What do you mean?'

'Not heal from cut.' Dog paused. 'Heal from punch.'

'What?' Justin couldn't fathom out what his friend was saying.

'Punched me.' Dog mimed a punch to the face. 'Four times. Told me heal myself.'

'What?' Justin nearly choked on his coffee. 'So, Jocky Diamond did this to you?' Justin asked. 'He punched you? Four times?' Dog nodded.

'Gordon Bennett, mate, he's lost it.' Justin knew Jocky was no good the first time he met him. 'I'm glad I didn't go.'

'Too shocked to heal,' Dog said, suddenly looking like a vulnerable child. 'Mind not straight. Couldn't heal. Jocky said go home.'

'He's freaking mental,' Justin said. Dog nodded and drew up the dregs of coffee through his straw.

'Not so epic then?' Justin asked. Dog shook his head in agreement.

****

"These abilities, dear One, are for all. They are unattached to whether you are deemed good or bad. They care not if you use them for so-called admirable or evil reasons. Obtaining the abilities isn't about your competence or skill level, or how kind you are. It's not about your strong work ethic or how much good karma you think you've amassed. They leave aside your bank balance, qualifications, and education. They ignore how much you have sacrificed. They care not for your background, class, creed, age, sex, or the colour of your skin.

You are mistaken if you believe that only the so-called good, virtuous, and benevolent will get these additional functions. Just as gravity does not assess your worthiness and record how many good deeds you have completed in order for it to work, these abilities operate in the same way, and will be available to everyone. There will be no discrimination, partiality, or favouritism, and you cannot secure these new functions with your riches and status.

My dear One, did you honestly think you could control who gets them and who doesn't? Did you believe you would somehow preside over them? No, you cannot. You shall all receive them. Every single one of you. The ministers and the muggers, the pious and the sinful, the egotistical and the timid. Every last one of you. That is how your game works. What is for one, is for all. Because ultimately, you are all One."

Chapter Nineteen

The front doorbell rang for a fifth time. He obviously wasn't giving up that easily and now held his finger on the bell. Dog didn't want to let Jocky in, but the noise was driving him insane. Dog's resolve ebbed away as he hid behind the sofa.

'Blow it!' he said. If Dog didn't answer the door, the neighbours would hear, if they hadn't already, and might come to investigate. He certainly didn't want them to see Jocky on his doorstep. Dog lived in a small row of terraced properties each with a ground floor shop and flat up above. There was the artisan bakery which sat below Dog's flat, a florist, a bicycle repair shop, and the other was being used as an authority-run drop-in centre, offering 24/7 support and advice to the Area One residents. When he first entered Area One, it had surprised Dog that there were still shops open and thriving. He'd since realised that even if you possessed the manifestation ability, it was far from consistent or reliable, and if people depended solely upon the ability for their food supply, they would no doubt starve to death.

A week had passed since Jocky had attempted to invoke the manifestation ability in Dog and slowly Dog's face was healing, the last of the bruising now a lovely shade of yellow. He'd avoided Jocky so far, but in a place like this, Dog knew that he must face him sooner or later. Dog sighed and came out from behind the sofa. He would answer the door. The ringing stopped and Dog stood still. Maybe he wouldn't have to. Maybe Jocky had got the message.

'I'll come back tomorrow,' Jocky said through the letterbox. Dog's shoulders slumped forward and he shook his head. *Why doesn't he just leave me alone? I'm taking the batteries out of the doorbell,* Dog promised. Mind you, Jocky hammering on the door wasn't going to be much better.

Dog and Jocky had met a couple of weeks after Dog gained residential status for Area One. Normally Jocky wasn't his type of friend, being much older than his twenty-three years and with a wild, manic edge that scared Dog more than he cared to admit. But things were different inside Area One, and after Dog arrived, he found that he was bored.

After the initial exhilaration had subsided, new residents were suddenly hit with being in a very strange place with no friends or family. Away from home and all that was familiar, they were confined to living within a small area with completely different rules and norms. Every new resident inevitably experienced a period of 'Huh? What now?' All focus and energy were about passing the assessment and getting in. Once in, most felt lost. This was when many were vulnerable and sometimes regretful, not knowing how or if they would fit in. Feelings of inadequacy were rampant, and most wondered if they had it in them to master the abilities. No one really tells you how completely mind-numbingly boring it can be when you're currently a Sterile and trying your hardest to get the abilities on board, especially for a young man like Dog who was eager to do amazing things. They don't tell you it can be hard to give up your friends, family, job, and home and be transported into a world that only has potential going for it. Of course, the potential is out of this world, but until it's mastered, it's still only potential. You may get the abilities, you may not. It's possible, but not guaranteed. All these things suddenly dawn on you during the first few days and weeks, and it can be tough. And this is the exact time that Jocky liked to pounce and befriend people, bringing them into the fold – his recruits. The authorities did their best to link up every new resident with a support group and mentor to help them with the integration process. But still, some inevitably fell through the net.

Even though Dog could only cope with Jocky in small doses, finding him a bit weird and full of himself at times, he still hung out with him. Jocky had tapped into the abilities, and Dog was not alone in finding that hugely magnetic. After all, it was the reason why every resident was in Area One. Quarternaters were especially mesmeric, and Steriles flocked to these people like moths to a flame.

For the fourth day in a row, Dog squatted behind the sofa with Jocky banging on the door. It was getting beyond a joke. Dog had hoped Jocky would leave him alone. It was clear he wouldn't. Dog felt defeated. He stood up and walked to the front door. If nothing else, Jocky was a source of entertainment, of sorts.

'Man! At last!' Jocky said as Dog opened the door. Jocky pushed passed Dog, strode into the lounge, and sat down on the threadbare, dark-brown, corduroy sofa. Dog sighed as he closed the door and followed Jocky.

'Tea, white, four sugars,' Jocky demanded as he crossed his legs wide, man-style. Dog rolled his eyes.

'Sure.' Dog made his way to the kitchen and came back minutes later with two mugs of steaming hot, strong tea and handed one to Jocky.

'Cheers.' Jocky gulped down his hot tea without a flinch. 'So, how's it going, mate?' Jocky ignored the fact he'd been banging on Dog's door for days.

'Yeah, okay,' Dog said, blowing on his tea.

'Haven't seen you for ages, man.' Jocky drained his mug. 'Nice cuppa. You haven't been for your training sessions.' Jocky put the empty mug down on the brown-and-orange swirly carpet.

'Yeah, I know.'

'You gotta do it, man. It's so freaking cool. I've got four new recruits. But Betsy, the old girl Joan, and your mate, what's his name?'

'Justin.'

'Yeah, Justin. Well, they've all scarpered. And now you.' Jocky held open his hands. Dog looked down, not knowing if he wanted to restart Jocky's training. 'I know you had a bit of a bumpy start...' *Yeah, due to you,* Dog thought. '...but you can't give up at the first hurdle. You gotta get back in the saddle. Take the bull by the horns. It's better than hanging around here.'

'Yeah, I know.' Dog sipped his tea.

'Well then, what are you waiting for? Next session is tomorrow night. You coming?'

'Maybe.' Dog bit his bottom lip.

'What? Spit it out.'

'I'm not sure about the whole group thing,' Dog admitted. In truth, he didn't like the idea of a repeat performance in front of an audience. 'It's not my thing,' Dog said.

Jocky paused as he reflected. If he was going to rise to power in this place, he would need all the followers he could get. And he liked Dog; he reminded Jocky of his younger brother, although Dog could be a bit of a wimp sometimes.

'Look, man, why don't you come over to mine tomorrow morning and I'll teach you the abilities on your own.' Jocky gave Dog his best smile, which still looked smarmy and shady. Dog's eyes lit up, because despite Jocky, he did want to get the abilities under his belt.

'Yeah, epic!'

'Good man.' Jocky smiled inwardly. He had plans for Dog. A general always needs a second in command and Dog was proving to be nice and malleable. Jocky knew he'd have to tread carefully with Dog and not scare him away, so he'd rein in the punches. For now. Slowly, slowly, catchy monkey. It wasn't Jocky's usual style, but he was willing to make an exception.

The next day, Dog went round to Jocky's three-bedroom Victorian house and wondered, not for the first time, how Jocky had wrangled it from the department who allocated housing inside Area One. Dog pressed the brass doorbell and in seconds, saw Jocky's unmistakable form through the stained-glass panes in the door.

'Hey, man. Come in.' Jocky opened the door wide and Dog went in. It was a handsome house, packed with period features, and had obviously been cherished by the previous owners. To Jocky though, it was a place to sleep and more importantly, it was his office and command centre.

'Cheers.' Dog followed Jocky through to the kitchen at the back of the property. It had large French doors leading out to a sunny and neglected courtyard garden.

'Tea?' Jocky asked, filling the kettle.

'Great, thanks.'

'Jasmine, Earl Grey, Oolong, or normal?' Jocky asked with no hint of sarcasm. Dog frowned, confused. They spoke at the same time.

'Are you...'

'They were here. Leftovers.'

'Oh, right. Normal please.' Dog was pleased he hadn't finished his sentence. No doubt it would have ended with regret and more punches.

'Cool, man.' Jocky made tea and then led the way down to the basement. It was Jocky's favourite room in the house. He liked the idea of his operation being controlled from a basement, hidden out of view. It wasn't your typical damp, musty, leaking basement room. Oh no, this was a stylish, immaculately renovated, blue-walled, wooden-floored type of basement. The sort of basement James Bond would approve of. At one end there were a few chairs and a table where Jocky gave his training; at the other end sat three cream leather sofas.

'So man, you fancy getting some of these talents, eh?' Jocky asked.

'Of course. Like everyone I suppose.' Dog sipped his tea. 'I haven't been able to get anything so far.' Jocky smiled a smile that said, 'I have.'

'Not got the touch, eh boy?' Jocky gulped back his hot tea. Dog shrugged. He hoped he would get something soon, otherwise what was the point of being here. It was so exasperating. That was another thing they didn't tell you about this place. It was so damn frustrating. Frustrating and boring.

Jocky started by trying to get Dog in touch with the manifestation ability. Dog began by focusing his attention on a toy Dinky car. He's not sure why he selected that item, apart from having a vague memory of his granddad giving him one when he was a little boy. Anyway, it didn't work. He switched to a football and failed again.

'You're not trying, man!' Jocky vented his irritation. He wasn't a natural teacher.

'I am!' Dog shouted back. After a few deep breaths Dog tried again, but this time with a golf ball. It didn't happen. The more Dog laboured, the further away it got. Annoyed at himself for not getting it, Dog stopped with his arms folded.

'Let's get you some motivation, man,' Jocky said, and messing around, pretended to throw a punch at Dog, who ducked. Dog was stunned and came up, eyes blazing at Jocky.

'I'm kidding, man. Don't panic,' Jocky said as he held up his hands. They stood facing each other, glaring. Then quite unexpectedly, Dog heard Jocky's thoughts. They were blue, derogatory, and aimed at Dog. *My God, I think I just heard Jocky's thoughts. I think I just done it.* Dog's stomach flipped with nervous exhilaration as he continued to look at Jocky.

'What you staring at, man? I was kidding; don't get so uptight,' Jocky said. Dog didn't know what to say. Why was he keeping quiet about the Thought Reading? Surely Jocky would be pleased. But Jocky was unpredictable, even on a good day, and sometimes Dog didn't trust him. Well, most of the time Dog didn't trust him. After the shock of hearing Jocky's thoughts, Dog closed down. It was all he could summon for the rest of the session.

'Don't worry, man. You'll get it,' Jocky said as he saw Dog to the door. 'Come back Sunday night. We'll crack it then.'

'Sure. Cheers.'

'No worries. Got to get you up to speed, soon as. Things to do. Things to achieve.' Jocky rubbed his hands together and stared off into the distance. Dog raised a questioning eyebrow. 'It'll be cool,' Jocky said after seeing Dog look at him. Jocky didn't realise it would take so flaming well long to get his army in place.

'Sure.' Dog turned and raised a hand goodbye as he walked down the path to the front gate. 'See you.'

'Sunday, man.'

Dog walked home, a mix of emotions. With his mind on his first ever Thought Read, Dog bumped into an elderly lady coming out of the bakery below his flat. It was rare to see any elderly person inside Area One. Dog wasn't sure why that was. Maybe they couldn't be bothered or perhaps the idea of the massive change was just too great, who knew. Dog apologised to the lady, and even though the woman smiled at him and said 'Never mind' out loud, her thoughts said the complete opposite. Like Jocky's thoughts earlier, they were coarse and far from what Dog would imagine an elderly lady saying. Surprised, Dog burst out laughing, which prompted another torrent of abuse for him in her mind as she rolled her eyes and stormed off. *Oh my word! This is epic!* Dog shook his head as he made his way to his flat.

The next day, the Thought Reading ability appeared again. Dog was on his way to a clearing in the forest that had wooden benches positioned to take in the picturesque views. As he passed the first bench he heard, 'Hello, sexy.' Dog turned towards the young woman who was sitting alone, seemingly enjoying the sun. She smiled sweetly and he returned the smile. *Did she actually talk to me?* Dog wasn't sure. 'Nice smile too. Yes, I think I probably would.' This time he was looking right at her face. Her lips never moved once. Dog stifled a laugh. *It's happening again.* He walked towards the bench furthest away. 'Cute. Definitely husband potential,' he heard. *Blimey!* Dog changed his mind about sitting down and walked straight on, euphoria and laughter fizzing inside him.

The following morning before he made his way to Jocky's, it happened again in the bakery. He was standing in the queue behind a couple who were waiting to be served. The woman was making all the selections and the man clearly did not agree, because Dog could hear him. Dog edged forward to check the man's face and, like the others, his lips were sealed. The man just smiled inanely at his wife as she made all the wrong choices. Dog sniggered and the man turned around.

'I agree, the sourdough bread is better,' Dog mouthed. The man raised his eyebrows as he realised what Dog had done and then shrugged in defeat, pulling a caught-in-the-act face. There was little place to hide in here and no point getting angry. Everyone wanted the abilities, and that inevitably meant being on the receiving end too.

As Dog made his way to Jocky's, it was clear he would need his help. The thrill Dog felt was tinged with apprehension, and as soon as Jocky opened the door, Dog burst out, 'I can Thought Read.' Jocky instantly went into high alert with the news, emptying his mind. He would have to be careful around Dog now.

It was a sacrifice Jocky was willing to make, because he had his plan – an army of loyal followers, all able to access the abilities to some degree, with him being the best, obviously. They would be unstoppable, invincible. Once

Area One was under his control, he would lead them out into the world. Now that is where Jocky saw it getting very tasty indeed. With these abilities and his army, he knew he could rule the world. No one would be able to touch him. And then everyone would know exactly why he was named The Untouchable.

'Cool, man.' Jocky high-fived Dog, who wasn't really into the whole weird greeting thing, but joined in, such was his mood.

'Once you've cracked one, they'll all come flooding in.' Jocky led the way to the kitchen.

'I can't wait,' Dog said, grinning as he remembered. 'I need your help controlling them though. It's completely epic. And a bit scary.'

'Sure thing, man. Tea?'

'Great, thanks.'

'Jasmine, Earl Grey—'

'Normal please,' Dog chipped in.

'Cool. We'll get this, then get down to work.'

As Jocky and Dog met regularly over the weeks, Dog got to sample the four abilities. Due to his lack of belief in his own capabilities, he found Manifestation the hardest. So far he'd only experienced it twice: once he materialised a small bottle of beer and the other time a pain au chocolat, not as good as the bakery's downstairs though. He'd have to work on that. It's funny how if you didn't get clear and specific, the universe filled in the gaps for you. To date, Thought Reading was his most successful ability, and he'd had some success with Seeing and Sensing. As with everyone, the abilities appeared only occasionally, which was just as well. Dog could clearly see how easy it would be to panic and freak out. It was especially true when Dog had a Seeing and Sensing episode together. That was way over the top and not something he wanted to repeat any time soon.

Dog had just manifested the beer and he and Jocky were taking a break. Jocky had been thinking about his younger brother Little Davey, who hero-worshipped him. For some reason, at the sight of the beer, Jocky started to feel a deep-rooted sadness and rage that his brother would never get to experience having a cold beer. His mind then darted to one of the most painful memories of his life.

Jocky was twelve and Little Davey was eight, and on this particular Saturday night when their dad arrived home from a day spent in the pub, he was in a foul mood – far worse than usual. Maybe he'd lost on the horses again or someone had spilt his drink, who knows. Or perhaps it was just because. Once he'd given their mum a fractured rib and Jocky a black eye, he started on Little Davey. This was unusual. He rarely gave out to Little Davey, but something was different about their dad today. In the past, he always stopped after a few punches had been dished out, with the lion's share going to his wife. Not today. Today the lion's share was unloaded onto Little Davey. God only knows why. Little Davey was the old man's favourite. With his face contorted and mask-like, he rained down on Little Davey, his eyes black, glazed, vacant. Shouting obscenities, spit flying from his mouth. Their mum screamed and begged him to stop hurting her baby. It was water off a duck's back. Jocky jumped onto the old man, kicking him and pulling at his arms to try and stop his fists flying into Little Davey's body. No one knew why he laid into Little Davey so hard that day. Something had snapped inside him. His punches pounded. Feet in boots slammed into flesh. Little Davey sobbed and curled into a ball. Until Little Davey's body lay motionless. A couple of seconds passed before the old man realised something had changed. He looked at Little Davey, then to his wife, then to Jocky. Coming to, registering, with eyes that were wide and mad; a face that was twisted in horror. He ran from the house. Then the screech of sirens sounded, coming closer.

Little Davey died two weeks later. Their mum blamed Jocky, and he was left to make sense of that day and all the years of abuse he'd suffered at the hands of his father, the man who was meant to be his protector, his hero. On top of everything, his mum now hated him. She made Jocky a target for her displaced rage, guilt, and hatred. The fact that his father was never caught only added to Jocky's pain. His twelve-year-old battered brain and crushed spirit made no sense of it at all. So he swallowed it up and crushed it deep inside him, leaving it to poison and contaminate every fibre of his being.

Dog felt the intense emotions from that day. He saw the turmoil Jocky had lived and felt the pain from years of abuse. He knew the deeply buried warped and gnarled agony that was locked inside Jocky's mind, body, and spirit. The emotions and feelings were overwhelming, the sensation was physical. Pain like nothing he had ever felt before. Raw, coarse, heavy, depraved, like a tsunami threatening to knock Dog off his feet and wash him into oblivion.

'Arghhhhhh!' Dog dropped to the floor, overcome.

'What's up, man?' Jocky went over to Dog.

'Boy. Small. Beaten.' Dog pushed out the words. He lifted up his head and his eyes met Jocky's. 'You were there. Much younger.'

'What?' Jocky sat down. He thought he knew what was happening to Dog, but didn't know how much he'd seen or felt. Dog was not only feeling Jocky's emotions about that whole experience, he had the scene running in his head. After a couple of minute's deep breathing, the emotions began to subside and the images vanished.

'Holy crap!' Dog said, breathing as though he'd run a marathon.

'What happened, man?' Jocky asked. Dog told him what he'd felt and the film playing out in his mind.

'That was us.' Jocky looked faraway. 'Happy families, eh?'

'I thought you could only see the present or the future. I didn't know you could see past situations,' Dog said, gobsmacked. He yawned, suddenly feeling overwhelmingly tired.

'Me too, man. Me too,' Jocky said.

After that, Dog's perception of Jocky altered. Yes, Jocky could be wild, aggressive, unpredictable, and downright frightening, but Dog understood where it all came from. And as they worked together, Dog got to read more of Jocky's thoughts and sense his emotions. Those times weren't easy for either of them, but it bound them together in a way that wouldn't have been possible outside of Area One. In those brief moments, Jocky lost his steel protection and became open, confused, lost even. As soon as the abilities had subsided in Dog, Jocky erected his guard, cleared his mind, and they continued with their work. It took some getting used to for Jocky, who was more used to being closed and the one calling all the shots. Through the abilities, Dog was able to catch glimpses of the real Jocky, and it was only for the fact that Dog reminded Jocky so much of Little Davey that Dog was still in one piece. Anyone else who tried to go that deep inside Jocky would have run scared, or failing that, Jocky would have ripped their heart out.

****

"In the beginning you will mostly experience one ability at a time, and the growth of that ability will be gradual and incremental. It will be vital for you to heighten your awareness so that you understand when the abilities are online and active, and how they are developing. If you do not strive for this awareness, you could be in turmoil with another's thoughts and emotions, believing they are yours, when really they are not. You may also see events, believing they are events in your own individual life, when really they are someone else's.

As you develop with the abilities, you will be able to pick up more than one person's thoughts or feelings. For example, you will hear two people at the same time, then three perhaps, then maybe a group of ten. The thoughts of a whole country, then the whole world, then finally the One. The same will apply to sensing the emotions of others. You will expand until you know everyone's emotions, all being felt simultaneously.

With the Law of Seeing you will firstly begin to see one event at a time, which may or may not be directly related to your life. Then you will grow to see more at the same time. Events in your life, overlaid with events in another's life. Moments in the past, combined with moments in the future. Events from this lifetime, intertwined with events from past, future, or parallel lifetimes.

This is the natural evolvement of all the Laws you have summoned. And it is the phase before all thoughts, emotions, and seeing become One."

Chapter Twenty

'We need to take action,' Jocky said as Dog came into the kitchen. Jocky had been awake since the early hours of the morning.

'What do you mean?' Dog asked as he ruffled his hair, still half asleep.

'They've got Keene.'

'Who have?'

'The security services. They got him in the night.'

Keene was one of Jocky's unknowing and unsuspecting Diamond Army recruits. So far, Jocky had six: Keene, Eyes, Wolf, Brains, Tommy, and of course, Dog. All selected for their malleability and enthusiasm for the dark side. None of them knew they were trying out for his army, because Jocky worked on a need-to-know basis.

Dog rubbed his hand over his face, trying to wake himself.

'Eyes came round this morning to tell me. Half past two. I was not happy, let me tell you,' Jocky said. A cruel smile spread across his face as he remembered Eyes's reaction when he hauled him in through the front door by the scruff of his neck and shoved him hard against the wall.

'I didn't hear anything,' Dog said, confused.

'Yeah, well. Eyes was at Keene's place last night. They'd had a few drinks and Eyes fell asleep in the toilet apparently. The secret service scum barged in and grabbed Keene. By the time Eyes knew what was going on, they'd thrown Keene into the back of a van and were off.'

In Jocky's world, everyone needed a nickname, unless of course he deemed your real name cool; then you were allowed to keep it. Eyes's real name was Howard and was nicknamed Eyes by Jocky because of his large brown eyes. Dog knew Jocky well enough now to know that he would never allow the name Howard anywhere near his mouth. Jocky liked the names Keene and Dog so they were permitted to remain unchanged. Dog, whose real name was Oscar, had changed his name at school and it had stuck.

'Why did they take him?' Dog asked.

'They don't need no reason.'

'But what can we do against them?' Dog said. Jocky smiled and tapped the side of his nose.

'All in good time.' Jocky left the house without another word.

Dog yawned and went over to the kettle. Recently he'd been spending more time at Jocky's house as Jocky taught Dog the way of the abilities. It was finally paying off and Dog was progressing. He was even helping Jocky out with his training courses, which were mostly attended by males with a certain wild edge. Dog smiled as he thought of the motley crew that was drawn to Jocky's courses, wondering how on earth some of them had made it through the Chryso in the first place. Thinking about it, maybe they hadn't. Not legally anyway. That was the difference between Jocky's courses and the authority approved ones. Jocky asked no questions and taught the abilities regardless, but in return he demanded your unswerving and unmitigated loyalty.

'Right, listen up.' Jocky stood in front of the five young men sitting in his basement room. Dog, Eyes, Wolf – nicknamed because of his copious amounts of thick dark hair – Brains because he had two degrees, and Tommy, who was allowed to keep his real name because it had a certain gangster ring to it. Jocky's talent was definitely not creative naming. 'By you turning up tonight, you're committed. No going back, right?' Jocky stared at each in turn, threatening them to disagree. They all nodded their accord. Jocky saw it as a test for them. If they proved themselves, these five would form the core of his army.

'I've got someone on the inside who's helping us, so it should be a doddle.' Jocky smiled, thinking back to what he'd done to wheedle out the information from Daisy. It hadn't been hard. She was a willing participant and definitely worth staying up half the night for. Eyes sniggered.

'Nice one, Jocky.' Eyes had read Jocky's X-rated thoughts. Jocky fixed him a fearsome look and immediately Eyes held up his hands. 'Sorry, sorry,' Eyes said quickly, trying to focus on something else. You had to be so careful in here. Jocky rapidly cleared his mind and went on to tell the boys of his plan.

'So we'll hit it when the guard is distracted. It's one of their quiet times. My person inside will open this door here at 3.10 tomorrow morning.' Jocky pointed to the hand-drawn map he'd attached to the flipchart stand. 'Keene's cell is the first on the right, just inside this door. She'll open the cell door and warn Keene prior. Now, has everyone got that?' They all nodded. 'Remember, we're doing this for our brother. He shouldn't be locked up; he's done nothing wrong. Are you with me?' Jocky held up his fist. The others followed.

'Yes!' they cried in unison.

In the early hours of the morning, they made their way on foot to the Bruce Temperance Institution and waited in a wooded area for Daisy to open the door.

'Right, you lot. Clear your minds,' Jocky instructed. They closed their eyes.

'Oh wait, I can see him,' Brains whispered loudly.

'I said clear your minds!' Jocky said, regretting that he'd brought all five along. Maybe he should have come on his own. It was their first proper job and they undoubtedly needed more training.

'It's Keene.' Brains opened his eyes. 'I can see him, Jocky. Inside the building.' Jocky finally realised what he was talking about.

'Can you see where he is?' Jocky asked.

'He's inside, sitting on his bed, dressed.'

'Good.' On second thought, maybe this was just what was needed, to test their mettle, see who could cut the mustard. Jocky grinned smugly at the progress his army was making. They would be bulletproof. 'What else?'

'His cell. It's exactly where you said it would be. See that door? It's the first cell on the right.'

'Well done, man.' Jocky smiled. So Daisy had come through. He wasn't one hundred percent sure about her. One night had obviously done the trick. 'Right, let's all relax again. We've got a few minutes before we move out.' After several minutes, Jocky checked his watch. 'Okay, show time. Brains and Tommy, you stay here. Wolf and Eyes, just outside the door. Dog with me.' They'd all been given their jobs earlier that night and knew what to do.

'You'll be alright.' Jocky stared at Dog. 'And Tommy, stop your complaining. We need men at each point.' Tommy and Dog hadn't opened their mouths. Jocky was Thought Reading. 'Does everyone know what they need to do?' They submitted. 'Good.' Jocky checked his watch again. 'On my say so. Go!' Keeping low, they moved into position. As Jocky approached the door, it opened and Daisy appeared. She beckoned them inside.

'Quick, you've got no more than five minutes to get him out. I couldn't get you any longer.' Her friend was currently distracting the security guard who was meant to be watching the cameras. Hopefully, she had also pushed pause on the recordings. Daisy unlocked the cell, turned to kiss Jocky full on the lips, and then ran away as fast as she could. She had to be somewhere else if it all kicked off. Jocky pushed open the cell door.

'Blimey! I didn't believe she'd do it. I thought they were stitching me up,' Keene said as Jocky and Dog strode into his cell.

'You alright, man?' Jocky walked over to Keene and patted his back. He flinched. 'You alright? Did they do something to you, man?' Jocky had heard the stories. Keene looked dark around the eyes, haunted almost. He lifted his top to reveal four red, square marks on the front of his body, more on his back. 'What's that?' Jocky asked.

'They tried to get me to talk.'

'What about? You haven't done anything wrong.'

'Whether I had the abilities. About anything really,' Keene said. Jocky's eyes blackened with rage.

'They did what?' Jocky's voice was low and thick as he held onto his anger.

'I didn't tell them anything. They said they would do worse.' Terror and tears filled Keene's eyes.

'Son of a...!' Jocky shook his head.

'Come on, let's go.' Dog had tried to check if anyone was coming using the abilities. He couldn't get anything; he was far too tense, especially after seeing Keene. If they caught them, who knew what was in store for them all.

'I'll go first,' Jocky said. He edged out of the cell and looked down the corridor to see two guards running towards them. Jocky moved back into the cell, slamming the door shut. He closed his eyes and held out his empty hands. In a millisecond, two guns appeared, one in each hand.

'Jeez!' Dog said.

'Oh my...' Keene said.

'We've got company. Keep behind me. I'll cover you both.' Jocky pulled open the door and stepped out, aiming the guns at the guards. 'Run!' Jocky screamed at Dog and Keene.

'Drop your weapons!' one of the guards shouted.

Keene saw the open door and ran; there was no way he was staying there a moment longer. Dog began to follow, but turned just in time to see the guards unleash their taser guns on Jocky, who dropped to the ground, body rigid with thousands of volts being delivered via thin copper wires. Jocky's face contorted, his eyes pleading, frightened and powerless. Dog spun round and ran as fast as he could out of the building. He knew there was nothing he could do for Jocky and he would only end up getting caught if he stayed.

Running out of the building, Keene stirred the others and soon they were racing back to Jocky's house, careful to enter through the back via the neighbour's gardens. They headed straight to the basement and collapsed on the sofas.

'Jeez! That was close,' Eyes said.

'Yeah, what happened to you two?' Dog looked at Eyes and Wolf. 'You were meant to be at the door as backup. Fat lot of good you were.' Dog pushed his hands through his hair. The night had not gone to plan. Wolf looked sheepish.

'I thought you said the coast would be clear?' Eyes was angry.

'Jocky's contact said that, not me.' Dog glared at Eyes.

'Anything could have happened to us. Just look at the state of Keene. We would have been next.' Eyes was jittery after their near miss.

'Jocky is already next,' Dog said to Eyes.

'Yeah, I know.' Eyes remembered they were minus one. He was only glad it wasn't him. Brains and Tommy looked at each other; they'd been the first ones to run for it.

'We've got to get him out,' Dog said.

'That's risky.' Keene didn't want to go anywhere near the BTI ever again.

'He risked it for you.' Dog pointed at Keene. 'And they've got him because of you.' Dog said.

'I know,' Keene said, feeling guilty. 'But you don't realise what they do to you in there.' He stood up and lifted up his top to show the marks of his torture.

'Jesus!' Wolf said. There was no way he was putting himself in line for any of that. As soon as he could, he was getting as far away from these people as possible. Maybe even leave Area One altogether. This whole thing was not matching up to his dream, in any which way. Brains and Tommy shook their heads in disgust, maddened at the BTI staff that had inflicted this upon their brother.

'It isn't some normal sort of prison or hospital you know.' Keene pulled down his top. 'Once they get a sniff of the abilities, they start on you. And I don't just mean questioning either.'

'Look, I know you had a bad time, Keene, but even more reason for us to get Jocky out and save him from the same fate,' Dog said. He wasn't going to leave Jocky in that place. No way.

'That's true. He would do it for any one of us,' Brains said, siding with Dog.

'I'm in,' Tommy said.

'Me too,' Eyes said. Dog looked at Wolf, who nodded without looking Dog in the eyes. Wolf wasn't doing it. Once he got out of here tonight, he'd be gone. Dog looked at Keene, who sighed heavily.

'Alright,' Keene said. 'But if it looks like we're getting in too deep, I'm out.' Dog wasn't happy with Keene's lack of commitment.

'Right then. So we'll meet at my flat tomorrow evening. Keep your heads down. Keene, you'd better come and stay with me. They'll probably be watching your place. No doubt they'll be watching this house as well, so we'll leave the back way.' They left Jocky's house and scattered.

'Has anyone heard from Wolf?' Dog asked. It was after dark the following evening as they sat in Dog's small lounge, minus Wolf.

'I knocked on his door on the way over and there was no answer. Definitely no one in,' Eyes said.

'What's he playing at?' Dog checked his watch and frowned.

'Do you think they've got him?' Eyes said. Dog paused for a moment, thinking. He nodded slowly. Eyes could be right.

'Jeez, you're right. They could have him,' Keene said. The thought added to Keene's anxiety. Being held in the BTI was awful, and he'd do anything to avoid a repeat performance. He'd have to be extra careful if he was going to help with the breakout of Jocky. And it was still a very big 'if' in his mind. As Keene brooded on Wolf's possible capture, the 'if' turned into a definite 'no way'. *It won't be long before they have us all,* Keene thought.

'That's not going to happen. Do you hear me?' Dog stared at Keene, who quickly snapped back to the room and wiped his mind clear as fast as he could. 'Too late, I heard you.'

'Huh?' Keene said. *What did he hear?* Keene was suddenly worried. *Christ, I hate this bloody place.*

'You said, "It won't be long before they have us all", right?' Dog's eyes bored into Keene, who inwardly breathed a sigh of relief.

'Right,' Keene said.

'Okay, we've got work to do,' Dog said as he addressed the boys. 'While we plan the breakout we'll need to keep honing our abilities.' Dog remembered Jocky's impressive manifestation of the guns. 'And we need to find out where they're holding Jocky.'

'And if they've got Wolf,' Keene added.

'Yeah, and that's just for starters. We also need to get someone on the inside to come onto the team.' Dog didn't know if Daisy would help them or even how to get hold of her.

'Can we really do this?' Brains asked. It sounded like an impossible task.

'We have to. Somehow, we have to,' Dog said, stepping into Jocky's role as leader of the pack.

Chapter Twenty-One

It didn't take long for Hudson to realise what he was involved in. Exactly one hour after Dr Emmett Brown left his room, Ms Judy Payne bustled in, a small, thin, nervous woman in her late fifties holding a clipboard.

'Oh, it's not locked,' Judy said as she entered Hudson's cell. Shortly after Dr Emmett Brown had left, a guard came along and unlocked the door, peered in, and said, 'I'll leave it open now.' Hudson wasn't sure what to do. Should he make a dash for it? No, it was too dangerous without knowing the quickest, safest route out. Instead, he sat on the bed trying to recall his mental health training.

'Orders from Dr Emmett Brown,' Hudson explained to Judy.

'Yes, yes, quite,' she said.

'Hudson Story, pleased to meet you.' Hudson held out his hand.

'Ms Judy Payne, pleased to meet you too.' She adjusted her tortoiseshell glasses and consulted the list attached to her clipboard. 'Right, Mr Story, follow me.'

'Oh, Judy, please call me Hudson.'

'Very well, Hudson.' She glanced down at the clipboard. 'I'm Ms Payne though,' she muttered.

'Right. Sure.' He was suitably told. Ms Payne gave very little eye contact and had a habit of smoothing out invisible creases in her high-collared white blouse.

'Follow me.' Ms Payne walked at speed out of the room, down the corridor, and through two sets of security doors. Hudson tried to catch the codes, but she was fast and covered the security pads with her clipboard. 'This is the Bruce Temperance Institution, named after the professor who opened it. He's not with us currently.' Hudson could barely hear her as she stormed ahead. 'The building is broadly divided into three wings that are formed into a U-shape with a lovely courtyard garden at the centre.'

'Right. Nice,' he said. Ms Payne stopped suddenly to check her clipboard and Hudson almost ran into the back of her.

'Ummm. Yes. I'll show you the key areas today. Now let me see. The C-Wing first, I think. They should be finished...' Ms Payne trailed off.

'Does the C stand for anything?' Hudson asked. Ms Payne gave Hudson a rare moment of eye contact and hesitated.

'The C-Wing is for our high-risk individuals. We also have the R-Wing for medium risk and then there's the B-Wing for low risk.' She looked down at her list.

'Do the letters stand for anything?'

'They're named after birds. Bruce Temperance was an avid birdwatcher,' Ms Payne said, consulting the all-important list.

'Oh, nice.'

'Yes, quite. Right, let's introduce you to the C-Wing.' She gave a distinct sigh and strode off. 'You were being held ... ummm ... I mean you were staying in our B-Wing, Mr Story.'

'It's Hudson. Please call me Hudson, Ms Payne.'

'What? Oh yes, quite.' She checked her clipboard again, as if she couldn't find her way through life without it.

'There is a building attached to B-Wing used for staff accommodation. I'll take you there later. And part of B-Wing is used for holding people until we've assessed and categorised them.'

'Right.'

'Then they are either released or moved to another wing.'

'Released? Okay.' Hudson doubted anyone was ever released.

'A small selection ... errrrr ... they're chosen to help us in the department called ... errrr ... Special Projects. It's located in a dedicated section of C-Wing.' Ms Payne speeded up and Hudson virtually broke into a jog.

'What's Special Projects?'

'Dr Emmett Brown can fill you in on all the details.'

'Okay.' *Special Projects. Sounds interesting*, Hudson thought.

'Over to C-Wing now.' Ms Payne slowed, leant towards Hudson, and whispered, 'These patients are high risk.' She shook her head in a shame-on-them manner.

'Right.' Hudson didn't know what to say or think. Ms Payne reminded him of so many people working in the mental health field, clueless about the people in their care. A feeling of déjà vu washed over Hudson and he sighed.

Ms Payne ticked her list, tapped the security keypad, and waited for the door to click open. As they walked down the short corridor and stepped into the common room of C-Wing, a man shouted out loud, 'It's coming! The end is coming!' Hudson turned to see a half-naked man with a large spider tattoo on his chest running towards them with two male nurses hot on his trail.

'Oh, my word!' Ms Payne held up the clipboard to protect her like a shield.

'Get him!' one of nurses yelled at Hudson.

'What, me?' Hudson turned to Ms Payne.

'Yes, quick. Catch him.' Ms Payne edged behind Hudson for cover and nudged him forward.

'Yes, you donkey, get him.' The nurse bent over with his hands on his knees trying to catch his breath as the half-naked man continued to run around the room, leaping over and around chairs and tables shouting, 'The end of the world is coming!' Other staff had now locked all the doors leading from the common room. As Hudson ran after the tattooed man, he wondered what on earth he was doing. This didn't bode well for the rest of his time here. Eventually, Hudson cornered him and just as he went to grab his arm, Hudson heard from one of the male nurses, 'Careful, he's got the sedative.' Mr Spider Man was hiding it in his hand and unleashed the full syringe into Hudson's arm.

'I think we should keep schtum. Think of the paperwork.' 'Anyway, he's safely locked up now.' 'Till the next time.' Voices swam around Hudson. He couldn't work out where they were coming from. 'He's been out for ages.' 'Do you think he's okay?' Icy water splashed over Hudson's face.

'Urghh!' Hudson opened his eyes.

'That was very unprofessional, Nurse Tindell,' Ms Payne chastised one of the male nurses now holding an empty cup.

'All yours,' Nurse Blake Tindell said as he left the room.

'Here, let me dry you off.' Ms Payne patted Hudson's face dry with a clean cotton handkerchief.

'Thanks.' Hudson slowly pushed himself up. 'What happened?'

'Well, one of the patients'—Ms Payne lowered her voice—'nasty piece of work he is, got loose. And you saved the day.' Hudson's foggy mind began to recall the half-naked man with the spider tattoo.

'The man the two nurses were chasing?'

'Yes.'

'But why am I...?'

'He sedated you.' She pushed her glasses up her nose and sniffed. 'Heaven only knows how he got the drugs and syringe.'

'Blimey!'

'Quite.'

After two cups of coffee and several chocolate biscuits, Hudson felt more awake and they continued the tour, although following Hudson's ordeal, Ms Payne deigned to shorten it. She was far from happy, as it totally disrupted her tightly timed schedule and forced her to make ugly lines on her paperwork.

It had been a depressing first day and later, as Hudson lay on his bed in the staff accommodation section, he realised he would have to find a way to get out of the Institution. Perhaps even out of Area One entirely. He had no idea how yet, he just knew he couldn't stay.

The next two days were less momentous with Hudson having a basic medical (which he passed), meeting some of the staff (definitely a case of the lunatics running the asylum), and having a laborious overview of the BTI's administration processes. This last part had Ms Payne in ecstasy, meticulously crossing every *t* and dotting every last *i* on her precious clipboard. If there was a significant other for Ms Payne, Hudson knew they would not have it easy. Now for his fourth day, Hudson had been handed over to Dr Sandra

Knutt for his first taste of caring and dealing with the Institution's patients.

'What makes them high risk?' Hudson asked Dr Knutt as they made their way to C-Wing.

'What?' Dr Knutt punched keys on a keypad for one of the secure rooms. The door opened on a frail old woman, sedated and strapped to a bed. As they stepped into the room, the stagnant, sour air hit Hudson and made him cough.

'What makes them high risk?' Hudson looked at the lady, who was making audible noises, aware that people had entered her room.

'Oh, you know.' Dr Knutt walked briskly to the end of the woman's bed, picked up the notes attached to a clipboard, and read them intently, flicking through the pages. 'Right, basic checks. Empty the urine bag, check the catheter, change her diaper, that's about it.'

'Should we bathe her?' It was obvious to Hudson the woman was in dire need of a wash.

'What? Yes, of course,' Dr Knutt said. 'Nurse Harper will do that in a moment. You can assist her.' She held the woman's thin limp wrist to check her pulse. *How long has she been like this? What on earth had she done to deserve this?* Hudson thought as he looked at the woman. She was probably someone's granny. Out of the corner of her eye, Dr Knutt saw Hudson staring at the patient, a distant look in his eyes.

'They can't all handle it in here you know,' she said.

'Surely there's a better way?' Hudson turned to Dr Knutt, who dropped the woman's arm and now lifted one of her half-closed eyelids. 'How long has she been like this?'

'Quite a while.'

'How long? This isn't right, you know.' Hudson couldn't curb his distress. 'If she can't cope, why don't you let her leave Area One and go back home?'

'We can't do that.'

'Why not?' Hudson didn't understand. 'Surely people like this could leave? Get transferred to one of the facilities outside of Area One? At least they would be closer to family and friends.'

'It's not that easy,' Dr Knutt said.

'Why? Why isn't it that easy?' Hudson was just about holding onto his rage.

'We did in the beginning. Well, not this one. But then...' Dr Knutt paused.

'But then what?' Hudson wanted to shake Dr Knutt.

'Some of them still had the abilities outside of Area One. Not everyone, just some.' She sighed and looked down at the floor, her mind travelling back to those chaotic weeks. *If he thinks this is bad, he should have been around then*, Dr Knutt thought.

'Oh, my...' Hudson clamped a hand over his mouth, realising the enormity of what Dr Sandra Knutt had just said. 'I thought people could only tap into the abilities inside Area One. I thought it was all to do with the environment, the location. That's what the government tell us. That's what they all say. That it's a portal. Some sort of energy portal. Here. Only found here. Everyone says that.' Hudson ran his hands through his hair. His eyes opened wide as his brain kicked into overdrive, extracting meaning from this staggering information.

'That's what we thought.' Dr Knutt suddenly looked tired. In seconds, dark circles and bags had appeared under her eyes.

'So you lied. You're lying. All of you. The authorities. The government. You tell everyone the abilities only ever work in Area One, within a specific location, a defined place. It's not true. You lied.' Hudson paced around, unable to keep still, his body filled with adrenalin.

'It seems that some who gain the abilities inside Area One have them forever, regardless of where they are.' Dr Knutt closed her ears to Hudson's accusations.

'Do you know what this means?' Hudson didn't really want an answer. He was trying to process everything. And anyway, she knew exactly what it meant. 'It means that it's not the place, it's the people.' As Hudson said the word 'people', his eyes stretched even wider. 'It's the people. Oh, my God. It's us. All of us. We're changing. Evolving. As a race. It must be that. It can only be that. Oh, my word.' Hudson felt lightheaded, as though he was floating.

'That's not strictly true. It does seem to be Area One that stimulates the abilities, but once gained, they can stay with you forever. No matter what the location.'

'Hold on, so what does that mean for the ones that can't cope and want to leave?'

'They can't.'

'They can never leave?'

'Never is a long time, Hudson.'

'Tell that to the prisoners you've got drugged and chained to the beds in this place!' Hudson was seething. Dr Knutt gave him a sideward glance.

'We're dealing with massive unknowns here, Hudson, just remember that. We're constantly exploring new ways of managing the situation, but we have a duty of care to everyone in this country. If a few have to be sacrificed for the peace and safety of the many, then so be it.'

'What? What the…? You cannot be serious.' Hudson glared at Dr Knutt, who shot daggers straight back at him. 'You heartless bitch!' Usually Hudson was not an aggressive person, but the Bruce Temperance Institution seemed to poke and jab at his deepest, darkest, shadowy places. Dr Knutt rolled her eyes in reprimand.

'I'll let that go, Hudson. It's your first few days and it's always a shock.' She replaced the woman's notes at the end of the bed. 'I didn't make the rules, just remember that,' she said. Carefully, she placed the fountain pen in her top pocket. 'Two thirty-seven can have her bed bath now. Nurse Harper will help you.'

'Two thirty-seven!? Two thirty-seven!? You give them numbers. Oh, my … Are you serious?' Hudson wrung his hands together angrily, mainly to stop him from strangling Dr Knutt. 'Jesus!' Hudson had been pushed to his limit. Dr Knutt gave Hudson a dirty look before walking out of the room with her head held high.

Hudson had already started gently washing Violet Buntiford's hands and arms, talking calmly and reassuring her, when Nurse Melanie Harper peered through the door's viewing window. Emotion caught at the back of Melanie's throat. It was a rare sight indeed to see someone gently and respectfully caring for a patient at the Institution. Opening the door, she walked in, and as Hudson turned around, she recognised him as the neighbour she'd been introduced to a couple of days ago.

'Hi. When they said you'd be helping, I didn't register the name.' Hudson put down the flannel and soap, peeled off his protective medical gloves, and went to the basin to wash his hands. 'I'm Hudson. Not sure if you remember?'

'Yes, I do. How's it going?' She saw something in his eyes that triggered her own bleak, raw memories. Melanie knew. She understood.

'Bit of a shock to the system, isn't it?' Melanie said.

'That's an understatement.' Hudson shook his head.

'Look, if you need to talk, have a coffee or something, I'm a good listener. I know what you're going through.' Melanie placed her hand on his arm.

'That would be great. How about tonight?' Hudson yearned for some friendly interaction. 'If you're free, that is?' She was the only kind person he'd met since being in here.

'Tonight? Okay. I finish at six. I could meet you then if you like?'

'Works for me. Can we meet outside of here though?'

'Sure. There's a little tea shop I know called Rose's Tea Shop. The owner makes the most heavenly cakes. And from scratch, even though she's an apt Manifester.' Melanie smiled fondly as she recalled the time Faith told her how she missed the whole baking process, weighing out the individual ingredients, the feel of butter and flour between her fingers, the comforting smells of cocoa, vanilla essence, and cakes baking in the oven. Faith had opened the shop manifesting all kinds of cakes and biscuits, and at first, it was a novelty. If a customer dreamt it, she would manifest it. Customers came from all over Area One to watch her in action, hoping her manifestation ability would rub off on them. But after a while, Faith admitted she missed the art and creativity, and went back to the old-fashioned way of baking. Although she did still manifest for a few hardcore Area One residents.

'Just what I need.' Hudson sighed, relieved at the thought of some home comforts.

'Great. Shall we continue with Violet?' Melanie asked.

'Dr Sandra Knutt called her Two thirty-seven.'

'I know. Most of the doctors and nurses use the numbers. There are a few of us who refuse and I'm one of them,' Melanie said firmly. Hudson's thirsty heart devoured its first sip of kindness.

'I shall follow your lead, Nurse Harper.' Hudson smiled. 'Do you know why Violet's here?'

'Not for sure. There were rumours that the people assessing her couldn't work out if she had dementia or if she had abilities and couldn't deal with them.' Melanie looked sad.

'So she could have dementia and they're leaving her like this?' Hudson was alarmed. 'What about her family? Does she have any?'

'I don't think so.' Melanie leaned closer to Hudson. 'That's why they can get away with it.'

'You are kidding me.' Hudson shook his head in disbelief. 'This place sickens me.'

'Me too. But I'm glad I can be here to care for her,' Melanie said as she checked the temperature of the water and put on her medical gloves.

Later that evening over a pot of tea and slices of bona fide homemade lemon drizzle cake, Hudson and Melanie got to know each other, and for the first time since his capture, Hudson felt like he'd found someone he could trust. He ended up telling Melanie about the break-in, Ziva, and his manifesting ability.

'Don't tell anyone about your ability, Hudson,' Melanie said in hushed tones.

'I told them during questioning,' he whispered back.

'You may not be safe, now they know.' She glanced around cautiously.

'Why not? Isn't that what this place is all about?'

'It's different for the staff in here, especially in the Institution.' Melanie decided to stop there. 'I'll tell you another time.' Hudson nodded and ate the last mouthful of cake, wondering what they would do to him. Every day his desire to get out of Area One was growing. *How utterly ironic.*

'Have you got any abilities?' Hudson asked in a low tone.

'I'm not sure. I'm pretty good at knowing other people's feelings and what's about to happen before time, but I've had these since I was a little girl. So they may not be the proper Sensor and Seeing abilities,'

Hudson leaned in. 'Do you know the abilities are not linked to the location?'

'I know,' Melanie said. 'I arrived just before they changed the policy about letting people leave Area One to go back home. It was mayhem. Everyone was running around like headless chickens, trying to find ways to get the situation contained.' Melanie scanned the tea shop, constantly vigil. 'We can talk about it another time.' Hudson understood and lightened the conversation by asking about Holmes Chapel, the village where Melanie grew up.

After tea and cake, they walked back to the staff accommodation block.

'So, tell me why I might not be safe now they know about my ability? What will they do to me?' Hudson asked.

'There was another nurse, a sweet girl called Charlotte, who joined just after me. She developed the Manifestation and Seeing abilities quickly after she arrived. Next thing, she's telling me they want her to work in Special Projects. I never saw her again.'

'Blimey!'

'Evidently they use a section of C-Wing for the Special Projects. Whatever they are.' Melanie shrugged. She hadn't been allowed inside that department.

'Did you try and find out where she went?'

'I asked our manager, who promptly told me to mind my own business.' Melanie stopped walking and turned to Hudson. 'You have to be careful in here, Hudson. Watch everyone. Trust no one.'

'Okay,' Hudson said. *Does that mean her too?* He hoped not. With her cute face framed by her neat blonde bob and crystal blue eyes, Hudson knew he'd have difficulty holding anything back from Melanie.

Hudson quickly learnt that Area One had two clashing sides. It was the brightest light you have ever seen and the murkiest black hole imaginable. It was fervent hope and deep despair. A place where every one of your dreams can be made real in seconds and a place where your most formidable fears are brought to bear. For many, Area One was paradise, the land of plenty.

For an unlucky few, it was purgatory, a place of cruelty and misery.

The next couple of weeks were a rollercoaster for Hudson as he worked at the Bruce Temperance Institution. There were times he could barely breathe and thought non-stop about how to escape. Then a wash of sadness would engulf him and the idea of leaving the patients to the uncaring many filled him with dread. In those moments, he was determined to stay. And occasionally, Hudson felt shards of hope pierce right through him as he dreamt about the astounding possibilities of Area One.

Within a short period, Hudson was emotionally wrung out. One particular grim day, Hudson witnessed something inconceivable – a doctor using a taser gun on a patient who was attacking another patient. If Hudson thought Violet Buntiford was a one-off, or the worst case, he was misguided, and today showed him that. After his shift, desperate for some gentleness and normality, Hudson went to Melanie's room. His need for closeness and tenderness won out and they ended up in bed together, all restraint lost. Relationships between the staff were forbidden, and although Hudson had tried to hold back from becoming romantically involved with Melanie, tonight he let comfort triumph over the rules. They spent a glorious few weeks as secret lovers until it began to weigh heavy on Hudson's mind. If they were watching him, which was highly likely, or about to whisk him away to Special Projects with his manifestation ability, Melanie could be in serious danger. He had to end it. If he was to protect Melanie, he had no choice.

'You're dumping me?' Melanie jumped up from the bed and stood with her arms folded.

'It's not like that. I'm worried I could be endangering you,' Hudson tried to reason.

'It's a risk I'm willing to take,' Melanie said. Hudson ran his hands through his hair. Maybe he shouldn't have let things go this far.

'I don't want you getting into trouble, Melanie. I couldn't handle it if something happened to you.'

'Don't you think I can make up my own mind?' Melanie's face turned from anger to sadness in seconds, and Hudson hated to see what he was doing to her. He stood up from the bed, went over to her, and wrapped his arms around her. Melanie let him.

'I don't want to hurt you,' Hudson said, smelling her lavender-shampoo hair.

'Then don't end it.' Tears welled in Melanie's eyes and ran down her cheeks. They'd had such a great few weeks together. The best. Hudson had made this whole Area One experience tolerable for her. For the first time in ages, Melanie felt hopeful. She'd been happy.

'It's not forever, just while we're both working at the Institution. You know after I've found out about my friends, I'm going to leave Area One? You did say that you would leave with me.' It was strange that Hudson now thought of his break-in companions as friends. The change occurred while working at the BTI, as Hudson realised what treatments they could be suffering. They hadn't known each other for long, but if it was within Hudson's power, he would find them and get them out. Melanie was quiet. 'You are still leaving with me, aren't you?'

'I will. One day. Soon.' Melanie sighed and sat down heavily on the bed. Why did everything have to be so hard? 'I'm afraid what might happen to some of my patients if I'm not here. People like Violet,' she said. Hudson sat next to Melanie and looked into her tear-stained face.

'We can take positive action from outside. Let people know what's going on. Expose the Institution for a start. We can do more good from outside. We can help put an end to the dreadful treatments they perform in here.'

'I know.'

'I can't put you in danger anymore, Melanie. I love you too much for that.' Hudson wrapped his arms around her and pulled her close.

'Do you?'

'Yes.' Hudson kissed the top of her head. 'Are we still friends?'

'Of course,' Melanie said.

****

"Such changes can never be confined. Because it is the energy that is changing, the underpinning energy of subatomic particles. The energy that charges through everything. That runs through your bodies, your world, and your universe, through everything and yonder.

No matter how tall the fences, how strong the cages, it can never be contained. It will unfurl and spread until it has touched every single atom and cell, every person, situation, and event. Then it will stretch through your galaxy, your universe, and into infinity. Your energetic shift will even encompass us, the Collective One, because as you transform, we all transform. We will metamorphose simultaneously, all moving in synchronicity. Dancing to the same tune.

You are beginning to feel the differences, even now. Surges of newborn energies, never felt before. Different frequencies and vibrations, currents and forces. Unfamiliar magnetism, pressures, and reactions. One minute soaring inside with zeal, the next, feeling tired and exhausted. Tingling shivers down your spine; lightheadedness; cold one moment, hot the next. This is all to be expected as the foundational energies alter. Many of you feel spent, worn out, and drained, as this version of the game you have played for thousands of years nears its conclusion.

Many have speculated, hypothesised, and guessed as to what might be happening here, but no one has understood the sheer magnitude of the transformation you are undergoing. People scrambling around trying to figure it all out, putting unnecessary meanings to it.

In recent years you have had glimpses into this new paradigm. Fleeting fractions of awareness and clarity, where you know exactly what is happening. Times when you almost comprehend. A flicker of enlightenment that hints at the truth. Then in a flash, it is gone.

This is a natural process, as your body and world integrate the energies and frequencies of these new Laws. No harm will come to you during this transition. Like the ski jumper who starts from standing, picks up speed, and finally launches into the air, you are near the end of the slope now, gathering speed, and are about to take off and fly. Don't be afraid of the sensation of speeding up; like everything else in your game, it is an illusion.

You are safe and protected as you make your evolutionary leap. Everything is unfolding as it should, just as you have planned, as you have designed."

Chapter Twenty-Two

'I think I've found Will!' Melanie came bursting into Hudson's room. His eyes shot open.

'Who? What time is it? Am I late?'

'No, it's ten past four. I just got back from my night shift. I couldn't wait to tell you.' Melanie kissed his messy hair and perched on the edge of the bed. They were still close, but had agreed to stick to being friends while they worked at the Institution.

'Four? Arrgh!' Hudson blinked his eyes, trying to wake.

'I've found Will.' Melanie was thrilled.

'Really?' Hudson pushed himself up and leant against the headboard. 'Where?'

'He's in R-Wing. Inmate number six thirty-four. I had to cover for someone who's off sick. I took him his supper and saw the tattoo on the inside of his left wrist. "The earth has music for those who listen." That's it, isn't it?'

'Yes! Wow! How did he look?' Hudson sat forward.

'Okay. Well, reasonable,' Melanie said, knowing that detainees could rarely be described as healthy and happy while inside this place. 'He's sporting a bushy beard now. And the best thing was, when I went to collect his tray, I called him by his name.'

'Not his number?' Hudson asked. Melanie shook her head. 'I hope no one heard.' Hudson was aware of the dangers for Melanie.

'I whispered it when I was close enough for him to hear.'

'What happened?'

'He looked at me and a smile crept over his face. Then he stopped and looked confused. I couldn't risk anymore, so I got out quick,' Melanie said.

'So he wasn't sedated or tethered?'

'No, just locked in the cell.'

'That's something I suppose.'

'What are you going to do?'

'I'm not sure yet. I'll have to think. Are you there for your next shift?' Hudson asked.

'Probably. The woman has got chicken pox so I might be there for a few days,' Melanie told him.

'Can't she heal herself?'

'Very few staff can.'

'Sterile?'

'I guess,' Melanie said.

'Thanks for this.' Hudson leant towards Melanie and kissed her soft cheek.

'You're welcome.' Melanie smiled; she liked his kisses. 'Think carefully about your next step and don't go doing anything stupid.'

'I'll be careful, I promise,' Hudson said. Melanie hoped so.

Without truly knowing how long Melanie would be covering for the other nurse, Hudson knew he had to act fast, his mind contemplating how to get Will out. Never in his life had he needed to think like this. Area One was changing him and not in ways that pleased him. The next day, Melanie seemed to deliver the perfect solution when she told him she would be covering the sick nurse's early shift, which involved escorting Will for his shower.

'Brilliant! That's it,' Hudson said. 'We'll only get one shot at this, so let's talk it through.' They sat in Melanie's room drinking coffee and eating chocolate cookies until late, working out their plan.

At 7.25 the next morning, Melanie made her way to Will's cell to escort him to his scheduled daily shower.

'Follow me. We're going to a different shower unit today,' Melanie said. She needed to be sure he would follow as she made her detour. As Melanie walked along the corridor, Charlie Burns in security was furtively admiring her form, watching the way she walked and appreciating the shape of her body in her uniform. He sighed wistfully. Charlie was deeply in lust with Nurse Melanie Harper and dreamt about her often. Ever since the day he accidentally bumped into her in the staff canteen and spilt his tea down her uniform. After his profuse apology, she told him not to worry. She was kind and gentle like that. Someone he could imagine taking home to meet his mum.

'Hold on.' Charlie screwed up his eyes as he watched Melanie pass the security door to the shower unit. 'Where's she going?' Charlie checked the daily itinerary on the computer system. All security personnel had details of every inmate's scheduled movements and according to his, inmate number six thirty-four was due at the showers at 7.30. 'Maybe she's lost.' Charlie knew Melanie was covering someone else's job while they were off sick.

Melanie held her breath as she walked past the shower unit and towards the fire escape door at the very end of the corridor. She knew the alarm was going to screech as soon as she opened it, and only hoped Hudson and Will would have enough time to run before anyone reached them. The plan was for her to accuse Will of having in his possession what looked like a gun. She'd tell them she wasn't about to find out if it was real or not, and would say the gun was obviously an unforeseen emanation of the manifestation ability in Will. It could and did happen. One minute a patient or inmate had no abilities. Turn your back for one second and – WHAM! Melanie didn't want to think what would happen to her if they found out she was lying. On the other side of the fire escape door, Hudson was waiting, trying not to look suspicious.

'Just a few more steps,' Melanie whispered to herself. Her hands were clammy, and sweat trickled from her armpits. Getting closer to the door, she turned to Will. 'Keep walking. Hudson is on the other side of this door.'

'Hudson?' Will's eyes lit up.

'Yes, he's going to help you—'

'Nurse Harper!' Charlie shouted, jogging down the corridor as fast as his unfit sedentary body would allow. Melanie and Will stopped in their tracks. Melanie's heart sank and she turned around, plastering on a smile. 'Nurse Harper, you've gone the wrong way. The showers are back here.' Charlie pointed to the door leading to the shower unit.

'Of course. Silly me.' Melanie began to walk towards Charlie and Will followed her. 'I was thinking it was B-Wing.' Charlie looked puzzled. 'What would I do without you?' Melanie stepped close to Charlie and touched his cheek lightly with her fingertips. His skin was hot and perspiring, a pink flush now spreading over his face. She knew Charlie fancied her. 'Thank you, Charlie.' She gave him her best smile. 'It's been such a stressful time covering these extra shifts. I need more sleep.' Melanie giggled flirtatiously and deliberately moved closer still, feeling the heat radiating from his body. 'I owe you a drink Charlie, my hero,' Melanie said as she moved out of his space and walked towards the shower unit door. Charlie wiped his perspiring brow and touched his cheek, right where her fingertips had been.

'I'll hold you to it,' Charlie called after her.

Hudson checked his watch for the umpteenth time. Something had gone wrong. It was now almost eight o'clock. Reluctantly he walked away, checking all around him, knowing that he couldn't hang around any longer without rousing suspicion. Melanie said nothing else to Will until he was back in his cell.

'We'll try again, Will. Don't give up hope,' Melanie said before she left his cell.

In one of the security control centres, Dr Sandra Knutt smiled to herself. She'd witnessed the whole show via the security cameras. Her morning reviewing security processes had promised tedium, but my, how that had changed.

'Well, well, well,' she said as her mind set to work. 'This morning just got very interesting.' She cackled out loud.

'They've moved him,' Melanie said in hushed tones. She kissed Hudson on the cheek and sat down opposite him at a corner table in Rose's Tea Shop.

'Where to?' Hudson mumbled with a mouth full of chocolate brownie. Hudson had arrived at the tea shop early after a horrendous day. What with the failed break-out and having to work alongside Dr Taser again, he needed comfort and cake.

'I don't know. When I went to take him his lunch, someone else was in his cell.' Melanie picked up a large chocolatey crumb from Hudson's plate and popped it into her mouth.

'Blimey!'

'I know.' Melanie sighed, licking her fingers.

'Someone's onto us. Do you think it's Charlie?'

'I don't think so. He wouldn't have the authority to move someone.'

'We need to keep a low profile,' Hudson suggested. He was worried they were getting too far down this bumpy track.

'Agreed.' Melanie poured herself a cup of tea.

The next day after work, as Melanie had coffee with Charlie in the staff canteen – that was as much as he was getting; she knew it wasn't him who'd blown the whistle on them – she excused her behaviour as sheer exhaustion, and Charlie tapped his nose and said, 'Your secret's safe with me.' Working for the Area One security service, Charlie knew all about exhaustion.

'It could have been anyone or no one,' Hudson said. Melanie didn't know if she was relieved or unnerved that Charlie hadn't told on them. She looked at Hudson with concern in her eyes. 'Don't worry. It may be a coincidence that Will was moved,' Hudson tried to reassure her.

'Maybe,' Melanie said. He was right. They both knew inmates and patients were moved all the time. Sometimes temporarily, sometimes permanently. 'So what do we do now?' Melanie asked.

'Sit tight, lie low,' Hudson said with more confidence than he felt.

'I could ask a couple of people I trust. Try and find out about Will,' Melanie said.

'No, you've gambled enough. We'll see if anything reveals itself over the next few days.'

No apparent clues jumped out to Hudson or Melanie regarding Will's move and as the days rolled by, they began to relax, believing it to be something and nothing. But Dr Sandra Knutt was biding her time and now she was ready to strike. She smiled to herself. 'See how he copes with this,' she said as she signed the authorisation papers for Hudson's secondment. The next day, Dr Knutt summoned Hudson to her office.

'Hudson, it's been agreed that you will work for a while in Special Projects.

Broaden your horizons a bit.' Hudson's face turned white and Dr Knutt laughed inside.

'Special Projects? What Special Projects? For how long?' Hudson was hit by her sucker-punch. It took all of his energy and control to suppress the rage he felt about the treatment of inmates and patients in B-Wing. Where would he get the strength to deal with Special Projects?

'I mentioned once before that we have to sacrifice a few for the many.' Dr Knutt stared at Hudson, enjoying his obvious discomfort. 'Special Projects is where that happens.' Dr Knutt had chosen her words deliberately and loved the fact she could make Hudson squirm.

'When?'

'Tomorrow.' She wanted to laugh out loud as Hudson looked like he'd been slapped around the face.

'Tomorrow?' Hudson's face turned ashen, and this only increased her desire to inflict more pain. 'Come to my office nine o'clock sharp. I'll brief you,' Dr Knutt said.

As soon as his shift finished, he rushed to Melanie's room.

'Oh, my word! Special Projects.' Melanie sat down wearily on her bed. 'She knows.' It all became clear. 'It was her.'

'What?' Hudson sat down next to her. 'Shoot! I didn't think of that. I was so shocked about going to Special Projects. My mind's been all over the place thinking about how I'm going to cope,' Hudson said. 'You're right. It must be her.'

'How are you going to get through it?'

'I honestly don't know. B-Wing is bad enough. God knows what Special Projects will do to me.'

'Hudson, you've got to look after yourself. I don't want you ending up as a patient in here.' Melanie knew Hudson was a kind, tender-hearted soul and not cut out for this place. He was similar to Melanie in many ways, although Melanie had an inner strength that belied her appearance.

'I'll be alright.' Hudson grabbed Melanie's hand and kissed it. 'I've got to be. I've still got people to find and I want to get both of us away from here.' Hudson felt more determined than ever to get out.

'Never mind about that. Just focus on you,' Melanie said. Hudson leaned over and kissed her on the cheek. Thank God for Melanie, otherwise he probably would be a patient by now.

The next morning, having got little sleep, Hudson walked to Dr Sandra Knutt's office with purpose. 'If she thinks she'll break me, she's got another thing coming,' he muttered to himself. His bravery instantly evaporated as Dr Knutt showed him the first special project and he ran from the room to throw up in the men's toilets, Dr Knutt revelling in his distress.

Dr Sandra Knutt hadn't always been this way. It had happened gradually over the weeks and months as she worked for the Bruce Temperance Institution. You see, the BTI had a way of getting under your skin and penetrating your whole being. It remoulded and changed you. A few escaped its claws, but most didn't, unaware of the surreptitious way it rewrote their programme, etching its collective pain onto their psyche.

Dr Knutt gave Hudson a few minutes and then found him out in the corridor taking deep breaths. He turned and gave her a hateful stare, as though she was to blame for all the suffering in the Bruce Temperance Institution. The sight in the room had repulsed him. Two people, a man in his forties and a woman in her thirties, lay in single beds, semi-conscious, with various electrodes attached to their bodies, hooked up to a myriad of machines that delivered specific electrical currents, waves, and pulses, causing their bodies to convulse and writhe, and doing untold things to their brains.

'Special Projects.' Hudson laughed cynically. 'A bit out of date with the treatments, aren't you?' he spat at her.

'As I've said, Hudson, we are dealing with the unknown here. We've had to test out all possibilities and yes, we're exploring methods that were used a while back.'

'A while back? That's a joke. More like centuries ago.' Hudson pushed his hands through his hair. 'Electroconvulsive therapy? Why don't you try lobotomies?'

'We have.' She knew those words would rile him further. Hudson looked at her as though she'd grown two heads. *Was she human? A real doctor? Someone whose raison d'être was about caring for and healing others? Had this woman even heard of the Hippocratic Oath?*

'You are rotten to the core, Knutt.' She didn't deserve the title doctor. Hudson squared up to Dr Knutt and poked his finger at her. 'You're evil.' His eyes blazed with fury. It wasn't in his nature to talk to someone like this and certainly not a superior at work, but this place got to him like nothing else.

'Look, Hudson.' She pushed his finger away and stepped back. 'The methods we use are not the ones used years ago; they have been updated.'

'Oh, whoop de do. Praise the Lord,' Hudson said manically. 'This whole thing would be laughable if it wasn't real.' Dr Knutt preferred Hudson when he was horrified and shocked.

'We have some of the best mental health doctors and professors working with us,' Dr Knutt said defensively. Hudson just laughed mockingly.

'Then God help us all.' Hudson shook his head and walked away. He wasn't staying there a minute longer.

'I want to see you back here tomorrow, Hudson. Nine o'clock sharp,' Dr Sandra Knutt said to his back. She was agitated.

'Whatever, Knutt.' In that moment, Hudson couldn't care less.

'Oh, Hudson, what are you going to do?' Melanie asked as she put her hand over his.

'I don't know.' After his first glimpse of Special Projects, Hudson walked for ages before sitting in Rose's Tea Shop for the afternoon, drinking tea and eating cake, waiting for Melanie to finish her shift. Hudson sighed with the weight of the world on his shoulders. 'I'll go back tomorrow. I've got to know if Trent and Devon escaped. And I need to see if I can find Will and Ziva and get them out. Even more so, now I've seen ... well, you know.' He took Melanie's hands in his. 'Then I'm going to get both of us out of here.' Melanie looked down. She wasn't sure she was ready to leave. It was tempting, of course it was. But what would happen to her poor patients? The very thought filled her with dread.

As much as the Special Projects unit disgusted Hudson, he was adamant he would stick it out until he could find his friends. Then he'd get the hell out of there and tell the world. He had to put a stop to it, and he couldn't do that from a cell inside Area One. But it was so tough. The sights he saw in Special

Projects, the suffering and the smells. My God, the smells. They were horrendous. And all in the name of saving the many.

'We've got to get to the root of why and how these abilities are developing in people. Then we can understand them, harness them, control them,' Dr Knutt told Hudson. 'Unless we crack this, the country – nay the world – will fall into cataclysmic chaos.' She was excessive to the last when justifying the torture. Hudson didn't believe it for one minute.

Most days it was an effort for Hudson to remember the amazing, beautiful side of Area One. His incredible vegetable moment and how that ability in itself could be used for good in the world. Never again would a living soul go hungry. And the way that Annetta healed and came back to Tate was overwhelmingly impressive. Hudson had also seen Faith, the tea shop owner, and her husband read each other's thoughts, and they were so close as a result of that ability. There was no doubt that used with love, care, and grace, the abilities could be breathtakingly positive. If only the authorities and staff of Area One would let it be so. Instead, they were intent on creating a dark, insidious side to this potentially celestial place.

'You lot are a bunch of animals,' Hudson yelled at Dr Knutt before he charged out of the Special Projects unit. Another day and another thing to rancour Hudson. It was becoming an unhealthy pattern. It was five days after his last storm out and he'd just been introduced to yet another woman, her head and body parts wired up to various machines. In many ways the sight was no worse than others he'd seen, yet this one caught him off guard. Hudson believed he'd seen every patient in the Special Projects unit and had ruled out finding any of the others there. Clearly he was wrong, because the woman in the bed was Ziva. Thinner and paler than before with dark circles around her eyes, but still her. Hudson wanted to punch Dr Knutt and her colleague, Dr James Shift. The urge to run over to Ziva, rip the electrodes from her body, pick her up, and run out was overwhelming. But he couldn't give the game away, so settled on leaving the two doctors in his angry wake.

'Hello, you. What are you doing over here?' Melanie said as Hudson jogged towards her.

'Can you take a break?' Hudson looked desperate. Melanie checked her watch.

'Yes, I'm due one soon. What's wrong?' Melanie said.

'Not here.'

'Okay, give me a couple of minutes.'

'I'll meet you outside the staff canteen,' he said.

'Sure.' Melanie nodded. Hudson bought them both a plastic cup of tea. 'What's up?' Melanie expected his usual rant about the injustices of the SP unit. It was a daily need for Hudson to help get the horrors out of his mind and keep him sane.

'I've seen Ziva,' Hudson whispered.

'Where?'

'In the SP unit.' Hudson swigged the plastic cup of tea.

'Gosh! Is she okay?' Melanie said, not liking the sound of that. Everyone knew the atrocities of the SP unit. Hudson shrugged, his body hunched forward.

'She's alive. I guess that's something.' Hudson sighed.

'Oh, Hudson.' Melanie rubbed his back affectionately. What he wouldn't give to be able to walk out right this moment and go back home. Few words passed between Melanie and Hudson for the rest of her break. They were unnecessary; she knew exactly how he felt. After he left Melanie, Hudson found Dr Knutt and apologised for his outburst. If he was going to help Ziva, he needed to be on the inside.

Over the next few days, Hudson kept a close eye on Ziva, and after seven days, she was put into what they referred to as 'consolidation', which meant they turned off the machines, stopped all electrical treatments, and tried to work out if her abilities had been altered in any way. In this phase, she was sedated, sometimes mildly, sometimes heavily, and often tethered. With Ziva in consolidation, Hudson decided that he had to make some positive moves towards getting her out. First things first, he needed to know whether she would recognise him. If he was going to get her out, he had to be sure she would come with him willingly. So when no one was around, he went into Ziva's room and walked over to her bed. No matter how long he worked at the BTI, he would never get used to the smell of the place. Noxious, sour aromas from all manner of bodily fluids and burnt flesh from the electrodes were mixed with feeble attempts to mask it with disinfectant and chlorine. It stuck to your clothes and hair, and hit the back of your throat, making you gag.

'Ziva? Ziva, it's me Hudson.' Hudson touched Ziva's arm lightly.

'Mmmmm.' Ziva looked mildly sedated.

'Ziva?' He shook her arm gently, trying to rouse her. 'Ziva, it's me, Hudson?'

'Huds...' Ziva mumbled, her eyes still closed.

'Ziva, can you open your eyes?' Hudson said louder now.

The door opened and in dashed a nurse carrying a stainless-steel kidney tray with a syringe. 'What are you waking her for? You'll have trouble on your hands if you do,' she said with a downturned mouth and eyebrows that were knitting together, showing her disapproval.

'Oh!' Hudson jumped and let go of Ziva's arm. 'Dr Knutt asked me to errr...' Hudson stepped away from Ziva and moved towards the door. 'I'll let you carry on.' Hudson opened the door and left. *Phew, that was close.*

A few days later and Ziva was back on her treatment, causing Hudson's rage to boil.

'She's not going to last if they keep doing this to her.' Hudson paced up and down Melanie's room. 'I can't let this go on. It's driving me insane.' Melanie didn't know how to help. 'I've got to think.'

The next day, as Melanie and Hudson drank tea in Rose's Tea Shop, Hudson came out with it.

'Melanie, I've got to change my plans. I know I said I wanted to find out about Trent and Devon and get both Will and Ziva out, but I've got to act now for Ziva. She won't make it if I don't.' Melanie leant across the table and held Hudson's hands, seeing the agony in his eyes and feeling the painful emotions in his heart.

'Oh, Hudson,' Melanie said. She was worried about him. 'But how? And when?'

'Soon. It means I'll be leaving. You know that, right?'

'I know,' Melanie said.

'You will get out of here too and come and find me, won't you?' Hudson asked. Melanie nodded, tears in her eyes. 'I've got an idea how to get Ziva out.'

'What is it?'

'I can't tell you.' Hudson put his hand on her cheek. 'I don't want you knowing. For your own safety.' Melanie nodded and brushed away her tears.

Days later when Hudson gave B-Wing patient Mr Spider Man a pack of cigarettes and lighter, he knew exactly what he was doing, and only hoped Mr Spider Man would follow through on his constant threat to 'torch the place to the ground'. Mr Spider Man's real name was Bobby Daltry, and he was responsible for plying Hudson with a sedative on his first day on the job. He was a well-renowned patient at the BTI who, in the early days, was viewed as a danger. After months in the SP unit, he was a shell of his former self. The treatments had wiped out any traces of his abilities and left him with coordination issues, extreme fatigue, and a plethora of other health problems to boot. Good old Special Projects unit. Most days he could barely walk or talk. Consequently, he was now classed as low risk and rarely locked up.

'Hi there, Bobby. Here you go, mate.' Hudson handed over the cigarettes and lighter to Mr Spider Man, who sat slumped in a high-backed, red PVC armchair in his room. 'This is a one-off and just between you and me, right?' Mr Spider Man's eyes opened and looked at what Hudson was offering him.

'Mmmm...' Mr Spider Man mumbled as he took the cigarettes and lighter.

'God, forgive me,' Hudson whispered to himself as he left Mr Spider Man's room. Hudson hoped he would have the strength to follow through with his ongoing threat and not end up falling asleep with a cigarette in his mouth.

Hudson hurriedly walked back towards the Special Projects unit. He'd already said goodbye to Melanie last night.

'Hudson, be careful.' Melanie looked at him with serious eyes. 'I don't know what they'll do if they catch you.'

'I know, I know,' Hudson said. They both had a good idea. Neither could voice it. 'See you on the outside,' he said, hoping she would follow him out. Most people thought it was difficult getting into Area One and didn't realise it wasn't that easy getting back out again. In fact, some would say it was nigh impossible.

'Soon.' Melanie bit her lip.

'I hope so,' Hudson said, knowing that now was not the right time to push. 'You've got my parents' address and number, haven't you?'

'Yes.' Melanie smiled sadly. She would miss Hudson like crazy. He was one of the few things that made sense in here. She knew she would leave one day. Not just yet though. The BTI had a bizarre knack of employing some of the most uncaring, unkind healthcare professionals she had ever come across. Most came here hoping the manifestation ability would hit them as soon as they stepped over the threshold, washing them with bounties of money and untold luxuries. Their motives were about gaining and getting, self and ego, and the people embodying these motives were not the nicest around.

'As soon as you get out, contact Mum and Dad. They'll know where I am,' Hudson said.

'I will,' Melanie promised.

'Look after yourself.' Hudson held Melanie close to him. She closed her eyes, drinking in the last few moments.

'Please be careful.'

'I'll be fine, honest.' Hudson pulled away and kissed her gently on the lips. They smiled, both worried about the other.

Minutes after Hudson had left Mr Spider Man's room, he hit the fire alarm, crossing his fingers it wasn't too premature. He didn't want innocent people getting caught in any fire. Then Hudson ran to find Ziva. He hadn't seen her for a day or so and hoped she was in the same room.

'Ziva, what have they done to you?' Hudson looked at the straps binding her wrists and ankles to the hospital bed. Her hair was greasy and lank, and her face unwashed and sweaty from the heat of the room. Hurrying over to her, he began unbuckling the straps. Sounds came from her mouth as she opened it, trying to form words.

'Water,' she managed.

'Alright.' Hudson rushed over to the table on wheels at the side of the room and poured water from the plastic jug. He held up her head, helping her to drink. Still woozy from the sedative, most of the water went down her chin and he wiped it with the bed sheet.

'We've got to get you out of here.' As Hudson untied her ankles, he noticed her dirty feet. Hudson dread to think the last time anyone gave Ziva a proper wash or let her take a shower. By the smell of things, it had been a few days.

Ziva felt strange, like an elephant finally released from its chain. She wobbled as Hudson helped her upright and swung her legs off the bed.

'I can't leave.' Ziva panicked at the thought of leaving the place she'd grown accustomed to. 'What's that noise?'

'It's an alarm,' Hudson said.

'I don't like it.' Ziva covered her ears.

'It will stop soon.' Hudson took Ziva's hands in his. 'Listen to me. I'm not leaving you here. I'm going to get you out.' Fear spread across her face.

'If they find out, they'll do them things to me again.' Tears welled up in her eyes and she shook her head. 'I can't do it again. Not again.' As she spoke, Hudson saw she had a tooth missing. He buried his anger, saving it for another time. Right now he had a job to do.

'Ziva, I'll protect you. I'm not going to let anyone harm you again, do you hear me?' Ziva looked at him questioningly. 'I'm taking you back home.' A smile flickered across Ziva's face. Her home, a place where she felt safe, where none of these frightening people could get her.

'Home?'

'Yes, home. Now I need you to do as I say, okay?' Hudson's heart broke to see what they'd done to her in such a short amount of time. *She shouldn't be here, or even in Area One for that matter.* Although why was he so surprised? Using the sheet and water from the jug, he quickly washed her face and hands, then got out clean clothes from his backpack. 'Put these on. You'll feel better.' He handed her the clothes.

'It's too hot.' Ziva looked at the tracksuit.

'It won't be outside; it's quite cool. And I don't want you catching a chill.'

He smiled to himself. 'I sound like my mum,' he mumbled.

'I want my mum.' Ziva's eyes overflowed with tears.

'I'll take you to her, as soon as you get changed.' Hudson gestured towards the clothes and then turned his back to give her some privacy. Once Ziva had changed, she sat back on the bed, unsure what to do next.

'Let's go. Do everything I say, okay?' Hudson said.

'Okay,' Ziva replied. Hudson took her small, unsure hand in his. Slowly he opened the door, checking up and down the corridor. All clear. If Mr Spider Man had gone the fire route, Hudson hoped all the patients were okay. Hudson couldn't care less about most of the staff, although that sounded dreadful. *Lord, what have I become?* He shook his head. Now was not the time for self-loathing. Hudson moved along the corridor, seeing the pandemonium outside through the windows. And yes, he saw smoke. People were running around, doctors and nurses moving patients and inmates to safety. Hudson's heart sank knowing he was to blame. Then the images that kept him awake at night surfaced and he remembered why he'd done it in the first place. Two people below caught Hudson's attention.

'Is that Melanie and Will?' Amongst the mass of people, he spotted their familiar forms. Hudson watched as Melanie guided Will away, looking all around her as she went. It was definitely them. *Melanie's helping Will escape.* Hudson's heart swelled with love for her and he prayed they would both be alright. Ziva started to shiver and Hudson jolted back.

'Come on.' Hudson led Ziva along the corridor to the stairwell. It was deserted. Hudson glanced at Ziva and wondered if she looked like an escapee. If someone only saw her from the back, she might get away with it. From the front, with her drawn face, it didn't look good. Hudson decided he would have to go to plan B and run away from the commotion. He had wanted to get swallowed up in the crowd, but no matter.

He led her down the stairs and out through the emergency door. Fire engines and people were racing around everywhere.

'This way, Ziva.' Hudson pulled her away from the hubbub, moving as fast as Ziva's thin and abused body would allow. Once they'd made it into a densely wooded area, Hudson slowed down.

'Let's stop for a while.' Hudson guided Ziva to a large tree trunk that had fallen and now lay on its side. They sat and Hudson reached into his backpack, taking out some water and fruit. Ziva hadn't seen fruit for ages.

'Here, have these to get your energy back.' Hudson handed her a pear and a banana. Ziva sat quietly eating the fruit, and Hudson smiled inwardly as he watched her enjoying them. Hudson had so many questions for Ziva, but for now they remained unasked. Hudson knew what she'd been through, and there would be time enough for that when he got her out to safety. One thing was for sure; as soon as he could, he was going to the press. People had to know the other side of Area One. *I won't let them get away with it any longer,* Hudson vowed.

Once rested and refuelled, Hudson packed up his bag and stood up. He held out his hand to Ziva and she took it.

'Follow me. I'm getting you out of here,' Hudson said as they made off. They broke through first perimeter fence without a hitch and were attempting the second when they heard a man shout out.

'Hold it, you two! Put your hands up!' A big, beefy security guard, who was as wide as he was tall, came towards them. Ziva, having been taught to obey over past weeks, immediately stopped and put up her hands. Hudson was stopping for no one and grabbed Ziva's arm.

'Run, Ziva!' There was no way they would get her; Hudson would make sure of it. They ran, with the security man following as fast as his burly frame would allow.

'Stop or I'll shoot,' the security guard said. He was quickly becoming breathless. Hudson was pleased; even with Ziva struggling, they could easily outrun him. 'Stop or I'll shoot,' the security guard repeated. A shot rang out, and Hudson felt Ziva's body slump to the ground. Without thinking, Hudson drew a gun from his jeans waistband and turned to shoot the security guard, hitting his lower right leg with the bullet.

The security guard fell to the ground, shouting out in pain. He was only one week into his new job and hating every minute of it; but this was the bloody icing on the cake.

With no time to think about the guard, Hudson turned to Ziva, who had blood on her chest and trickling from her mouth. Refusing to give up, Hudson bent down, picked up her tiny frame in his arms, and walked with her, as fast as he could. After a few hundred yards he had to stop. He lay Ziva down carefully on the ground, her breathing now laboured and shallow.

'Ziva? Ziva, can you hear me?' he whispered into her ear. Slowly she opened her eyes.

'Huds ... go on.' Ziva struggled to breathe, blood oozing from her mouth. 'Leave me.'

'Ziva, I'm not leaving you.' Hudson held Ziva in his arms.

'Over.' Ziva looked into his face, her eyes glazing.

'Ziva, no, don't go. You can fix this. Why aren't you fixing this?' Tears stung Hudson's eyes. 'Heal yourself, Ziva. You can do it, you know you can.'

'No,' Ziva said. 'Tired.'

'I won't let you go, Ziva,' Hudson said, scared at the thought of Ziva dying in his arms. It wasn't meant to end like this. He couldn't accept it would end like this. That *she* would end like this. 'I'm going to do it then. If you won't, I will.' Hudson would not abandon hope. 'Ziva, I see your body healed. I see the bullet melting away inside and all the damaged tissue healing and mending.' Tears dripped from his eyes onto her pale face, mixing with her blood.

'Tired.' Her voice grew quiet and croaky. 'Too much. Go.'

'Ziva, no! Don't leave!'

'No more.' Ziva closed her eyes and exhaled for the last time.

'Ziva, no, no, no!' Hudson cried, rocking her limp body in his arms. He was past caring that the Area One security would be arriving any second. In that moment, he hated Area One more than ever. The government and all the people involved should be ashamed of themselves. *I hope they rot in hell!* They don't care about the people that can't fit into Area One. Once they pass the assessment, if they fail to thrive, they should be allowed to go home, back to normal life, not be cooped up, detained, and experimented on. The authorities believed that if they found ways to control the uncontrollable, then they may be able to scale back the security. With costs for Area One spiralling out of control, they were desperate. They knew that running Area One was currently unsustainable and if they weren't careful, it would threaten the whole country's economic situation. But that was no excuse to betray your own people.

Ziva should never have been inside Area One in the first place. *Just because she couldn't cope. Why didn't they let her leave? What have they done to you, Ziva? What have they done?*

Hudson laid Ziva's body on the ground and knew he would never be the same again. They had robbed him of his dream that Area One could give people a better future. Instead, it had turned into an atrocious nightmare. He reached out and picked a white anemone flower from a plant next to him and placed it in Ziva's hand.

With little choice left, Hudson left Ziva's body. He had to get out. He had to tell the world what was happening, now more than ever. For Ziva. And for all the poor souls inside Area One that were being held against their will and against all that was humane.

****

"These new functions have the potential to be breathtakingly empowering and expansive. They have the capacity to lift your world from poverty, hunger, and hopelessness; slicing through the chains that imprison your people. They have the power to make real your phrase heaven on earth. But, conversely, while you have duality in your game, they also have the potential to bring you to your knees and pull you to a depth that your world has never witnessed. For what end they will be used is yet to be determined by you. It is you who writes the script of this play. You are in charge of the outcome. Will you choose to use them with love or with fear? Compassion or malevolence? Will you use them for expansive purposes, or to restrict and confine? Will you use them with an open, loving heart, or from a place of selfish greed? The choice is, as always dear One, yours.

Chapter Twenty-Three

Over the next couple of weeks, Dog and his crew, minus Wolf, honed their abilities and worked out their plan of attack. They knew the abilities came easier when you were sitting comfortably in your lounge, so they staged some pressurised situations. Firstly, they tried to manifest weapons on the run in the dark while being chased. The only person successful with this exercise was Dog, who managed one gun. Unfortunately though, he had to stop to get into the zone, which took eighteen seconds, then it took an additional ten seconds before anything appeared. It just wasn't good enough; they'd be toast by then. Next on the list was manifesting weapons as they were rugby tackled to the ground. This only produced bruises and hysterics. For the next drill, the barrel of Dog's gun was directed at their temples as they tried to ignite the abilities. Dog succeeded with one manifestation – a pizza cutter. Who knew what he was thinking. They also rehearsed seeing through walls and into buildings to ascertain threat levels. Dog, Tommy, and Brains were good at this, with Dog being the best. Although it was always going to be easy with no threat of capture or torture, unless of course the homeowner saw you squatting in their garden.

Overall, Dog was the most consistent with the abilities, probably due to Jocky's one-on-one coaching. Keene came out bottom in all of the exercises, his mind still filled with memories of his detention.

****

"Currently you mostly exist in three-dimensional space-time reality, but this is changing. As the new Laws integrate, you will begin to experience the environment around you in four

and five dimensions. That means, for example, that you will be able to 'see' and 'know' all six sides of an opaque box and inside the box simultaneously. You will be able to see and know all points concurrently, including the inner structure of solid objects and things obscured from a three-dimensional viewpoint.

Houses and their contents, viewed and known without going inside. The inner workings and organs of physical bodies, scanned before cutting them open. Disease inside people and animals, known without X-rays and invasive tests. The workings of machines, observed without taking them apart.

Hidden and imprisoned people, found. Fights played out behind closed doors, brought out into the light. Meetings in secure rooms, witnessed. With the dawn of these new Laws, no deed will ever go unnoticed again, and secrets will be a thing of the past."

****

Finally, it was the evening before the bust-out, as the five sat in Dog's small lounge. Dog had successfully tracked down Daisy, but she was unable to act immediately as she was laying low, convinced she was being watched. Once she'd established it was only Charlie Burns, the security services letch, ogling her and working himself up to ask her on a date – which prompted a firm 'no' from Daisy – she began searching for Jocky. Unfortunately, she found Jocky in the SP unit where security was high, and she couldn't see a way to get him out. As much as it pained her, Daisy left Jocky there. It was too risky to do anything. When Jocky was eventually moved, it was all systems go and Dog and his team got ready. Then an inmate escaped from the BTI and Jocky was moved again. Throughout, Dog worried about Jocky. He knew the side of Jocky that others didn't and the years of suffering he'd gone through. Dog wasn't sure how much Jocky could take and prayed it wouldn't be the straw that broke the camel's back.

With every set back, Keene sighed with relief and wondered whether he was subconsciously manifesting the hitches in their plan, such was his reticence to go anywhere near the BTI again. Now, at long last, they had Jocky in their sights. Daisy warned Dog that Jocky wasn't his old self, and that only fuelled Dog's desire to get him out. He'd seen what they'd done to Keene.

'Is everyone clear on what you need to do tomorrow night?' Dog asked the four. Tommy, Brains, and Eyes said 'yes' together. Keene nodded slightly, trying to keep his mind clear, knowing full well Dog was getting good at this Thought Reading malarkey.

'Come on, let's manifest the tools,' Tommy prompted, fidgeting in his seat.

'Calm down, Tommy.' Dog held up his hands. It had been Tommy's suggestion to manifest the weapons prior to leaving so they weren't trying to do it under duress. 'Let's do it sensibly, alright?' Dog directed his words at Tommy. 'We need something that's discreet and won't hinder us when we're moving. No torpedoes, machetes, or machine guns, alright?' Dog smiled at Tommy.

'Oh, mate,' Tommy whined. He was planning something memorable.

'It's got to be handguns; they're easier to hide,' Brains said.

'Yeah, I agree. We can't be carting around massive armoury. We'll never get the job done,' Eyes said. Keene remained silent, trying to keep his thoughts clear. He didn't like the sound of any of it. Not even the idea of getting revenge on the people inside the BTI appealed to him. It seemed far from sweet and gave him no pleasure at all. His longing to get away from Area One solidified. Keene was well and truly done with this so-called Promised Land. *They can keep the stinking rotten place.*

'Okay, let's go for handguns then,' Dog said.

Tommy capitulated. 'Suppose.'

'It makes sense. We don't want to go nuts and as Eyes said, how on earth do we get the heavier gear around? We can't. We're sticking to handguns.' Dog talked to Tommy, who looked away. 'Right, everyone ready?'

'Yeah, let's do it.' Eyes was eager.

'Sure,' said Brains.

'Okay,' Tommy said. Keene scarcely nodded.

'Right, let's go for it.' Dog had barely finished his sentence when two handguns appeared in Tommy's hands, one in each. Tommy burst out laughing as he felt the cold metal touching his palms and fingers. Dog, Brains, and Eyes took a moment longer to manifest theirs – one each. Keene couldn't rally anything, and he knew why.

'Here, mate, have one of mine.' Tommy handed a gun to Keene, who took it reluctantly.

'Thanks,' Keene mumbled.

'I think that will do us. So you all need to be back here tomorrow at midnight. We'll keep the guns here. Until then, keep your heads low and just chill out,' Dog said.

'How about one of these before we split?' Eyes said, and in that second, five bottles of beer appeared on the carpet in the middle of the room, condensation running down the glass.

'They're cold.' Tommy was surprised as he picked one up.

'Of course they are.' Eyes frowned at Tommy, who hadn't thought about temperature when he'd manifested food and drink in the past. Dog laughed and headed to the kitchen for the bottle opener. He could have manifested one, but there were only so many bottle openers one person needed. Walking back into the lounge, he saw a plate of caramel-iced ring donuts on the floor.

'It's gotta be done,' Tommy said, biting into one. 'Beer and donuts. Mmmm.' He was a funny one, that Tommy.

The next night they met at Dog's all dressed in black. Keene's mind was all over the place and he was fighting a losing battle to clear it. Dog talked through the plan one final time.

'All set everyone?' Dog looked at intently at everyone. 'Keene, you alright?'

'Sure.' Keene turned his mind quickly to his family dog, Buster, who had always been by his side as a young boy.

'If something's up, you need to say now,' Dog said. He was picking up glimpses of Keene's emotions and he didn't like what he was sensing. To be successful tonight, they all needed to be on top of their game. There was no room for chinks in the armour.

'Seriously, I'm fine. Just want to get the job done.' Keene rubbed his hands together unconvincingly.

'Okay then. But any doubts, you've got to say. I don't want anyone compromising this mission. Right?' Dog added.

'Right,' Keene said.

'If everyone's ready, let's move out,' Dog said.

They went on foot, avoiding the roads. Dog had persuaded Daisy to open the exit door and bring Jocky with her. In the early hours of the morning, Daisy opened the door as agreed.

'You're going to have to come and get him if you want him,' Daisy said. 'Quickly though.'

'What do mean?' Dog said.

'He won't come out. He thinks it's a trick,' Daisy said.

'Jeez!' Dog rubbed his hand through his hair. 'How far is it?'

'Not too far. He's in his cell. Fifth one on the left. Down this corridor.'

'Five down? We'll get caught,' Keene said. Fear flooded through his body, making him feel sick.

'No, we won't. We'll be quick,' Tommy said. He was fired-up and wasn't going to let anyone ruin his night of action.

'Come on then.' Dog beckoned.

'I'm going to scoot,' Daisy said. 'Good luck.' She began to walk away, then stopped and turned. 'Look, he's in a bad way. He's not the same.' She paused for a second, sadness mixed with tears in her eyes. She sniffed, turned, and jogged down the corridor. Daisy's words triggered Keene, and his mind recalled vivid memories from his time inside. Desperately he tried to bat them away.

'Okay, let's go.' Dog headed down the corridor with Tommy, Eyes, Brains, and Keene following.

'This is it.' Dog pushed open the cell door. Jocky was sat hunched in the corner of the room behind the door. Normally, his menacing aura made you overlook his thin stature. Now though, with his aura zapped away, he looked like a frail old man. Jocky slowly gazed up at the five young men who had barged into his space, his blank eyes unable to recognise them.

'Jocky, it's me, Dog.' Dog knelt down. Jocky's brow furrowed.

'Davey?'

'No, it's Dog. And Eyes, Brains, Tommy, and Keene. You remember us, don't you?' Dog asked. Jocky looked at the others as they stared at the shadow of Jocky's former self. 'Eyes, get the other side.' Together Dog and Eyes hauled Jocky to his feet, his slight body making light work for them. 'We're taking you home, Jocky. You've got your classes to run, remember? We've been practising, but it's not the same without you. We need our leader.' Dog rambled as he dealt with the shock of seeing Jocky. The word 'leader' activated something in Jocky's mind. He looked at Dog, then to Eyes the other side of him.

'I can walk,' Jocky said and shoved them away. Yes, that was it; he was the leader. It was coming back to him now.

'Come on then, let's get out of here,' Keene said, feeling decidedly queasy. Jocky went to take a step and stumbled.

'Drugs,' Jocky said. 'Pumped me full.'

'Lean on me,' Dog said. They left the cell with Dog virtually carrying Jocky and made their way along the corridor to the exit door.

'It's closed! It's locked!' Keene cried out as he banged and kicked at the door.

'Keep it down!' Dog whispered loudly. Entering the building had never been part of their plan. Now they were screwed. Tommy pushed on it with his shoulder. It was no good; the door was too heavy and solid, the locking system too stable. Keene's heart raced. He looked around for a way out, saw the fire bell, and smashed the glass, hoping it would release the door. The alarm sounded loud in their ears.

'What are you doing?' Dog stared at Keene. Before he could answer, another voice shouted down the corridor.

'Security! Hold it there! All of you! Hands ups!'

They turned to see an armed guard running towards them. Keene panicked, raised his gun, and shot the guard in his left hand. He was aiming for his chest, but with his hands shaking so much, he was way off target. The guard screamed, clutched his hand, and sank to the ground.

'Take down!' Jocky laughed manically.

'Keene, calm down!' Dog yelled, worried that Keene was putting them further in danger. Brains tried the exit door. It was still firmly locked.

'The door's still not budging! Quick, the other way!' Brains said. With none of them able to open it with their abilities, they ran down the corridor, around the injured guard, who tried unsuccessfully to grab Dog's leg, and then halted at a crossroads.

'Which way?' Eyes asked.

'Left,' Tommy said, guessing. Down another corridor.

'It's a dead end. There's no door! No exit! No way out!' Keene glared at Tommy as though he could kill him in that instant for making the wrong call.

'Let's go back the way we came in. The door has to open somehow,' Dog said. Dog and Eyes hoisted Jocky up between them. They ran back. The guard was still on the floor in agony. Dog unhooked Jocky, took out his gun, and whacked the guard over the head, knocking him unconscious. Grabbing Jocky again, they headed for the door. Keene tried it again. Still it wouldn't shift.

'Wait!' Tommy said, putting his arms out to stop everyone in their tracks. He closed his eyes for a couple of seconds. BAM! On the ground at his feet was a shoulder-fired rocket launcher. Jocky's eyes lit up, a glimmer of his old self.

'Jeez!' Keene said, feeling faint.

'Do you know how to use it?' Dog asked.

'Watch,' Tommy said. A smile spread across his face. He picked it up and aimed at the door. 'Get back! Turn around and cover your ears.' They drew back, and with their ears covered, Tommy launched the rocket. The sound was deafening and made mincemeat out of the door and surrounding brickwork. Outside, sirens shrieked and emergency vehicles skidded towards the scene in response to the alarm. Keene was first out through the hole and ran as fast as he could in the opposite direction.

'Keene! Wrong way!' Dog shouted. Keene ignored him and kept running.

'Keene, it's this way, man!' Brains called out after him. It made no difference.

'Leave him! Come on, we've got to keep moving!' Dog yelled. As they got through the hole in the wall, Daisy came rushing towards them. With smoke all around, she couldn't see and bumped into them, sending Jocky crashing to the floor.

'You've got to get out! They're coming for you!' Daisy yelled.

'Oi!' Jocky said, sitting on the floor rubbing his head. He was not fully with it. Dog and Eyes bent down to retrieve Jocky.

'Hold it! Throw down your weapons! Now!' shouted one of the heavily armed guards. Dog abandoned Jocky, grabbed Daisy, and thrust his gun to her temple.

'You drop your weapons and back away!' Dog screamed as he dug the gun into Daisy's flesh. She cried out in pain. Even through the drugs and the after-effects of the treatments, Jocky still mobilised a feeling of pride at his protégé and gave a lopsided smile.

'Dog! What are you doing?' Daisy said, terrified. She was the one that had helped Dog for Chrissake! She didn't sign up for this. Her mind snapped back to when she originally applied for the job. She remembered laughing and saying to her mum, 'How much real work will the security services need to do in Utopia?' Daisy believed she had secured an easy, undemanding little number in a place called heaven on earth. Being taken hostage was certainly not on her radar. This wasn't meant to happen, not to her.

'Just keep your mouth shut and you'll be fine,' Dog said through gritted teeth. He hadn't wanted to do it. Dog knew the guards wouldn't hesitate to open fire on them, but with Daisy close they wouldn't risk it, he was sure of it. She was one of them. They were getting in far deeper than he would have liked, but he was confident with their abilities, they could still turn this around.

'Hold your fire! Everyone!' someone in charge barked at the masses of security personnel that had now accumulated around the area. The guards stood down.

'Back away! Behind those trees! Now!' Dog shouted and pressed the gun hard into Daisy's temple again. Slowly the guards backed away.

'Come on...' Dog said as he edged his group along the outside of the building, looking for an escape route. There was nothing obvious. The guard's eyes never left Dog and his crew. Dog stopped. Everyone did the same. There was nowhere to go. Dog had to think. He had to clear his mind. Eyes sat a wobbly Jocky on the ground. All the abilities had deserted Eyes who, although he liked to live on the edge, felt this was pushing it a little. Brains tried to manifest something that would end this ordeal. He also drew a blank.

Tommy, on the other hand, was psyched by the whole thing. To him, it was like being in a real-life computer game, and he was well and truly tapped in and turned on to his abilities. Seconds after they stopped, two massive armour-plated barriers appeared in front of them, giving them instant protection.

'Whoa! Alright!' Tommy clapped his hands and dived behind one. Brains followed him, glad at least one of them still had it. Eyes helped Jocky to slide behind the barrier with Tommy and Brains, and Dog dragged Daisy behind the other one.

The situation had escalated to the head of Area One security services, then to Mike Tremblay, Head of MI5, and now included Doug Greenlake, Head of MI6. With a hostage situation and Manifester as part of the group, they would need all the resources they could get.

'They've manifested two armoured barriers and three shoulder-fire rocket launchers,' said the leader in charge of the security ground crew. He was on a conference call with Mike and Doug.

'They've done what!?' Mike said.

'There could be more weapons. So far, that's all the helicopter scan has picked up.'

'Give me strength,' Doug said as he looked up towards heaven. He knew the opening up of Area One had been a big rotten mistake. He'd felt it in his gut at the time. You don't just allow civilians into a situation that's totally unknown. What had he been thinking when he agreed to it? Doug had to remind himself that he'd had no choice.

'Have you identified the Manifester?' Mike asked.

'We're pretty sure it's the one who's taken the girl. He's still got her next to him with the gun at her side. His name is Oscar Hamilton. Goes by the name of Dog. He seems like the ringleader.'

'Have you taken any shots?' Doug asked.

'Not yet. The negotiators are still working on getting the girl out.'

'Keep working on that. I think we need to pull in some Manifesters of our own. Mike, have you got anyone suitable?' Doug said.

'I'll check and come back to you.' Mike said.

'Cheers,' Doug said. They ended the call. Doug knew it was time to inform the PM. He wouldn't like it and it served him right. This was the PM's fault, and Doug would make damn sure he remembered that, and that everyone and his aunt knew who was to blame.

'I can do better than this. How about a tank? We can flatten them and bulldoze our way out,' Tommy said with an insane look in his eyes. He'd already manifested two more rocket launchers.

'No!' Dog shook his head, but it was too late. Thirty feet away from them now stood a M1A2 Abrams battle tank.

'Yes!' Tommy shouted and shimmied his shoulders in celebration.

'You idiot!' Dog screamed at Tommy. The shock of the tank's appearance caused the armed security personnel to ready themselves with their weapons. 'Look what you've done,' Dog said.

'Cover me while I run to it,' Tommy said.

'No, you won't,' Dog said. Eyes and Brains jumped on Tommy and held him back. After a minute grappling, Tommy held up his hands in defeat. Eyes and Brains let him go.

'None of us are going anywhere near that thing. Do you hear?' Dog directed his words to Tommy, who nodded unenthusiastically. 'We'll end up starting World War III if we're not careful.'

'They said if we let Daisy go, they'd talk to us to find a resolution,' Eyes said, wanting it all to end now. He'd had enough of the edge for one day.

'They're liars!' Jocky screamed suddenly. He'd been quiet for a while, head slumped forward and eyes closed. They thought he was asleep.

'Look, we can still get out of this,' Brains reasoned. 'We just need to calm down. We must be able to get ourselves out of this.'

'Let me go, please. I'm sure they'll be more lenient. In fact, I know they will.' Daisy said, ruing the day she ever stepped foot in this godforsaken place.

'No! There must be another way out of this. We hold all the cards,' Dog said, nodding towards Daisy.

'Yeah, let's fight our way out. I'm jumping in the tank,' Tommy said.

'No!' Dog threw a stone at Tommy to distract him.

For the next twenty minutes, they went round in circles and came out with nothing. They couldn't see a way out that didn't involve causing mayhem, casualties, or getting shot themselves. Dog rubbed his eyes, and Daisy could see he was tiring of the whole thing.

'Dog, let me go. I think it's the best solution,' Daisy said. She was determined not to die here with them. Dog sighed. He couldn't think of anything else and didn't fancy their chances if they went with Tommy's idea.

'Right, okay.' Dog sighed heavily. 'We'll let you go. Without you nagging, I might be able to think straight and get us out of this.'

'I'll take her,' Tommy said, bored with the impasse and ready for action.

'No, you won't. I can go on my own,' Daisy said. She didn't want any of them near her.

'Let me give the signal then,' Dog said. The negotiators had already given the group a signal to use if they wanted to talk. Dog put down his gun and raised his hands to show they were empty. Very slowly, he stood up. Daisy followed his lead. She carefully walked from behind the barrier and towards the line of security personnel with their vehicles. As Daisy got close, a guard grabbed her and pulled her behind a car. Before Dog could duck away behind the barrier, a sniper hit Dog and he fell to the floor. Jocky's eyes shot open and he howled at the sight.

'NOOOOO!' Eyes shouted, knowing for sure he'd had enough. Jocky quickly crawled to where Dog lay. He picked up Dog's limp body in his arms.

'I've got you,' Jocky said. 'You're gonna make it. I won't let you die.' Jocky's eyes filled with tears, an unusual act from the person with a thick steel exterior.

'Christ!' Brains stared at the scene with his mouth open, hands wringing. 'This is meant to be Utopia for crying out loud.' Nothing seemed real. Time stood still. To Brains it was like being in a dream. Blood pumped in his ears; his heart thumped in his chest. For a moment, he didn't know where he was.

'Oh, my God! Oh, my God! Oh, my God!' Eyes looked at Dog. This was too much. *Shall I run? They'll shoot me. Maybe that's for the best.* He couldn't do time in here; it would kill him. *I wish I was dead.* He should have run with

Keene. *Why did I stay? Why did I come to Area One in the first place?* Eyes prayed to be out of this place, right now. His prayers were unanswered.

The shot silenced Tommy. Up until that point, it was a game he was playing. Now reality hit him and his whole body jerked backwards and forwards, tears creeping down his cheeks.

'I'm gonna save you. I'm not letting you go this time,' Jocky said as deep sobs swelled up from the depths of his soul. His whole body shook with suppressed emotion. 'I've got you, Little Davey, I've got you. It's your big brother here. I'll save you, Little Davey. I'll save you.' Jocky held his forehead against Dog's, tears streaming from his eyes onto Dog's closed eyelids.

****

"Money, time, physical ability, mental agility, and social standing will no longer be barriers to getting what you need, when you need it. This will trouble many who have built their games with hoops to jump through and obstacles to overcome. Those in perceived control and power have made up complicated rules for how you can get to a specific point or obtain a certain thing. Their rules, empires, and pedestals are beginning to collapse.

Thousands will run scared and some will attempt to prevent you claiming what is rightfully yours. But their authority will no longer hold up as they discover that you, too, can have everything they have, and more. All of you.

No age barriers, no class blockades, no education brick wall, no physical obstructions, no elitist hurdles. Not one thing will be out of your reach."

Chapter Twenty-Four

'Red Hawk to Silver Raven, can you hear me?' Doug asked. His stress levels were through the roof. Feeling sick to his stomach and as though someone was clenching his heart, he could barely breathe. 'Red Hawk to Silver Raven, come in,' Doug said. Still nothing. 'Silver Raven, come in!'

'Silver Raven to Red Hawk. The Dog is down. All under control. I repeat, all under control. Over and out.' Mike Tremblay took the radio from his mouth, rested it in his lap, and closed his eyes. Never in his life had he been so scared.

'Thank God.' Doug Greenlake turned off the radio and leaned back in his chair. Relief flooded his body. That was too close for comfort. They'd had a few close calls inside Area One, but this one had threatened everything. If Dog and his crew had gone just that bit further, who knows what would have happened. They couldn't afford to let these people with abilities have so much free reign. It was a bloody disaster waiting to happen. They were dealing with people who could manifest rocket launchers, guns, machetes, and tanks at a blink of an eye, for Chrissake! It had been the longest few hours of Doug's life, and for a moment he thought the tide had turned against them. He didn't dare think about what could have happened if they hadn't taken down the leader and captured the others. Minutes from now, they'd all be drugged up to the eyeballs, unable to call upon any of their abilities. *Thank God.* The prime minister marketed the place as some sort of Utopia. *Hell, more like it.*

Realisation about the destructive nature of Area One hit Doug like a ton of bricks, and contrary to his impenetrable exterior, he put his head in his hands and cried. He'd never cried before on duty and rarely in his personal life. Lack of sleep, heightened stress levels beyond anything he'd experienced, dealing with this abhorrence, and actioning the PM's impossible demands for Area One made Doug crack. Angrily he rubbed away his tears and reached for his cigarettes.

Chapter Twenty-Five

London, UK

The cellar room of the Sourcer Studio was made darker still with navy-blue painted walls and no natural light. The place was crammed with far too many people for the likes of health and safety. All were here by invitation only, responding to Hudson's call to action, bound by their common understanding of the drastic nature of Area One. Many had first-hand experience being inside Area One, whether through work, passing the assessment, or breaking in. The rest had been touched by Area One in other ways. Hudson took to the small raised stage at the front of the room and the audience quietened.

'Thank you for coming.' Hudson smiled. He hoped the people standing at the back and around the sides wouldn't be too uncomfortable. Nerves filled his stomach and to settle himself, he sought out the familiar faces in the crowd – Devon, Trent, and Will. Some days Area One seemed like a lifetime ago, sometimes it was as though he was still there with the smells and sights still lucid and alive in his mind.

'Like many of you, when I first heard about Area One, I was excited about the possibilities for humankind and our planet. I believed the abilities would allow us to grow and mature as a race. I naively thought that only good would come out of Area One, but I was wrong. And I had the misfortune of finding that out.

'As soon as the first ability appeared, everything on this earth changed forever and it will never be the same again. But the people in authority feign otherwise. They try to contain these abilities, control them, subdue them, medicate them, and electrify them out of people. They are mystified, groping around in the dark, as they authorise the most heinous abuses on our people. All hidden – or so they think. They patronise us with their belief that they know better. Bury their heads in the sand and pretend that the old rules to their old game still apply. They're wrong. The world has changed and so have the people in it. And their dominance is yesterday's news, irrelevant in this new environment.' Hudson spoke with passion. Cheers rose from the audience. 'Their guile and authority turn to dust in this new world. They are naive and ignorant, fooling themselves that their powers still remain.' Sounds of agreement washed around the room.

'I know what some scientists are now peddling – that this is a temporary blip, something that will correct itself over time. That we will go back to normal; whatever that is. They don't realise, this is no blip. This is us asking for these abilities and receiving them. This is humankind evolving and expanding. This is no blip. This is the law of human evolution playing out beautifully before our very eyes.' Hudson paused, his body tingling.

'A new paradigm has opened up. One where we can no longer be held to ransom by governments, leaders, and corporations.' Some took to their feet, roused. 'With the arrival of the Area One energy, we need nothing from these people, or from anyone else in a position of power. They have nothing to offer us which we cannot provide for ourselves. Their temptation and enticements no longer work. They have nothing to hold over us, nothing to barter with, nothing to trade.' Rowdy sounds of accord came from the audience. Hudson took a deep breath. He caught Trent's eye and Trent smiled at Hudson, giving him two thumbs up.

'A new world is forming. One where all needs can be met, where all wishes come true. People who try to withhold will lose their authority and power. Those who try to control behaviour with their manipulations will be washed up. It is a world where everything will be open, seen, and heard. All will be revealed to us: true thoughts, feelings, and actions. There will be nowhere to hide for the deceiver or defrauder. Liars and cheats will be outed. All seen, all transparent. Everyone will be unmasked. There will be no more secrets. Suddenly the world will be an even playing field.

'And not just for a chosen few. And not, as they would have us believe, within a specific location. No, this new world is extending to us all. The Area One energy is growing to include every single person and every centimetre of this planet. It's giving us the most profound freedoms ever. Freedoms that we could only dream about until now.' Everyone in the room was on their feet, cheering, punching the air. 'It is lifting us out of the old way of operating and into a new glorious world where abundance, openness, and transparency prevails. A world where you will never be beholden to another. A world of unimaginable possibility. Of equality. Of unity. Of Oneness.

'We are evolving, my friends. And there is no turning back.'

Exhilarated by the response, Hudson stood watching the audience as they smiled, cheered, and clapped. And in that moment, it reinforced the promise he'd made to himself – that he would never rest until Area One, and all that it meant, was respected and dealt with in a way that honoured the people of this planet.

****

"You now stand on the brink of a pivotal moment which contains potential for phenomenal miracles and at the same time, the potential for complete annihilation. It is time to choose your route, dear One. How will you unify these new Laws? What will become of your people, your world?

Use them for gluttony, hate, and revenge, and it will take you further away from all-that-you-truly-are. Such misery you will find, beyond any definition or experience you have ever had. You will be locked in fear, imprisoned in purgatory.

Use them for love, equality, and peace, and it will take you closer to all-that-you-truly-are. Such liberty you shall know. Beyond any definition or experience you have ever had. You will be free from limitations, living in pure joy, bliss, and abundance.

As the Laws take hold, the veils of illusion are dissolving.

What was hidden will now be seen.

Those who used cover will be exposed.

What was unsaid can now be heard.

Those who were silenced will have a voice.

What was desired can be realised.

Those who struggled can find greater ease.

What was off limits will now be accessible.

Those held back can now fly and soar.

What was suppressed can be avowed.

Souls who were lost will now be found.

The time has come, dear One, for you to start awakening to the truth of Who You Are.

YOU, *my child, are the* ONE.

YOU *are the* ONLY ONE."

Chapter Twenty-Six

Cannonball Run, USA

'What's going on, man?' Robbie Reeves yelled at his co-driver, Dexter Cane, who looked around him. It was dark, the road empty. He stared straight ahead and then turned to Robbie.

'We're off the freaking ground!' Dexter said. 'The car's actually off the road! We're hovering!'

'I know, I can feel it.' Robbie carried on driving. There was no way he would let up. They were on target to smash the current US Cannonball Run record, travelling from New York to Los Angeles. They'd done it before and now they were doing it again, and nothing was going to get in their way. 'We're going faster!' Robbie tapped the speedometer. 'Jeez, look at that!'

'Stop accelerating then!' Dexter accused.

'I'm not!' Robbie shouted. 'I've taken my foot off the gas and we're still going.' Robbie stared at the dials on the dashboard. 'We're increasing speed. We're freaking flying!' Robbie laughed out loud, banging the steering wheel, exhilarated and terrified at the same time. Dexter went quiet and looked across at Robbie, who was laughing demonically as they flew down the road.

'What's wrong with you?' Robbie said. Dexter sat motionless, staring at Robbie. 'Don't worry, Dext, we're definitely gonna smash the record now,' Robbie said. Dexter remained silent. 'We're fine, no one's around. Who's gonna know we had a little helping hand from the Big Guy upstairs?' Robbie laughed, loving the sheer madness of the moment.

'It wasn't the Big Guy upstairs,' Dexter said slowly. 'I did this.' He stared out of the front window.

'What do you mean?' Robbie said. 'You fixed the car to do this? That's amazing, man.'

'No, I didn't do anything to the car,' Dexter said. 'Well, not physically anyway.'

'What? You're not making any sense Dext.' Robbie shifted in his seat, now concerned that his co-driver was suffering from exhaustion.

'I made the car fly,' Dexter said.

'Riiiiight.'

'I was worried we couldn't do it in the time, so I wished the car would fly. Fast,' Dexter said, gradually grasping the situation. 'Just this minute, I wished for the car to fly. I prayed that it would fly.' Dexter turned towards Robbie. 'Then it did. It literally took off and flew.' Dexter laughed nervously.

'What?' Robbie said as he tried to wrap his mind around what Dexter had told him. 'Are you sure? You're just tired, man. We should stop for coffee.' Robbie started to get anxious for his buddy and went to apply the brakes. They didn't work. 'The brakes have gone!' Robbie loved the feeling of going fast, but not having a way of stopping a car that was picking up speed . . . that was an entirely different ball game.

'I'll ask it to stop.' Dexter closed his eyes, and two seconds later the car slowed, touched down on the road, and came to a complete stop. Dexter opened his eyes and turned to Robbie.

'Freaking hell, man!' Robbie said as they both sat staring at each other in complete shock, wondering if they were dreaming, hallucinating, or had died and gone to heaven.

****

Sussex, UK

'Rosie, where are you?' Rosie's mum, Chloe, frantically searched around her daughter's bedroom. *She was here just a minute ago.* Chloe had put her in time out. *Too much cheek for a six-year-old if you ask me.* Rosie was the headstrong but adorable only child of Chloe and Graham. Chloe checked under the bed again. Then the windows. *No, they're still locked.* The cupboards. *Nothing. Where is she?*

'Rosie? Where are you?' Fearful thoughts sprang into her mind. *Someone's taken her! She got out of the house and is wandering around the streets. No, that's impossible.* The intruder or Rosie would need to pass the kitchen to get out of the house. 'Rosie, where are you? Mummy's not cross anymore, come on. You can have some chocolate as a treat.' Surely that would root her out.

'I'm here, Mummy, in the kitchen,' Chloe heard her daughter shout.

'How on earth did she get there?' Chloe flew down the stairs and there in the kitchen, as bold as anything, was Rosie. 'Darling, how did you get here?' Chloe picked up her daughter and checked for injuries.

'I magicked my way into the kitchen. Isn't it great, Mummy? Lanier at school showed me how to do it. Can I have some milk with my chocolate?' Chloe put down her daughter, opened the fridge, pulled out the carton, and poured a drink for Rosie, all the while wondering what on earth was going on.

'What did Lanier show you then?' Chloe felt uneasy.

'He showed me the magic.'

'What do you mean the magic?'

'Well, it's when you need to move around and you don't want to walk. Like on the magic shows, when the lady goes into one box and magics to the other box.' Rosie took a gulp of milk, two hands holding the glass. She loved magic shows.

'So you sneaked out of your room when I wasn't looking?'

'No, not like that. It's when you travel somewhere and you don't want to go on the bus or in a car, you just want to be there fast.' Rosie drained her glass and put it on the side. 'Can I have some chocolate now?'

'Like when you run very fast.' Chloe didn't get it.

'No, Mummy, you don't understand.' Rosie faced her mum, hands on hips. 'Look, I'll show you, but you have to promise not to tell anyone. Not even Daddy, because Lanier says it's a secret and I promised not to tell anyone.' Rosie looked earnestly at her mother. Chloe wondered if she would have to take her precious little girl to the doctors; she was acting very strange. 'Do you promise, Mummy?'

'Yes, I promise.'

'Okay then. Lanier won't be my friend if he finds out I've told you.'

'I won't say a word. I promise.' Chloe had never seen her daughter like this.

'Right. Ready?' Rosie rubbed her little hands together. 'Stand right here so you can see properly.'

'Okay, I'm ready.' Chloe stood in front of her daughter.

'I won't go far.'

'Right,' Chloe said, still at a loss.

'Just outside into the garden. By the apple tree.' Rosie loved the apple tree, climbing it and picking its juicy fruit.

'Right,' Chloe said.

A flash of light radiated from her daughter, so quick and fleeting Chloe wondered if it had happened at all. Then Rosie vanished. Disappeared. Gone. Just like that.

'Oh, my...' Chloe felt faint and quickly sat herself down on a chair. Daring to turn, she looked out of the patio doors to see her daughter outside, jumping up and down by the apple tree, waving to her mum and laughing.

****

"And then there were five – the Law of Teleportation."

"Some of you profess this evolutionary leap is the end. And in some ways, it is. But it is only the end of living in fear, lack, and separation. It is not the end as defined and portrayed by your media and film-makers, a nightmare of fire and brimstone, the obliteration of you. It is the beginning of the end of your game. And a vital step to living closer to who you truly are. It is you becoming One again.

These five Laws come to you now because you have asked for them. You forget you hold the controls for this life, the world, and beyond. But you not only hold the joystick in this game called life, you also write the script and direct it all. You are the characters in the game, the owner of the company that produces the game. You are the designer, the engineer, programmer, and developer. You are the manufacturer, retailer, purchaser, and player. You are the critic and reviewer. You are the beginning, middle, and end. And you are everything in between and all around. It is all You, dear One. Every single thing. From the Big Bang, until now. You have created everything. Every situation, species, plant. All of it — You. That is how phenomenal You are. And there you were, thinking how small, insignificant, weak, hopeless, and unlovable you are. Oh, my dear One, you have no idea. If you could see what we see, know what we know, you would never again doubt or fear.

Because You are the Everything, the All, the Eternal Creator. Here at this exceptional time, to take part in one of the most incredible evolutionary leaps towards Oneness. All of which is at your command and control.

It is time for your union, your completeness.

Time to step into your magnificence and own your greatness.

It is time to be all that you can be. All that you have ever been — THE ONE."

www.estellecranfield.com

Made in the USA
Coppell, TX
15 January 2020